Where It All Began

Lorana Hoopes

ISBN: 153728813X
ISBN-13: 978-1537288130

DEDICATION

To my husband, Dean, who allowed me to write late at night.
To my three children who are the inspiration.
To Ryann Woods who continues to inspire characters.
To Amy Rutledge who let me bounce ideas off her.

CONTENTS

ACKNOWLEDGMENTS

I want to say thank you, first and foremost, to you the reader. I know this isn't an easy topic, but if we don't speak for the unborn, who will?

Thank you to Tim Gephart who took a chance on my first book "Heartbeats" and let me know that men connect with this book too.

Though this is technically the second book in the series, don't worry if you are reading it first. You can then read Heartbeats to find out more about Callie's story.

10% of all proceeds from the Heartbeats series will be donated to pro-life organizations. You can follow my website, www.loranahoopes.wordpress.com, to see a list of which organizations your purchase has supported. If you have a favorite, please contact me and I'll make sure to add them to the list.

1

When it all Began: Mesquite, Texas 1980

I touched the white paper that had been burning a hole in my pocket all day and took a deep breath. Though I hadn't had the courage to read it earlier, I knew that I would have to sooner or later. Pulling it out, I unfolded it and scanned the words. My heart sank. What were we going to do? We couldn't have a baby right now; we were both still working on getting our careers started.

I could hear Peter opening and closing drawers in the bedroom. He was such a creature of habit that I could almost see him pulling on his blue plaid pajama bottoms and buttoning up the shirt. Next he would pull back the crisp white sheets, making sure they were exactly half way down the bed; then he would climb in. My heart thudded in my chest, and I bit the inside of my lip. *Should I tell him now?* Folding my fingers around the incriminating paper I had brought home and taking a deep breath, I exited the bathroom.

"Hey babe, is everything all right?" Peter looked up at me as he finished pulling back the comforter on our queen sized bed. Exactly half way, and then he ran his hand over it to crease it.

I shook my head, blinking back tears. Stepping closer to him, I slowly held out my right hand and opened my fingers to reveal the paper.

He tilted his head at me; confusion gleamed in his brown eyes, but then he followed my gaze down to my outstretched hand. He picked up the white paper, and his eyes scanned back and forth. "I don't understand; how did this happen?" He plopped down on the bed and turned wide eyes up at me.

I sat down beside him and picked at a thread in the comforter. I couldn't meet his eyes, and my throat was so dry. "Peter, you're training to be a doctor. You know how it happens."

He closed his eyes and shook his head, "No, I know that, but we were always careful."

"Not careful enough, I guess." I forced my eyes from the comforter to his face. "I knew something was off; I just felt weird, so I asked them to run a pregnancy test at work today. What are we going to do?"

A sigh escaped his lips as he ran a hand across his forehead. "I don't know. We both work too many hours to raise a baby right now." He trailed off and lowered his eyes to the paper again. "Let's sleep on it and discuss it later." He folded the paper carefully – as if it were contaminated – placed it on the nightstand, and crawled into bed. Right now, for him, the discussion was over.

I nodded, but his words didn't ease my anxiety. Instead of the advice I sought, I had received dismissal. A little part of me had been hoping that he would be excited and propose, but he wasn't. He seemed unenthused, to put it mildly.

As I walked around to my side of the bed, I blinked back tears. Climbing in beside Peter, I stared at the white popcorn ceiling. No answers resided there, but it was something to focus on as questions charged through my mind. *Could we raise a baby right now? Will I have to give up my career? Would I be happy if I did? What will my parents say?* Peter let out a soft snore, and I glared at him. Men had it so easy. They never had to worry about pregnancy and how it was going to change their lives.

I entered the hospital the next morning in a daze. My mind had raced through questions and pondered possibilities until past three in the morning, and when the alarm went off at six am, I felt like I had just fallen asleep.

As I shuffled down the hallway, I rubbed my eyes. They burned from lack of sleep. The training room door loomed on my right, but just as I touched the handle, the door swung inward. Raquel bounded out, nearly colliding with me before stopping short and squinting her green eyes at me. "Whoa, what's up with you? You look like you were hit by a train."

I shook my head, swallowing the lump of emotion lodged in my throat. I couldn't talk about it yet, not even with my best friend. I had to at least decide how I felt about it first. Raquel took the hint and wrapped an arm around me. "Don't worry. Whatever it is, I'll be by your side." I nodded, thankful for the support, and followed Raquel back into the training room. We took a seat around a back table as Nurse Hatchett, as we called her, entered the room.

She was a large German woman. Her tight blond bun demanded compliance, and her harsh brown eyes scoured the crowd, looking for the victim of the day – the student she would focus on and correct relentlessly. "Today, we will be practicing blood draws on the bags in front of you. Your job is not to screw it up, because if you do, that's a life you may not save."

"Nothing like fear to motivate you," Raquel whispered under her breath. I nodded, but not even Nurse Hatchett could garner all of my attention today. My mind veered back to the possibilities of my more current problem. Maybe I could find time to have a baby and still go through nursing school, or maybe I could take a year off. It wouldn't be that long, and I could always go back.

A fist pounded on the table, and I jumped. "What are you doing?" Nurse Hatchett's eyes bored into my own; her large paws sat on either side of my equipment. My eyes darted around, not sure at first what she meant, and then realized I had poked my bag in the wrong place.

"Sorry," I stammered as heat flamed across my face.

She folded her arms and leaned back. "Your patient just died. Don't be sorry. Do it right."

I nodded, shaking my head to clear the invading thoughts. I had to focus, or I'd get kicked out of the program, and a baby really wouldn't matter. Raquel squeezed my arm in reassurance as Nurse Hatchett stomped off to terrorize the next student.

I existed through the rest of the day, with no clear memory of anything I'd done. Though I'd managed to focus on work, it hadn't really been conscious. I'd been operating solely on auto pilot. Relief flooded my body as I pulled into the apartment parking lot and saw Peter's car. Maybe we could finally talk about this pregnancy so I could get my brain back.

The smell of pasta greeted me as I entered the front door. Peter stood in front of the white stove, stirring a pot. He turned at the sound of my footsteps and smiled, "There you are. Just in time, the spaghetti is just perfect."

"Okay." I hung up my purse on the rack just inside the door and shuffled into the kitchen. Peter had already set our small dining table, so I pulled out my chair and sat down. A minute later, he loaded my plate with spaghetti. Though enticing, the smell neglected to clear the other thoughts from my mind. I looked up at him as he pulled his chair into the table across from me. "So, did you think any more about the baby?"

He wrinkled his brow and frowned, "Let's not discuss that right now. It was a long day; let's just have a nice dinner, okay?"

I bit my lip, but nodded. Why didn't he want to talk about it? How much longer would he wait? I ate the spaghetti and listened to Peter rattle on about his day, but my mind cycled a million miles away. What kind of mother would I be? Would it be a boy who took after Peter or a girl who resembled myself?

"Sandra, Sandra," he was shaking my arm.

"Sorry what?" I shook my head and forced my eyes to focus on him.

"I was asking you which direction you think I should go: Emergency Medicine or surgery?"

"Umm, I'm not sure. Which do you like more?" I twirled my fork aimlessly on the plate. *Really? This is what he wants to discuss right now?* A much bigger elephant filled the room. A tiny spark of aggravation flickered in my heart.

"Well, Emergency Medicine would probably be more exciting; you know never knowing what's coming in, but surgery would pay better. Of course, I'm not in it just for the money, but wouldn't it be great to get a Porsche like Dr. Rhodes?"

The spark ignited. I dropped my fork and glared at him. A Porsche would never be a good family car. "Do you even want this baby?" A tightening sensation squeezed my heart, and the words spilled out, barely more than a whisper.

He sighed and scratched his chin. "I don't know. I mean I want to be a father someday, but I don't know if now is the right time. I'm not saying for sure yet, but maybe you should look into an abortion."

My jaw dropped. "Abortion? But Peter, this is our child. Yours and mine." I couldn't abort my own flesh and blood, could I?

He threw his napkin down on the table, "I know. I know. Look, this is why I didn't want to talk about it yet. Just give me some time to think, okay?" He shoved his chair back, causing it to tip and clatter to the floor. I jumped, clasping my hand to my mouth as he stalked out of the room.

The agitation flamed, and my hands clenched. Tears pooled in my eyes. I thought babies brought people together, but this one seemed to be tearing us apart. Blinking the tears away, I grabbed the plates and rinsed them in the sink before throwing them in the dishwasher. The sound of the TV reached my ears, and I rolled my eyes. The agitation turned into ire. A huge problem needed discussing, but he was watching football on TV.

I stomped out of the kitchen – past Henry sitting on the couch – to the guest room. A bed, nightstand, and dresser were the only real furniture in the small room, but what I was looking for was in the closet. Opening the sliding door, I pulled out my easel, paints, and a canvas. I wasn't sure when it had actually started, but painting had become a cathartic therapy for me. After setting the easel up, I opened a jar and shoved a brush inside before bringing it to the stark white canvas. I wasn't surprised to see red splashes appear. It seemed to match my mood perfectly.

Two hours later, my irritation had calmed down, and I had an angry piece of artwork covered in reds, browns, and blacks. Sighing, I screwed the lids back on the paints and took the brushes with me to wash them in the kitchen sink.

The living room was quiet now; Peter must have gone to bed. I washed the brushes, dried them, and then headed to the bedroom myself.

He was indeed lying in bed with closed eyes, but I could tell from the uneasy cadence of his breathing that he was still awake. After brushing my teeth and changing into pajamas, I crawled in my side of the queen-sized bed. As I pulled the stark white sheet to my face, I could almost feel the tangible chill in the space between us in the bed. Once again I found myself gazing at the ceiling, searching for answers it couldn't provide.

When the alarm went off the next morning, I turned it off and held my breath. Silence met my ears: no shower, no TV, no kitchen noise. I rolled over and sighed in relief that Peter's side of the bed was made up, and he was clearly gone. The previous night had been too tense, and I didn't want that same feeling this morning. I needed to have my head in the game today. After dressing, I curled up with a cup of coffee on the leather couch and watched the news before heading to work.

Raquel waved from across the room as I entered the training room. "You look better today," she said when I sat down beside her.

"Really?" I raised an eyebrow. "I don't feel any better. Look, let's talk at lunch, and I'll tell you what's going on." The door swung open, and Nurse Hatchet stomped in carrying an armful of bandages.

"Today you will be working on wrapping. You'll use this skill often, so be sure and get it right." Her eyes found mine, and I cringed inside. She tossed a few bandages on our table, and we began wrapping. The routine movements were oddly cathartic, and I found my mood lifting as I wound them around and around.

"Hey, come on," Raquel tapped my arm, "It's lunchtime." I put down my bandage and followed her out of the room. The hospital cafeteria was two floors up and down the hall. Though there weren't many people in this area of the hallway, Raquel still managed to draw the eyes of every man we passed. With her long black hair and emerald eyes, Raquel defined beauty and turned heads wherever she went. She smiled and waved at the men, and I shook my head.

The cafeteria was just getting busy, but plenty of open seats remained. We grabbed the silver metal trays and picked up a salad and a drink from the buffet area. "Are you going to tell me now?" Raquel asked as we waited in line to check out.

I glanced around, shaking my head. "Wait till we sit down; there's too many people here." After paying the cashier, we crossed through the sea of conversation to the far side of the room where a few empty tables sat alone.

"Okay, seriously, why the secrecy?" Raquel asked as she put her tray on the grey Formica table.

Setting my own tray down, I pulled out the hard plastic chair. A deep breath and a glance around assured me that no one was listening; I didn't want the gossip. I leaned in to keep my voice from carrying, "I'm pregnant."

Raquel's eyes grew wide. "Is that a good thing?"

"That's the problem," I sighed. "I don't know. I mean I always thought kids would come after marriage, but the more I think about it, the more the idea grows on me. But I'm not sure Peter feels the same way. He won't even talk about the baby, and the one time he has, he said we both work too much."

Raquel bit a chunk of her carrot stick. "That is tough," she said between bites, "I guess I can see his point. This program does take a lot of time, but I can see yours, too, even though I know I'm not ready to be a mother. So what are you going to do?"

Sighing, I picked at my salad, "I don't know; I really don't know."

Peter's car was in the lot when I got home, and I braced myself for the strain I was sure was still there. Sure enough, Peter glanced up as I entered, but then turned his face back to the TV. Clearly, he was not ready to talk tonight either. I sighed and crossed to the kitchen.

After throwing together some food for dinner, I ate in silence and then retired to the guest room. I took the canvas from the night before and laid it on the beige carpeted floor, leaning it against the dresser. Then I removed another blank canvas from the closet. This time my painting took on hues of blue, and when finished, it also perfectly mirrored my melancholy mood.

Peter still sat glued to the TV. He spared not even a passing glance as I passed through the living room to clean the brushes. After changing into pajamas and brushing my teeth, I lay in bed and placed my hands on my abdomen picturing the baby. I envisioned myself running after the chubby legs or going for long walks pushing a stroller. As a smile pulled at my lips, I realized I might really want this baby.

2

When Push Comes to Shove

Peter still wasn't talking to me the next day or the day after, and I was steadily running out of canvases. Though painting proved therapeutic, we'd have to discuss this baby soon, or I would have no place to put all the art. As we drifted apart, thoughts of raising the baby on my own invaded my mind. I stared into my cereal bowl, watching the cheerios swim and imagining a toddler munching on them.

"How would you feel about a weekend at the lake?"

The sound of Peter's voice shattered my daydream. I blinked and raised an eyebrow at him. "I think we need to discuss this baby first."

He put his fork down and ran his hands along the table beside his plate. "Yeah I've been thinking about that. I just don't think we have time for a baby right now. I think you should just have an abortion and move on."

Silence descended on the room. My heart dropped. Could he be serious? "I don't know if I can do that. I've been thinking too, and I think I might really want to be a mother."

Peter scowled from across the table, "But I just said I'm not ready for kids."

Anger fueled inside me. "You also haven't been talking about the baby for a week. I have been thinking about it non-stop."

"It's not a baby, right now." His face reddened, and he slapped his palms on the table top, causing my bowl to jump. "Stop calling it that. It's just a clump of cells."

My mouth dropped open. "Peter, we learned about human development. We both know that isn't true."

He shrugged and folded his arms across his chest. "It's mostly true. It's not like it could live by itself right now, and seriously with our schedules the kid would always have to be in daycare, Sandra. What kind of life would that be? We should wait till we have more time and can be good parents."

I closed my eyes and took a calming breath, "I don't want to kill this baby, Peter."

When I opened my eyes, he was staring at me, rage fueling his eyes and distorting his features. "You have two choices," – his voice, cold as ice, cut to my soul – "You can get rid of the pregnancy or raise it alone. I'm not giving up my career." He pushed back from the table, sending his plate and my bowl clattering to the ground. Then he stormed out of the apartment. The slam of the door reverberated down my spine.

His empty chair mocked me as the silence set in, and tears filled my eyes. If those were the choices, then so be it. I grabbed the fallen dishes and threw them in the sink. Returning with a towel, I mopped up the milk that had spilled on the floor and begun spreading out. Then I yanked my purse from the bar and pulled out my checkbook and a notepad. I began writing down the bills, rubbing my temples as the list grew. How would I ever be able to afford a baby on top of all the bills? The numbers swam together as the tears threatened to spill over. Would my parents help? Probably not, they had been disappointed when I had let Peter move in; they would probably be angry about a baby out of wedlock. No brother or sister to turn to, I was an only child. All that left was Raquel. A light went off in my head. Maybe Raquel would let me move in with her. If I split the rent, surely I could afford a baby. I scooped up the checkbook and notepad, throwing them back in my purse, and hurried to the bedroom to get ready for work. Lunch could not come fast enough today.

"So, let me get this straight," – Raquel said over the noise in the cafeteria that afternoon – "You want to try and have this baby even though Peter wants you to have an abortion?"

"I can't bring myself to have an abortion, but I can't pay the bills and cover the baby alone, unless I had a roommate maybe." I stared into Raquel's eyes, hoping she would get the hint.

Her eyes widened, "You don't mean come live with me and bring a baby?"

"Well, it would only be for a little while until I got a better paying job. I could help with rent, and I'm sure the baby would be no trouble." The words tumbled out of my mouth in a rush.

Raquel shook her head. "Look, I like you, Sandra, but I like men too. Having a baby would totally ruin my image. How many men do you think want to stay the night and be woken up by a crying baby? It's why I had my own abortion a few years ago. I don't do kids."

Her words pierced my bubble of hope, and my jaw dropped, "You had an abortion?"

Raquel shrugged, "Yeah, it wasn't a big deal. I had a little too much to drink one night and hooked up with this really cute bartender." Her eyes sparkled at the memory and then refocused on me. "I guess we forgot to be careful. Anyway, as soon as I found out, I went and had it taken care of."

Her callous words coursed over me, and my forehead wrinkled. I'd always thought I was pro-choice, and if Raquel had had an abortion, then maybe they couldn't be that bad. A seed of doubt erupted in my chest and began strangling out my desire for the baby. "Did it hurt?" The words came out small and quiet.

"A little for a day or two, but then I had my life back, so it was worth it. Look, you have to make up your own mind, but maybe Peter is right. Wait until you guys are settled in your careers, and then you can have some kids if you still want them."

Raquel's words collided with Peter's ultimatum, and together they began to make sense in my head. After all, if I couldn't move in with Raquel, I really was out of options, and, as Raquel said, we could always try again later. A small voice insisted that this wasn't right, that abortion was murder, but I pushed it aside. The thought of abortion had taken root, and the knowledge that Raquel had done it caused it to grow. Ending the pregnancy would be the easiest option, and no one would ever have to know besides Peter and Raquel, and they would never tell.

As soon as I opened the door that evening, Peter rose from the couch, folding his arms across his chest. The anger still radiated off him. "Well, have you decided what you're going to do?"

Sighing, I set my purse down on the coffee table. Had I decided? Even though the abortion made sense, I still didn't want to do it, but what choice did I have? "I'll do it," I said softly, and an icy cold sensation trickled through my veins.

A smile broke out on his face as his posture softened. He crossed the room and embraced me. "I knew you'd see it my way and make the right decision," he said into my hair.

I nodded against his chest, but a seed of doubt remained. I just wished I knew it was the right decision.

3

Down the Path of No Return

A few days later, I stood in the parking lot of a small nondescript brick building. It didn't look fancy, but surely that didn't matter. My heart galloped in my chest like a wild stallion, and I took a deep breath to calm my nerves. As I walked up the sidewalk to the front door, I fully expected lightning to strike me when I touched the door handle, and when it didn't, I pulled the door open. The air inside was much cooler than the summer heat outside, and a shiver shimmied down my spine as the air conditioning chilled me. "Can I help you?" To my right, a girl with short blond hair and an ear full of piercings, sat behind a desk.

"Um yeah. I'm Sandra Baker. I have an appointment." As I crossed to the desk, my throat constricted, and ice coursed through my veins. I shivered again and swallowed the bout of nausea that clawed up my throat and threatened to choke me.

"Right, here's your paperwork. Have a seat, and we'll call you back in a minute." The girl handed over a clipboard and some forms, and I took them to a nearby chair and sat down. As I picked up the pen, my hand began to shake. Closing my eyes, I took a deep breath. *It'll be okay. It'll be okay.* I played the mantra over and over in my head, though it did nothing to stop the freight train roaring in my heart. Somehow I managed to force the pen down and write information on the form. I had no idea if it was correct or not. A door opened, and my eyes flicked up. A hardened woman with steely grey eyes and a clipboard met my glance.

"Sandra Baker?"

The lump in my airway grew, and I swallowed it down and nodded. My legs shook as I pushed up from the chair and stumbled in her direction. Weights like anchors pulled on them. Were they even part of my body? A screaming erupted in my head, urging me to flee, and I froze. My eyes tore about the room, but there was no one screaming. *What am I doing?* I turned to flee, but then I remembered Peter's ultimatum, and the fact that I couldn't raise this baby alone. It's for the best. The mantra started again and propelled me to the waiting woman. Up close, she was even more harsh looking. Ice for eyes, no smile, a don't-mess-with-me aura, hair pulled back in a tight brown bun. Executing a nearly perfect three-point turn, the nurse spun as soon as I reached her and marched into the back. Shoulders down, I followed, even as a small voice pounded in my head to turn around.

The nurse turned into a tiny room with a bed, a stool, a hard plastic chair, and a tray with instruments. "Undress from the waist down and put this on," the nurse said as she picked up a gown off the tray. She shoved it unceremoniously into my arms, and then she left the room.

The cold sterility of the room tightened the fear on my heart, but somehow I managed to pull off my clothes and fold them on the chair. I slid on the paper thin gown, wrapping it around my body. I shouldn't be here. I thought about bolting, but what good would it do? Instead, I climbed up on the bed, the paper crinkling beneath me. Surely, something in the room would calm my nerves. I glanced around, but there was nothing on the stark white walls, not one picture. No beaches, no calming words. Just a harsh white. Why did the walls present nothing calming? Surely other women felt the same anxiety.

A knock at the door arrested my attention, and I jumped. An older man with bushy white eyebrows and a wrinkled forehead entered along with the hardened nurse. I waited for a comforting word, but none came.

"Lay back," the nurse pointed. I acquiesced and focused on the white tiled ceiling. No comfort there either. "Legs up." I positioned my legs in the cold, metal stirrups and shivered again.

"Am I going to be awake?" I asked as the fear squeezed ever harder.

"Yes, did you think we would put you out?" A sharp stare from the icy eyes.

That was exactly what I had expected. I didn't want to be awake for this. If I got up to leave now, would they let me? A sharp sting caused me to suck in my breath.

"That was a local anesthetic. It will help."

A weight like a stone rolled on my chest, and it grew hard to take a breath. I squeezed my eyes shut, but that only intensified the sound of the clanking metal instruments. I opened them and began counting the holes in the tiles. One, two, three, "Ouch!" Tears filled my eyes as the pain intensified. Why had no one warned me about the pain?

"Hold still." A cold hand held my legs apart, and the freezing sensation crawled up my leg. Then the scraping started. I bit back the screams, though moans escaped, and tears flowed freely down my cheeks now. Scrape, tug, scrape, tears, moans, scrape, tug. My hands clutched the side of the bed. The scraping stopped, and I sighed with relief. Surely this was almost over. Then the whirring started, and my heart stopped. More suction, more tears, and still no comfort. The sound stretched to eternity; the pain never ceased. And then it was silent.

"You can get dressed now," the nurse said, and they left the room. The doctor had never spoken; I didn't even know his name. How different from all the doctors I worked with, who always introduced themselves. I tried to sit up, but my body fought me. The feeling of being punched repeatedly in the abdomen kept me prone. Then the guilt crept in. What had I done? A feral moan reached my ears. *Was that me?* And then a baby's cry echoed throughout the room. My eyes darted about, but I was still alone. The cold returned and hungrily licked up my body. Crossing my arms, I hugged my own shoulders, wishing I had never entered this vile place.

After some time, I managed to force my body into a sitting position. My head pounded like a drum and my stomach ached as though I'd lost a terrible boxing match. Nausea bubbled in my belly as I stood, and I clasped a hand to my mouth to keep the contents in. My shaky legs barely held my weight as I struggled to calm my quivering hands and redress myself. The nurse re-entered just as I finished.

"Come with me." She pivoted and marched out the door.

I followed, pulling my shirt close around my neck and using the wall for support. The feeling of being naked and exposed lay on my shoulders like a coat. Would everyone know what I had done? Would it flame on my chest like a scarlet letter? I suddenly knew exactly how Hester Prynne must have felt in the novel I was forced to read in High school.

The nurse opened a door on the left. "Take a seat. You have to wait at least an hour before we can release you."

I nodded and entered the room. The door clicked closed. Nothing but hard plastic chairs and three other women filled the room. One woman nonchalantly read a book, but the other two mirrored my feelings. One girl, probably only in her teens, sat rocking with her knees at her chest. Her dark hair covered some of her face, but her vacant brown eyes stared at nothing. The other woman, a young Hispanic who appeared about my age sniffled softly into a tissue. Tears streaked her face. I sat down in the chair one away from her, but the girl did not even glance at me. Her eyes also focused on nothing.

As I studied my brown hands clasped together, the questions barraged me again. *Why did I let Peter talk me into this? Will this massive guilt ever go away? Will the child ever forgive me?* The cry of the baby came again, and my head popped up. I glanced from one woman to the next, but they appeared to hear nothing. Was I going crazy then? The cry grew louder, and my body began to shake uncontrollably. *I must be going mad.* I jammed my fingers in my ears to block the sound, but the cry echoed in my head. I couldn't seem to stop the sound. My hands found the side of my head and squeezed. Black dots swam before my eyes, but finally the noise grew silent.

The nurse came in, and the woman with her book exited. How could she be so calm? Had she not had the same procedure? Why had no one told me about this guilt? Was it not normal to feel so much guilt? Or the pain? The pain in my stomach but also in my heart. Pain I had never felt before. Emptiness.

The blond girl went next, but not by herself. Two nurses carried her from the room. She never once looked at anything. Her wild eyes remained vacant. I wanted to talk to the Hispanic girl, but how do you strike up a conversation after you've done the unthinkable? Then the Hispanic girl left, shuffling as a zombie after the nurse, and I was alone. Why had Peter not come with me? He said he'd been too busy, but he should have been here. This was his idea. He'd given me the money like a prostitute and sent me to do the dirty deed myself, and I hated him for it. The silence in the room pressed in on me, and I swallowed. The room began to spin and my breath . . . I couldn't get a full breath. Nothing but shallow gasps. I tried again, clawing at my throat. What was happening to me? My eyes grew wide as I struggled, but the darkness won.

When I opened my eyes again, I was no longer in the small room. I blinked a few times, taking in the cream colored walls before realizing I was home in my own bed in a pair of pajamas. How had I gotten home? I pushed back the covers and sat up, but immediately the room spun. Slamming my hands to the side of my head, I waited for the room to stop turning. When it finally stilled, I pushed myself off the bed. As soon as my feet touched the floor, I nearly crumpled from the pain. A burning sensation blazed through my abdomen, and I wrapped one arm around my stomach. The other grasped the wall, and slowly I limped down the hallway and into the living room where Peter sat on the couch watching TV. He glanced up as I entered.

"Hey, how are you feeling?" he asked, before returning his eyes to the black box.

My eyes narrowed, and I glared at him as hatred fueled in my heart. I bit back the hateful words I wanted to spew and took a breath, "How did I get here?"

"Evidently you passed out, and they called me. We still need to go back and get your car."

"No," – I shook my head as the nausea reared up again – "I never want to see that place again, so find someone else to drive it home, or they can have it towed, and I'll pick it from the tow place."

Peter wrinkled his forehead, "Don't be silly. It's just a few minutes down the road. We'll get it when you feel better."

"If I ever feel better," I whispered as the grief pulled at my heart, and the tears tumbled down my cheeks again.

Peter rose from the couch to comfort me, but his touch only ignited the nausea and repulsed me. I shook him off and limped back to the bedroom, shut the door, and crawled back into bed. Pulling the covers up over my head, I closed my eyes, wishing I could redo today and make a different decision.

At some point Peter came in to offer me dinner, but I couldn't eat. I wasn't hungry; I wasn't sure I'd ever be hungry again. He didn't come back that night, and I was glad. The mere sight of him stirred the seed of hatred, and the thought of his body next to mine made me cringe.

The cry of a baby woke me some time later, and I glanced around. A tiny baby in a blue sleep suit lay at the foot of my bed crying softly and flailing little arms. Was it a boy then? I reached for the baby, but my arms continually fell short. The cries grew softer and softer, and my heart squeezed tighter and tighter. And then they stopped, and the baby regarded me with empty dark eyes. A guttural scream reached my ears, and I snapped my eyes shut and clapped my hand over my mouth.

Drenched in sweat and tears, I slowly re-opened my eyes, but there was no longer any baby. There was no baby. I had killed him. I curled into a ball as racking sobs wrenched my body. When there were no tears left, I touched my stomach and the pure emptiness consumed me again. I had killed my own flesh and blood, for what? Convenience? I couldn't go on like this, and I couldn't get back to sleep. How could I deaden the pain?

The image of the small stash of liquor Peter kept for parties jumped in my mind, and I limped my way into the kitchen. He was snoring softly on the couch as I passed, and the hateful thoughts that jumped in my mind surprised me. I shook my head and continued limping along. A few more steps landed me at the little chest. Opening the door, I took stock of the offerings. I had never been a big drinker, so

I had no idea what I was looking at or what each tasted like. Rum, Tequila, Gin, Whiskey, Scotch, I played a quick mental game of "Eenie-Meenie-Miney-Moe" and grabbed a bottle, closing the door softly and shuffling back to the room.

I sat on the edge of the bed, staring at the bottle. Would it help? Unscrewing the lid, I lifted the clear liquor to my mouth, took a deep breath, and swallowed. Fire burned my throat as the liquid slid down, and my eyes watered. I coughed and slapped my hand over my mouth. Had I woken Peter? I held my breath, listening, but no sound came back. I swallowed the fire completely and then tilted the bottle up and downed another large gulp. When the bottle was half gone, the glorious numbness finally set in. I screwed the lid back on and placed the bottle in my nightstand drawer, covering it up with pajama shirts. I crawled back in the bed, closed my eyes, and let the spinning room rock me to sleep.

It was late when I woke the next day. The apartment was quiet, and though I wasn't really hungry, the alcohol mixed with the lack of food created an unpleasant sensation in my stomach. I pushed myself up, grimacing at the amount of pain still coursing through my body, and repeated the previous night's limping expedition to the kitchen.

Nothing appealed to me, so I finally settled on a bowl of cereal. It was easy, and hopefully it would soothe the swirling sensation in my stomach. The walk to the living room proved even slower, as the hand holding my abdomen now had to hold the bowl of cereal, but finally I made it. I sank onto the brown leather couch and clicked on the television. Pictures flashed, but I saw none of them. The sound, however, was better than the silence. The silence scared me as the cries of a baby always seemed to come in the silence.

When the cereal was gone, the sensation in my stomach waned, but as it did, the pain in my heart returned along with the need for a drink. I limped the bowl to the sink and then back to the bedroom where I rescued the bottle and downed another fourth. It was nearly empty. I had no idea how often Peter checked the stash or if he'd even know if a bottle was missing, but I decided I better replace it and buy some more.

I shrugged on a cardigan, not bothering to brush my teeth or my hair. I didn't care what anyone thought about me, as long as they didn't know my secret. Clutching the cardigan high around my neck, I grabbed my wallet and limped out of the apartment.

A liquor store sat a few blocks up, and I thought I could make it, but about halfway there, the pain blossomed in my stomach. The sun beat down, causing beads of sweat to pop out on my forehead. If anyone peered out their window, they would probably wonder why I was wearing a cardigan in the summer heat, but I didn't care; the layers helped me hide.

By the time I reached the store, sweat poured down my face, and I couldn't stand up straight. A small bell announced my entrance, and the clerk, an older man in a short sleeved t-shirt, raised his eyebrows as I entered. Avoiding his gaze, I dropped my head and pulled the sweater closer. Because I had no idea what I was looking for, I grabbed the first few clear liquors I saw and carried them to the front.

"Are you having a party?" the man asked kindly, scanning the bottles.

I chanced a quick glance at him and then returned my attention to my wallet. "Something like that," I said as I fumbled with the zipper. Forking over the money, I picked up the brown paper bag and tucked it under my arm. The bell jingled again as I exited, and taking a deep breath, I began the trek back toward the apartment.

By now, my stomach was screaming at me, but I kept pressing on until the cry of a baby stopped me short. I closed my eyes briefly before looking around, expecting to see nothing like the last few times the phantom cry had come, but this time I saw a young mother playing with a small child in her front yard. Somehow that hurt even worse as the reminder of what I had done to my own child seared my heart again. Gritting my teeth against the pain raging in my abdomen and now my heart, I quickened my pace to escape the "accusing" cry. My vision blurred as tears built up behind my eyes, but I blinked them away until I reached my front door. Then they came back with a vengeance, causing me to fumble with my keys at the front door.

"Are you okay? Do you need some help?"

A glance to my right revealed a man with dark tan skin watching me. I sniffed, "No, I'm fine. It's just allergies," and jammed the key in the lock again. This time it clicked into place and opened the lock. "See? But thank you."

I shuffled inside as quickly as I could and closed the door, leaning against it as the tears overwhelmed me. I let them come, pouring down one after the other. I couldn't have stopped them anyway; I was like a leaky faucet. When they finally tapered, I dropped my keys on the entry table and wiped my eyes with the free hand. The aching pain fueled the need for a drink and a nap, but I had to make it there first. Tucking the bag close to my stomach so I could hold the contents and my abdomen, I limped to the bedroom.

When the door opened, my eyes tore around in search of a hiding place. Peter was such a minimalist that the bed, dresser, and nightstands were the only furniture in the room. I could hide one bottle in the nightstand, maybe two, as the one residing there currently was nearly empty, but where to place the others? I quietly cursed my neatness as no piles existed to hide them under or behind.

As I pulled open the nightstand drawer, I realized I could probably fit two bottles there, so I plucked one from the bag and placed it next to its friend. Then I sank to the floor and peered under the bed. Only our slippers were there, but maybe if I put the other two close to the wall and my slippers in front, they wouldn't be easily seen. I pulled them out of the paper sack and situated them against the wall.

A key in the front door grabbed my attention, and I quickly shoved the bag under there as well. I'd have to retrieve it later. I stripped off my cardigan and tossed it under, and then I crawled into bed, pulling the covers up over my ears. Peter's steps came down the hallway, and I wished I'd had time to sneak another drink. I couldn't talk to him right now. I squeezed my eyes shut, hoping he'd either think I was asleep or that I needed more space.

"Sandra?" Hesitation colored his voice, but it didn't ease my hatred of him. "Sandra, I'm really sorry you are feeling badly. Liam and I went and got your car, so it's back in the parking lot for when you have to go to work on Monday." I held my breath; surely if I was quiet he would go away. He sighed, "Okay, I'll leave, but I'm going to make lunch, and I hope you'll join me." His footsteps receded, and I sighed. Would I ever be able to forgive him? More importantly, would I ever be able to forgive myself?

Saturday turned to Sunday, and I stayed holed up in the bedroom as much as possible. When I heard the front door close and knew Peter was gone, I would venture out to get a small bite of food. It still held no taste, but the sensation of being hungry was slowly creeping back in, and my stomach would grumble in complaint.

To Peter's credit, he hadn't bothered me again and was either sleeping on the couch or somewhere else. I didn't care as long as it wasn't with me in the bed.

I had finished the first bottle of liquor and was already halfway through the second. I hoped I wouldn't have to make another trip to the corner store, but the liquor seemed to be the only thing getting me out of bed in the morning and to sleep at night.

4

The Slippery Downward Slope

When the alarm went off Monday morning, I glared at it. Could I make it through work today? Did I even want to? If I didn't go, what would I do for money? The questions paraded in my mind even as I forced my legs out of bed.

Immediately, I opened the nightstand drawer for another drink. The quenching fire burned down my throat, giving me the courage to get up. I pushed myself off the bed and shuffled to the closet. The pain was less today, almost manageable.

I perused the closet and reached way back on the shelf for a pair of sweats and an oversized shirt. I wanted to hide in the layers and bagginess. Thankfully, I was still in the training program where casual dress was still allowed. I wasn't looking forward to the day I had to wear the rather tight-fitting scrubs.

The blue button-down shirt hung from my body, but I still felt naked and exposed. I turned to the bathroom mirror, shocked by my appearance. Pale, splotchy skin covered my face, and my hair looked oily and grimy, but I had no time for a shower today. After splashing a little water on my face, I patted it with a towel, and decided I didn't care. I hastily pulled my hair up, securing it with a clip, and then I turned out the light and left.

My car was sitting right where Peter had said it would be, but my feet wouldn't move to it. Images of where I had gone the last time I sat in it flooded my mind, stirring a feeling of nausea. I closed my eyes and began to count. The sound of my heart pounding in my ears almost drowned out the numbers, but as I neared fifty, it began to lessen. My hands stopped shaking, and my feet finally stumbled to the car.

I had loved this car. All through college, I had begged my father for a dark blue mustang, but he had always said no – they were too frivolous – but on my graduation day, it had been waiting for me outside.

My fingers touched the door handle, remembering the first day when I drove it until it completely ran out of gas. My father had had to come and bring me gas, but he had been smiling when he showed up. Images of Raquel and I with the windows down and the music blaring replaced that one, and then images of Peter and I scrunched in the back seat beneath foggy windows. But the image of the clinic lasted longer. The cold sterility of the place invaded my mind, and my hand flew back as if burnt. I would have to get rid of this car as soon as I could. I'd just have to tell my father I needed something more reliable. Surely, he would understand.

After several more minutes and a few deep breaths, I was able to open the door and climb inside. As soon as the door shut, the car began to squeeze in on me, and black spots impeded my vision. I dropped my head in my hands and tried to slow my breathing. *Just get me to work.*

That's all I ask. Just get me to work. I can take care of the car after work. The dots faded, my breath slowed, and I put the car in drive and headed to the hospital.

As I pulled into the parking lot, the panic hit again. Surely everyone would be able to see what I'd done just by looking at me. Why hadn't I called in sick? My pager buzzed and Raquel's number popped up. I had to make it inside before she sent a search party looking for me. Taking a deep breath and swallowing the large lump of fear, I exited the car and forced my feet toward the entrance. Each crack in the sidewalk I passed increased the pounding of my heart in my chest as I crept closer to the door. Beads of sweat broke out on my forehead and tumbled into my eyes, burning. I wiped the sweat away and pulled the door open.

The cool rush of air conditioning engulfed me, causing a shiver, but it didn't cool the fever burning inside of me. No one yelled accusations at me though, and slowly the pounding softened. I kept my head down, weaving my way through the halls to the training room. Sweat had broken out on my palms even in the cool hospital, and I ran them down my pants before opening the door.

I closed my eyes against the onslaught of judgement I knew was coming and stepped inside. No conversation stopped. No one screamed in horror. Slowly I opened my eyes. No one was even looking my direction. Relief flooded my body, and I slunk to an open table at the back of the room. Though no one was staring at me, I still felt exposed, and I shrunk down in my chair as much as possible.

Raquel entered the room a few minutes later, and her eyes scanned the tables, widening as we locked glances. She crossed the room quickly, "What happened?"

"What do you mean?" I asked, pulling the collar of the shirt even tighter around my neck.

Raquel raised an eyebrow. "I mean you look like crap. There are dark circles under your eyes, your hair barely looks combed, did you even shower? And you're wearing clothes two sizes too big for you. What's going on?"

My eyes dropped to the table as my finger scratched something on the surface, and I wished she'd stop asking. Though I knew it was only because she cared about me, I had no desire to talk about the dirty deed I had done, at least not yet. "Nothing." A glance out of the corner of my eye indicated she wasn't buying it. "I just didn't sleep well." Raquel pursed her lips and shook her head but said nothing. I swallowed a tiny sigh of relief.

"Look, I know you don't want to talk right now," Raquel said that afternoon when class had ended, "but I'm here if you ever need me." Worry surfaced in her bright green eyes, and tears filled my own in response. The pain, still raw, flared anew.

"I'll tell you soon," I whispered, hugging her and then hurrying out of the hospital and to my car before the floodgates opened. As I closed the door, the tears won and spilled down my cheeks. Would this ever end?

As soon as the tears ebbed enough for me to see, I backed the car out, heading to the nearest used car dealership. I parked by the front door, and a man with a pot belly and a mustache came out to greet me. The last button on his Hawaiian shirt didn't cover his enormous belly, and dark hair poked through. The small name badge on his shirt read Jerry. Swallowing my disgust, I wiped my eyes and exited the car.

"How can I help you?" he asked, scratching his belly and causing his shirt to rise, exposing even more flesh and hair. I forced my eyes to his face.

"I need to trade this car in for something else," I said.

He drew his eyes together, tugging on his mustache with thick fingers, "What's wrong with it?"

"Nothing, I just want something different." I crossed my arms and rubbed my palms up and down my biceps.

"Well, what do you have in mind?"

Turning, I scanned the rows of cars. I didn't honestly care, but a small, silver, four-door caught my attention. "How about that one?"

He followed my finger, and his eyebrows arched up. "You want to trade a Mustang for a Ford Taurus?"

"I just want something reliable that won't cost me more than the trade-in. I don't want monthly payments."

"Are you sure there's nothing wrong with your car?" He scratched the rotund belly again.

"Just memories I no longer want."

"Oh I hear that little lady." He winked at me. "Okay, follow me, and we'll get you set up."

I cringed at his word choice and familiar gesture, but followed him inside.

The dealership was small and dark, even with rows of windows as the outer wall. A few other smarmy salesmen glanced up as we entered, but no one bothered us.

Jerry sat down at a cluttered desk, shoving the papers spread out on his desk onto the floor. A fake potted plant sat behind him, and a picture of what I assumed was his family rounded off the rather impersonal area. I stared at the two vinyl chairs across from the desk, afraid of what might be growing on them, but I took a breath and sat down on the very edge, careful to touch as little as possible.

Thirty minutes and a stack of signed papers later, he handed me the keys to the Ford Taurus, and I exited the stifling building. I opened the door of the car and slid inside. The grey interior matched the exterior, but it was comfortable, and it looked and smelled clean enough, so as long as it drove fine, I'd consider it a good trade.

By the time I got back to the apartment, Peter's car was parked outside. After putting the car in park, I turned off the engine. *Do I go in or wait for him to leave?* I chewed on my right thumbnail and tapped the steering wheel with my left. *Who knows how long he'll stay; I might as well go inside.* Sighing, I grabbed my purse, locked the car, and entered the apartment.

The smells of dinner accosted me as I stepped inside, and I paused. My stomach rumbled, but was I hungry enough to see Peter? He stepped out of the kitchen just then and stopped short at the sight of me.

"I made dinner," he said softly, "I hope you'll join me." His eyes darted back and forth across my face. His normally strong shoulders slumped in defeat. A spark of sympathy flickered in my heart, and I nodded. "Yeah?" A flicker of hope danced in his eyes. I could only nod again; I didn't trust myself to speak.

I followed him into the kitchen and sat down at the table. Peter placed a plate of grilled chicken and vegetables in front of me, and while my fork mechanically brought the food to my mouth, my mind whirred a million miles a minute through future possibilities. *Can we get over this? Will the guilt go away if I just give it enough time?* The sound of Peter's voice discussing his day hummed in my ear, but I couldn't muster much more than a nod or "hmm" in response.

After dinner, I helped with the dishes, but the proximity to Peter began to churn the nausea that had developed in my stomach over dinner, and I quickly retired to the bedroom for the evening. A small drink quieted the pain, and after returning the bottle to its hiding place, I closed my eyes, letting the darkness overtake me.

The sound of crying snapped my eyes open. I slapped the empty bed beside me and shot up. A tiny baby, wrapped in a blue blanket, lay at the foot of my bed. The little hands waved, and the tiny mouth wailed. I reached for the baby, but again my arms only brushed the blanket. The baby stopped crying and turned sad brown eyes on me. The grief in the tiny orbs seared my heart, and tears rolled down my cheek. It must have been a boy then. I'd now had two dreams of the baby wearing blue. The baby faded away, but the echo of his cries remained. I pulled the sheet over my head. "Go away. It was my choice; I don't need the guilt." The echo slowly tapered off, but sleep was slow in returning.

I slapped the alarm the next morning, eyes still closed. When the incessant beeping stopped, I rubbed my face. My eyelids felt like stone slabs glued to my face. After getting them open a tiny crack, I pulled the nightstand drawer open and felt around for the bottle. Clasping the neck, I unscrewed the lid and brought the bottle to my lips for my morning ritual.

When the fire had burned down my throat and created a nice buzzing in my head, I managed to fully open my eyes and roll out of bed. I shuffled to the closet, but everything still looked too form fitting, so I threw on another pair of sweats. I cringed at the puffy eyes and the splotchy face staring back at me from the mirror. It was no wonder Raquel had caught on that something was wrong, I wasn't even sure I recognized myself.

The hospital loomed a giant steel beast as I pulled into the parking lot, and I dreaded entering. There were too many people, too many eyes. I counted the cracks in the sidewalk this time as I approached – fifty-four – and then the lines in the floor on the way to the training room – sixty-two.

I was early enough today that a few empty tables remained at the back. I slunk to the farthest one and tried my best to disappear.

"Uh oh, was it a bad day?" Raquel slid in the chair beside me, looking immaculate as usual in her dress pants and Guess shirt.

I stopped chewing my rapidly disappearing thumbnail long enough to nod, "I'll tell you at lunch." Nurse Hatchett entered the room then and began her lecture on disposing of needles. I tried to focus on her words, but the image of the baby kept appearing in my mind.

"Come on; it's lunch," Raquel nudged my arm, and the baby vanished for the moment. I followed her down the hall, my stomach churning at the thought of telling Raquel what was going on. Raquel had seemed so nonchalant about her abortion; she couldn't have gone through anything like what I was facing.

After standing in line for food, we headed to a far table. "You had the abortion, didn't you?" Raquel asked as we sat down. My eyes widened, and my jaw dropped.

"Is it that obvious?" I whispered, glancing around to make sure no one overheard.

Raquel smiled, "To me it is. You've been acting weird, so I figured you must have decided on abortion. You certainly don't have that pregnancy glow about you, but aren't you glad you have your life back?"

I dropped my eyes to the Formica table top and shook my head. "It's been horrible. The procedure was awful; there was so much pain afterwards; and . . ." – I raised my eyes to her – "I keep hearing a baby cry, but then there's nothing there. But the dreams are the worst."

Raquel raised an eyebrow, "Dreams? What dreams?"

"Dreams of the baby. He just stares at me and cries, and I reach for him, but I can't ever touch him."

"Him?"

I shrugged, pushing my food around on my plate. "I guess it's a him; the baby has been in blue both times I saw him, so I'm assuming my baby would have been a boy. Did you never have dreams?" A vein of fear ignited and began to course through my body. What if there was something really wrong with me?

Raquel shook her head slowly. "No, I never had dreams, and I never heard phantom crying. You probably have just been thinking about it too much. You need to let it go, and realize you have your life back now."

I nodded, but the words fell on loose sand and blew away. Maybe I was overreacting, but Raquel didn't hear the cries; she didn't see the baby. But she was right; I did need to get on with my life. I had made my choice, and even if I regretted it now, I could do nothing about it. The question was though, how did I go on about my life when I was being haunted by my child?

Raquel continued to pour affirming words into my head over the next week, and slowly they began to take root. The physical pain diminished, and the nights remained blissfully dream free, thanks to the alcohol coma I practically put myself in at night. I even started thinking that maybe Peter and I could work out, with time, so I was disappointed when his car wasn't at the apartment when I arrived home.

As I was locking the car, a small pink ball rolled up to my feet. I picked it up and looked up to see a little girl with brown braids staring back at me. She held her chubby hands out for the ball and smiled. Breath caught in my throat. I tried to smile back, but the grief gripped me, tightening its vice grip on my body again.

A woman carrying a baby approached, "I'm so sorry. Karen, I told you to keep the ball in our yard." As she was speaking, the baby cried, and a tiny hand waved. The dream flooded back, shredding the dam I had built, and I fell to my knees. The pebbles in the asphalt bit into my skin, but I couldn't move. The little girl stepped back, reaching for her mother's hand. "Are you alright?" the woman asked and pulled her daughter close to her with her free hand.

"I'm sorry," I whispered, rolling the ball to the girl. The girl scooped it up, and the trio turned quickly, leaving me on my knees in the parking lot. My body shook as the grief clawed through it once again. The darkness began to cloud my vision until a hand landed firmly on my shoulder. I forced my eyes upward. The same man from a few days before stood beside me, staring down with gentle brown eyes brimming with concern.

"Can I be of assistance?" He extended his other caramel hand to help me up, and I accepted.

"I'm sorry," I managed when I got to my feet. My knees still shook beneath my pants, and cold tendrils gripped my stomach. "Thank you."

"Can I walk you to your door?"

Though I didn't know him, his voice soothed my raw nerves like balm on a burn, and I nodded. I took his arm, grateful for the help, and pointed out my apartment. My hands were still shaking when we reached the door, and the keys tumbled out of my grip to the ground. He picked them up, holding them out to me. I shook my head and pointed to the middle silver key. Understanding my silent request, he inserted the correct key, turned the lock, and opened the door.

"Will you be alright now?" he asked. I nodded, though his raised eyebrows told me he didn't necessarily agree. "My name is Henry. I live in 2B. If you ever need anything, you come knock, okay?"

I grasped his hand and squeezed. "Thank you," I whispered. He nodded, and after a final look, he turned away.

I entered the apartment, shut the door behind me, and sank to the beige carpeted floor. How was I ever going to get over this? If just seeing a baby sent me into a tailspin; how was I ever going to continue to be a nurse? Then, as if on cue, the phantom cries started again. I slammed my hands over my ears and rocked back and forth, willing the sound to go away, but instead it grew louder. My heart accelerated, and a weight fell on my chest. The air wouldn't come; I clawed at my throat, but the darkness crowded in, pressing down like a vice until it won.

"Sandra? Sandra?" A hand was shaking my shoulder. I snapped my eyes open, but there was no cry. There was only Peter staring at me with wide frightened eyes.

"Are you okay?" Peter asked, "What happened?"

"I'm not," – my head shook – "I am definitely not okay."

5

When Sorry Isn't Enough

I lay on the brown leather couch, staring at the ceiling. I didn't want to be here, but I had agreed with Peter after the mini-breakdown to try something. His solution had been to introduce me to one of his doctor-friends, a psychologist named Dr. Munch. At 45, he was nearly twice my age, and not being a woman, I figured he would not understand my issue, but here I was lying on his couch anyway.

"So why don't you tell me what's been happening?" he asked as he sat in a chair across from me and pulled out a notepad.

"I lost my baby, and now he's haunting me." I glanced over, but he showed no reaction. His calm brown eyes returned my gaze.

"Go on," he said.

"That's it." I wasn't telling this man about the abortion. "I hear phantom cries, but there's no baby there, and sometimes I have dreams where I see the baby but can never touch him." His pen began scratching on his paper, unnerving me. Was he writing that I was crazy? "It's affecting my work and my relationship, and that's why I'm here." I took a deep breath, expecting some kernels of wisdom to flow out of his mouth and heal my pain, but he simply stared back at me.

Unease set in and filtered through my body, "Don't you have anything to say?"

"That isn't how it works," he said and raised his eyebrows.

"So what am I supposed to do? I can't keep going on like this." I crossed my arms over my chest.

"Well, I don't think you've told me everything, and that would be a start. I think you should also look into a support group, but I'll give you some positive mantra exercises, and I'll see you again when you're ready to be honest." He stood and walked to his desk.

Heat and anger flared within, and I sat up, "That's it? That's all you can do for me?"

"It takes time to heal." He held out a piece of paper. I snatched it and, still shaking, stomped out of the door. The slamming door brought a small semblance of satisfaction. Peter jumped, and his eyes widened. He opened his mouth to speak, but quickly closed it. Instead he stood and took a tentative step in my direction.

"All done?"

I glared at him and shoved the paper in his hand. "That was a waste of time." Pushing past him, I flung the outer door open. Behind me, a sigh, but then footsteps.

The car ride home was quiet, uncomfortable. As soon as Peter parked, I opened the door and hurried into the apartment, making a beeline for the bedroom.

My hands were still shaking as I locked the bedroom door and as I opened the nightstand drawer. The bottle smiled at me from its snug bed, and I jerked the lid off, downing a large swig. A knock on the bedroom door caused me to jump, spilling a little. I cursed at the wasting of the liquid courage.

"Sandra? Are you okay in there?"

I rolled my eyes and shook my head. "I'm fine. Just leave me alone for now." Silence descended, and then his footsteps receded. I tilted the bottle again and hugged my knees to my chest. The fire spread from my throat to my toes. After recapping the bottle, I placed it back in the nightstand and curled into a ball. Maybe I could just drink the pain away.

When the alarm went off the next morning, I sighed as I turned off the buzzer and reached for the bottle in the nightstand. Almost empty. It was going too quickly. *I'm drinking too much, but I can give it up when the pain goes away, when the dreams stop.* I put the bottle away and threw on some clothes for work

As I drove home that evening, I hoped Peter wouldn't be there. After a long day of work, the tense evenings zapped any strength remaining. I just wanted him to be gone or for things to be the way they had. The decision seemed to change from moment to moment, but the former seemed much more likely. Sighing, I pulled in next to Peter's car; another tense night loomed ahead of me. I grabbed my purse, locked the car, and stepped to the door. The key had just touched the golden lock when the door swung open, and a beautiful woman I didn't know met my stare.

"Oh, I'm sorry," – she raised a perfectly manicured chocolate brown hand to her smooth throat – "You scared me." Her white dress shone against her darker skin, and her long smooth hair glistened like an onyx.

The keys clenched in my hands; my knuckles turned white; and I narrowed my eyes. "I'm sorry, but who are you?"

Peter appeared behind the woman's shoulder. His eyes darted

between the two of us. "This is Sheila. She's an associate at the hospital. We were studying for exams." His words tumbled out in a stream, and I ground my teeth together.

"Nice to meet you, Sheila." I pasted a smile on my face and stuck out a hand, which Sheila cautiously shook back. "Now, if you're done studying, I'd like to spend the evening with my boyfriend."

Sheila's eyes flashed, hardening at the implication. "Of course, I'll see you tomorrow," she said to Peter, laying a hand on his chest. Then she glided past me, sashaying her hips as she left and leaving a floral scent in her wake.

I stepped over the threshold and slammed the door behind me. Ice flooded my body, and my nostrils flared. "Are you cheating on me?"

Peter crossed his arms across his chest and leaned back. "Nice to see you too; no, I am not cheating on you. She really was here to study with me, but could you blame me? You can't even look at me, much less let me touch you."

My jaw dropped as heat flared all over my body. "Are you kidding me? You forced me to kill our child. You have no idea of the guilt that I face every day. The thought of you touching me just brings back the memory, and what if we got pregnant again? Would you encourage me to have another abortion?"

He threw his hands in the air. "That's not fair."

"Fair?" I screamed, my voice rising in pitch. "Was it fair that you made me go to the clinic alone? Was it fair that I had our child cut out of me or that I'm haunted by dreams of him?"

Shock colored his face, and he crumpled to the floor, bringing a shaking hand to his mouth. "It was a boy?"

The rage burning inside fizzled at his reaction, but my body remained steadfast, and I crossed my arms, "I think so. Every time I see him in my dreams, he's wearing blue."

He ran his hand across his face and turned hollow eyes up at me.

"We would have had a son?"

My eyes narrowed, "Are you saying it would have been okay if it were our daughter?"

He blinked, "What? No, I guess, I just . . . What did we do?" He dropped his head in his hands, and compassion flowed over me. Maybe he was finally feeling a small portion of what I had been battling.

I crossed and sat down beside him. "We did the unthinkable." I rubbed my arms, but no comforting words flowed from my mouth. He reached for my hand and squeezed it. I leaned into him, hoping that this time it would be different, that this time the nausea wouldn't rear its ugly head, that maybe we could move on, but as soon as his arm went around me, the familiar churning began. I swallowed the sensation as long as I could, but as the turmoil grew, the need to detach myself won out. "I need to change clothes." I stood and rushed into the bedroom.

As soon as I closed the bedroom door, I leaned my head against it and swallowed repeatedly. The sickness began to subside as I breathed evenly. Pushing myself off the door, I crossed to the nightstand and uncapped the bottle. A sip of the fiery nectar sated the nausea. Another cooled it completely. A third created the welcoming fog, and the sensation slowly faded away. I smiled. *That wasn't too bad; I just needed a few sips, and, surely with time, it will get easier.*

After changing into comfy clothes, I rejoined Peter in the living room. He smiled and opened up his arm to cuddle on the couch. Forcing a smile in return, I swallowed and sat down beside him. He pulled me close, wrapping his arm around my shoulder. The alcohol helped me relax for a while, but when Peter's hand caressed my shoulder, the nausea ignited, and when he cupped my chin to kiss me, it enflamed. Putting my hands on his chest, I pushed back with tears in my eyes. "I'm sorry," I said and hurried back into the safety of the bedroom. As I crawled under the covers and curled into a ball, the flame sputtered and died out. A solitary tear rolled down my cheek.

Sometime later a knock sounded at the door. “Sandra? Can I come in?” I crawled out of bed and opened the door for him. Shoulders slumped, Peter stood on the other side. He flashed a weak smile. “I can’t do this anymore, Sandra.” My eyes blurred with tears, but I nodded. He was right. It had been weeks, and I still couldn’t forgive him or myself. I stared down at my hands and then up at him.

“Where will you go?” As much as I hated him for pressuring me into the abortion, a part of me still loved him.

“Liam’s offered to let me move in with him for a while until I decide where I want to go.” He scratched his fingernail against his pants as if scraping off a crumb. When he met my eyes, tears glistened in his as well, “I wish it could have been different,” he whispered.

I bit the inside of my lip to stop the flow of tears, “Me too.” He reached out and squeezed my hand, and then he brushed past me and walked to the bedroom. I decided to give him some space and wandered into the hallway and then into the guest room. The canvases I had painted before the procedure silently accused me of never coming back to them. No desire to paint surfaced, so I packed up the paints, put the canvases and easel back in the closet, and shut the door.

After leaving the guest room, I wandered into the kitchen to busy myself with the dishes. The sound of Peter packing in the bedroom reached my ears, and I sighed as the melancholy filled me. I had been so sure that Peter and I would marry; we had always been so good together. The memory of the first day we met popped into my mind.

We had been waiting for the same drink at a local coffee shop, and when the barista called the order we both reached for the cup. “Sorry,” our voices said in unison. He let go, giving me the first drink, which I took to a nearby table. A few minutes later he sat down beside me. “Can I join you?” His smile had caused my heart to stutter, and I had nodded. As we drank our coffees, we discovered we were working at the same hospital. Peter was interning to be a resident, and I was just starting the nursing program. It had been love at first sight for both of us. We exchanged numbers and went out the very next night. We'd been almost inseparable since then, until now.

I guess there are some things you can't get through together. I washed the lipstick off the last glass, and ire flared briefly again. It wasn't my shade, but what did it matter? He was free to date Sheila or whomever he pleased now. After placing the dishes in the blue rack to dry and wiping my hands on the checkered towels, I wandered back to the bedroom to check on Peter.

He stood in the closet doorway, surveying the holdings. At the sound of my footsteps, he turned to face me, the Hockey jersey I had given him last Christmas in his hands. Defeat weighed down his shoulders. He folded the jersey and placed it on top of his other clothes in his large black suitcase. After zipping it up, he turned downhearted eyes on me. "I'm really sorry," he sighed, "If I had known, I would never have pressed for an abortion. Maybe we could have done it, found the time I mean, to raise a baby."

I knew he was trying to apologize, but his words cut like a knife and only deepened my regret in killing our child. *Why couldn't you have given the thought a chance before I ended our child's life?* A lump formed in my throat, and I clenched my hands at my side. He was waiting for me to say something, but the words wouldn't come. All I could do was nod.

Sighing, he picked up his suitcase and walked past me, out the bedroom door. Rooted to the spot, I listened for the click of the front door; only then did my body release my feet. I sank to the floor and wrapped my arms around my knees. The beige carpet swam like a muddy sea before me. Silence descended, and I let the grief wash over

me in waves. Then I spied the remaining bottle, a life raft, under the bed and grabbed it. After unscrewing the cap, I took a long sip and allowed the fire burn my pain away.

6

I expected the next few weeks to be hard, but a relief descended in not having to see Peter. Peter was gone, my car was gone; almost nothing remained to remind me of the "procedure" months ago, and I felt like I was slowly beginning to heal. The phantom crying hadn't returned, and the liquid nectar at night kept the dreams mostly at bay or at least kept me from remembering them.

"Let's go get some drinks tonight," Raquel suggested as we finished the day. I grabbed my purse from the locker and shut the door. The sound of liquor excited me, even though the thought of dressing up and hanging around strangers held no appeal. I agreed only because it had been some time since we had gone out.

When I got home, I peeled my clothes off and rummaged in my closet. Though not looking for romance, I deserved a little dressing up, so I pulled on a simple black dress and applied a little makeup before heading back out to meet Raquel at a nearby bar.

The full parking lot forced me to park further from the door than I would have liked, and I swallowed my apprehension as I hurried past the few people lounging in the lot. Something about the bar crowd at night always rattled my nerves. Raquel stood waiting for me at the front entrance in a sparkly white dress.

"Well, I feel underdressed," I said looking down at my dark dress.

"Nah, you're good. It's nice to see you looking better," Raquel said as we flashed our IDs and entered.

I smiled. "It's nice to be feeling better." We maneuvered through the smoky crowd up to the bar. Then my heart froze, and my feet melted into the floor. Peter sat at the bar with his arm around Sheila. Her hand lay on his thigh, and their heads were just inches apart. I shouldn't have been surprised; I had seen the way he had gazed at her that day and the glass with the lipstick, but a part of me had hoped it wasn't true.

"Sandra," Raquel tugged on my arm and then stopped. She turned to me, face as white as a sheet. "Let's just go somewhere else."

"No, it's fine," I shook my head. "I just wasn't expecting it is all."

Peter looked up at that moment, and his eyes grew wide. His arm slipped off Sheila as a red flush crawled across his face. Noticing his change in demeanor, Sheila turned. As she saw me, a malicious smile spread across her features.

"Look just order, and I'll go find us a seat," I said to Raquel, forcing my feet to move and heading further back to an empty booth. I brushed the crumbs off the table and sat down on the wine colored pad. I wasn't really angry at Peter, more confused. How long had he been cheating on me then? I shook my head. It didn't matter; we would never have made it.

Raquel plopped a large Pina colada down in front of me. "I'm so sorry. I had no idea he'd be here."

I peered up at her. "Did you know he was with her?"

She bit her lip and dropped her eyes, turning her glass in a slow circle on the table top. "I'd heard some rumors today, but I didn't see how telling you would make you feel any better."

I nodded my head and picked up the drink. "It doesn't matter. Here's to a girls' night out." I tipped the drink back, downing half of it. Raquel raised her eyebrow at me, but followed suit. One drink turned into two, and then a couple of handsome men bought our third and fourth drinks. Raquel's eyes began to glass over. "Come on, let's go home," I said, taking her arm.

"What? No, the fun is just getting started," she slurred.

"Not for you. You've had too much." I pulled her toward the door, but she shook my hand off her arm.

"No, you're just no fun anymore. Ever since you . . ." I slapped my hand over her mouth to keep the condemning words from escaping. Rage burned inside me.

"Don't say another word," I hissed. "I am trying to keep you from doing something you'll regret."

She pulled my hand from her mouth, her eyes afire. "I didn't regret mine, remember?" she whispered, and that was all it took. Rage erupted inside.

"Fine, do what you want." I turned around and stormed out of the bar, my cheeks flaming. As I walked to the car, the cool night air chilled my anger, and I realized she was right. I didn't do anything fun anymore. I went to work, and then I went home. I rarely ever left the house for any other reason. This was the first time I had been out in ages. As I climbed into my car, I decided I would go out more. If Peter was moving on, maybe I could too, as long as it was with someone else.

Back at my apartment, I climbed into bed and closed my eyes, only to open them minutes later to the sound of cries again. A baby boy about six months old was lying next to me in the bed. He reached out a hand and smiled, and I reached for him. My arms had always fallen short before, but this time I was able to hold him. I wanted to hate him for the guilt he brought; I knew I'd done a terrible thing, but maybe he was coming to see me for a reason. Maybe relief existed in acceptance.

Tears flowed down my cheeks as I studied his perfect features. Warm brown eyes peered at me from his chocolate skin, and his toothless smile began to mend my broken heart. The baby cooed, but all the words sounded eerily like mama. My breath caught at the words, and then tears streamed down the baby's cheeks. There was no cry, just the echo of mama as the tears tumbled down. I pressed the baby to my chest to comfort him. Somehow, I would tell him how sorry I was, and then my arms were empty. I stared at my hands, nothing; the bed next to me, empty. Tears fell down my cheeks as well; my baby was gone; Peter was gone; and I had nothing but dreams to look forward to.

I woke up the next morning determined to be different. I still ached over what I'd done, but being able to hold the baby had somehow allowed me to accept some of the consequences of my decision. I knew I couldn't go back, though I wished I had made a different decision, but I could enjoy the dreams of the baby whenever he came. It might hurt my heart, but it would also be the connection to the child I had lost, and somehow I would make sure he knew how sorry I was.

Raquel was waiting for me when I arrived in the locker room at work to clock in. She rushed to me, chagrin all over her face. "I am so sorry," she gushed. "I'd had way too much to drink. I didn't mean what I said."

"Stop," I held my hand up, and she paused, pursing her lips together. "You were a jerk last night, but you were right. I haven't been any fun lately, and I'm sorry."

"Really?" Raquel squeaked.

"Really," I nodded. "I've decided I need to try and get on with my life."

"How much so? I mean are you willing to try dating?"

I raised my eyebrow at her and crossed to my locker to load my personal items for the day.

"Hear me out. Philip has a single friend who's very nice. Just come on a double date with us and see." Philip was the chiropractor that Raquel had been dating for a few months. I had to give him credit; he'd lasted longer than most of Raquel's flavors of the month.

I closed the locker and turned around, "Okay."

Raquel shook her head and smiled, "I'm not taking no for an answer. Wait, did you say okay?"

I returned the smile and shrugged. "I said okay." She enveloped me in a giant hug, squealing in my ear. "Alright, alright," I said pushing her off. "You're excited, I get it."

"You have no idea," she said. "Tonight, my place, seven pm."

I agreed and headed to the front desk for my assignment. Thankfully I wasn't in pediatrics or labor and delivery today. Those proved the hardest rotations for me. The day flew by uneventfully and before I knew it, I was standing in my closet trying to decide what to wear on a blind date.

I hadn't been on a date in years. Peter and I had been together for three years, and we had met at a coffee shop. With no idea what this guy even looked like, I pulled a simple blue dress off the hanger and shimmied into it. After applying some lip gloss and pulling my hair up, I decided I looked good enough.

As I pulled into Raquel's apartment parking lot, butterflies began to swarm in my stomach. What if this man nauseated me like Peter had? *Maybe I can return home and pretend I forgot. No, Raquel would never believe that, and she'd never stop nagging me.* Sighing, I parked the car, grabbed my purse, and smoothed my dress before walking up to Raquel's door.

The door swung open just as my hand hit the wood. "You made it," she smiled. "I was afraid you were going to flake on me."

I gazed down at my feet as a blush spread across my face, "I thought about it."

Raquel laughed and pulled me inside, "Well, I'm glad you didn't. Come on in; Philip just called to say he and his friend were on their way. Do you want some wine?"

Relief flooded my body; it wasn't my normal drink anymore, but surely the alcohol would work the same. "Yes, a tall glass; lead the way." I shut the door behind me and followed Raquel into her immaculate kitchen.

Raquel's father owned several hospitals in the area, and Raquel had never been wanting for money. The marble countertops had probably been cleaned by a maid just that day. I ran my hand across the tan, speckled surface, wishing I had the money Raquel did. Maybe if I'd had the money, I wouldn't have had the abortion. I shook my head to clear the thought as soon as it emerged; I'd never get through this date if I kept thinking about that. A wine glass filled with red liquid appeared before me, and I tipped back the glass. The comforting fire didn't accompany this liquid, but it still seemed to infuse me with courage.

"Woah, try not to get drunk before dinner," Raquel laughed. "Since when did you get so good at holding your liquor anyway?"

My face flushed as I surveyed the now half-empty glass. "Sorry, I guess I'm just nervous." Inside, my heart sped up. *Would Raquel buy that? I'll have to be more careful.* I picked the glass up again for a dainty sip, and a knock sounded at the door.

"Ooh, they're here," Raquel squealed. "Do I look okay?"

I smiled as Raquel bounced on her toes. Her black dress hugged her figure and set off her pale skin and green eyes even more than normal. "You look radiant."

I placed my glass on the countertop and followed Raquel to the door. As the door swung open, my breath caught in my throat. Standing beside Philip was the man from 2B who had helped me the day of my mini-breakdown. What was his name? All I could remember was that it started with an H. Would he remember the breakdown? My throat constricted at the thought.

"Hey baby," Philip said, embracing Raquel and planting a kiss on her lips before turning to his friend. Philip was just as immaculate as Raquel. His perfectly combed dark brown hair completed his rugged good looks, and his button down shirt and chinos appeared freshly pressed. "This is Henry; Henry, my girlfriend Raquel."

Henry stuck out his hand, but his eyes focused on me. My heart thudded loudly in my chest, and I brought a hand up to cover the noise. "Pleased to meet you ma'am." Raquel tossed a conspiratorial wink at me before smiling and returning the handshake.

"Please come in," she said. "This is my friend Sandra."

Henry crossed the threshold, and my heart froze. Would he tell them he knew me or how we met? His smile widened, and my heart began to melt. Somehow, it comforted me.

He stuck out his hand as if we'd never met, "Pleased to meet you, Sandra." His brown eyes twinkled, putting the ball in my court. I could play along or tell them the truth; he had given me the choice.

I swallowed as my mind weighed each option. I didn't enjoy lying to my friend, but she didn't know about my drinking either, so I guess I'd already been lying to her, and telling them about my mental breakdown before dinner certainly held no appeal. Besides, Henry was being very nice to let me save face. I took his hand and returned the smile. "It's nice to meet you, too."

"Okay, small talk over," Philip broke in. "We have reservations, so we better get going."

"Thank you," I whispered to Henry as we followed Raquel and Philip out of the apartment. He smiled and nodded and then held out his arm in a lead-the-way gesture.

We all piled into Philip's red BMW to make the trek to the restaurant. Raquel and Philip caught up on their day in the front seat, which gave me the chance to speak quietly to Henry in the back. "Why didn't you say you knew me?"

He smiled. "I'm going to guess that wasn't a good day for you, and probably not a usual one. Why would I call attention to a time that was obviously hard for you?"

Those days were more regular than I would have liked, but I smiled and nodded. There was something about Henry. I observed his open face, trying to figure out what made him seem so different. He was handsome, but not model handsome. In fact, one eye looked a little larger than the other. His teeth weren't perfectly straight, but that didn't affect his warm smile. His suit was nice, but didn't appear overly expensive; it made me wonder how he and Philip were even friends. Of course, I felt the same way about Raquel and myself sometimes, but we had been friends since meeting in college.

As we pulled into the restaurant's parking lot, Henry touched my arm, "Please wait here and let me get your door." I raised an eyebrow at him, but did as he asked. When the car parked, he got out first and then came around to my side of the car, opened the door, and held out a hand to help me up. I smiled as I took his hand. How long had it been since a man had held a door open for me? It seemed to happen less and less as feminism grew and women demanded equal treatment. While I agreed women should get paid the same if they did the same job, I did miss the chivalrous gestures that men used to do.

We walked into the upscale restaurant and Philip relayed his name to the hostess, who sat us immediately. A white cloth covered the table, and a candle centerpiece emitted a romantic glow in the dim restaurant. I reached for my chair, but Henry beat me to it and pulled the chair back for me. I flashed him another smile before sitting down. Then he pushed my chair in before taking his own seat. Raquel raised an eyebrow at me, but I just shrugged in response.

The delicate paper menu held only a few choices, and my eyes widened at the prices. I should have thought to ask where we were going before I agreed. I didn't have the money to spend so much on dinner, especially since Peter had moved out, and money was much tighter. My heart thudded in my chest as I quickly scanned for the cheapest item on the menu; even the side salad was nearly fifteen dollars. *How do people afford this? Well, the salad comes with bread and a bowl of soup, so at least it should be enough to fill me up.*

The waiter, clad in a white dress shirt and perfectly pressed black pants, appeared just as I laid the menu down. "Have we had enough time?" he asked politely, glancing at each of us before focusing his attention on Philip, who took the lead in ordering.

"Yes, we'll have two glasses of your finest red wine and two plates of the steak and lobster, grilled medium well." He handed his and Raquel's menus to the waiter.

"Very well," the waiter nodded and turned his attention to me.

I swallowed, "Um, I'll have the side salad and the tomato soup."

The waiter cocked his head, "Will that be all miss?"

My face flushed, and just as I was about to answer, Henry jumped in. "Yes, and the same for me please." He handed our menus to the waiter.

The waiter nodded, "Yes, sir, and anything further to drink?"

Henry glanced quickly at me; I shook my head slightly. "No, water will be adequate for now, thank you."

As the waiter turned away, I regarded Henry. Who was this man, and why was he being so nice to me? He caught me staring and shot me a small wink as he picked up a piece of bread.

"So, Henry, what do you do?" Raquel asked, nibbling her own piece of bread.

"I'm in sales," he said. "Not glamorous, and I don't save lives like you all, but I do get to meet some interesting people."

"Was that how you met Philip?" I grabbed a piece of bread for myself.

Philip laughed, "No, we actually met at the gym. It turns out, we both like racquetball."

"Well, I need to freshen up," Raquel said pushing back her chair. Immediately Henry pushed back his chair and stood. Raquel and I both gawked at him. "Um, Sandra, will you come with me?" she stammered. I nodded, but before I could push back my chair, Henry was pulling it out for me. I smiled up at him and then followed Raquel to the bathroom.

As soon as the door closed behind us, Raquel whirled to face me. "He seems nice, right? I mean a little odd with the standing thing just now, but nice, don't you think?"

I smiled at her, "Actually, yeah he does, and the standing thing just now was him being chivalrous. At military balls, all the men at the table stand anytime a woman gets up from the table. It's a sign of respect."

Her eyebrows knitted together, "Really? How do you know that?"

"My dad was in the military. He always told me growing up how a man should treat a lady and being chivalrous was one of his big points. I've never actually met a man who does it outside the military though, but it kind of makes me feel special." Warmth flooded my body at that realization.

Raquel turned to the mirror and pulled out her lipstick. "I wish Philip would do that for me, or even open my car door like Henry did for you. Maybe not every time, but once in a while would be nice."

I nodded absently. This new feeling of appreciation and lack of nausea distracted me. Could I be developing feelings for this man or was I just reacting to the kindness he had shown tonight? I sat down on the plush red couch and then peered around as the realization that a couch resided in the bathroom sunk in. Above me, an elegant chandelier hung from the ceiling. The counter gleamed with white marble, and the walls were painted gold. White tile shone on the floor, and even the stall doors were white with gold trim. This restaurant bathroom was nicer than any I had ever seen.

Raquel finished touching up her makeup, and we returned to the table. Henry stood as we approached and again helped me with my chair. Our soup and salads arrived a moment later, and everyone reached for a fork, except Henry. Out of the corner of my eye, I noticed his hands folded on the table, his eyes closed, and his head bowed. Realizing he was praying, I put my own hands down and waited for him to finish. It seemed the respectful thing to do and a small way to say thank you for his kindness to me. Only when he picked up his fork did I follow suit.

As we finished the appetizer, Philip and Raquel's meals arrived. I tried hard not to stare at the beautiful plate, but the tantalizing smells of meat tickled my nose, and though I was no longer truly hungry, my stomach complained a little that it wasn't getting the delicious food accompanying the aroma. Henry and I each took another slice of bread and smiled at each other. Had he ordered the same to be nice or was he short on cash like I was?

The talk turned to Philip's practice and the crazy stories from the hospital while Raquel and Philip finished their dinner. Henry and I listened in a companionable silence.

Then the waiter returned. "How was everything?"

"It was very good," Philip spoke up before the rest of us could say a word.

"Wonderful, now there is no rush, but how would you like to handle the bill sir?" His eyes jumped from one person to the next. I blanched and swallowed.

"I'll take ours," Philip said, pointing to himself and Raquel.

"And I'll take ours," Henry jumped in. I shot him a relieved smile. A few minutes later the men paid the tab, and we headed back to Philip's car. Though still early fall, a chill had descended while we dined in the restaurant, and I shivered as it breeched my skin.

"I have a coat in the car," Henry whispered.

"I'm fine, really," I smiled up at him even as I hugged my arms tighter around myself. Little goose bumps popped out on my arms.

When we reached the car, he opened my door before climbing in his own side. He passed his brown leather jacket to me, and I smiled gratefully, pulling the jacket up to my neck. The smell of leather and sandalwood tickled my nose, and I inhaled deeply. I missed the masculinity.

During the quiet ride back, I stole subtle glances at Henry. He seemed so nice; could he be genuine? And even if he was, could I handle male companionship again? Before I could completely sort that thought out, we arrived back at Raquel's apartment.

"I'd love to stay babe, but I have an early day tomorrow," Philip said, giving Raquel a quick kiss. She sighed up at him, but relented and crawled out of the car. Henry followed suit and then opened my door.

"It was a pleasure to meet you," Henry executed a little bow at Raquel and then at me. "I sure hope we can meet again." His eyes stared directly into mine.

Heat crawled across my face, "I'd like that." Henry climbed into the passenger side of Philip's car. As the men drove off, I realized I still had his jacket in my arms. A little smile tugged at my lips at the thought that I'd have to see him again to return his jacket.

"So do you think you'll see him again," Raquel teased.

"Maybe," I smiled, "I think I'd kind of like to."

I hugged her goodnight and returned to my own car. My heart fluttered as I replayed the night in my mind on the drive back.

As I entered my apartment, I hung Henry's jacket on the coat rack by the front door and smiled as I changed for bed that night. It wasn't until I was in bed with my eyes closed that I realized I hadn't taken a comfort sip from my stash.

7

Understanding A Loving God

The sunlight filtering in the window woke me the next morning. I yawned and stretched, realizing I had actually had a decent night's sleep. No dreams, no crying baby, just silence. Blessed silence. Better still, I felt no burning need for a drink this morning.

Smiling, I rolled out bed, dressed, and shuffled into the kitchen to make a cup of coffee. On my way, I passed the brown leather jacket, and my heart warmed. Something about Henry was definitely affecting me, and I couldn't wait to find out what it was.

As I was putting the grounds in the coffee maker, a knock sounded at the door. I glanced at my watch, *who could that be? It's only 9 am.* After pushing the button on the coffee maker, I crossed to the front door.

No one was visible through the peephole, so I turned the lock and opened the door cautiously. A bouquet of beautiful flowers lay on the stoop. I poked my head out as I retrieved the flowers, looking quickly left and right, but no one was to be seen. Whoever had dropped them had disappeared without a trace. I brought the flowers inside and shut the door.

In the kitchen, I pulled down a vase from the top brown cupboard. After filling it with water, I unwrapped the flowers, placing them inside. A small white envelope poked out from the top of the pink carnations and white daisies. Plucking the envelope, I opened it up. A handwritten note stared back at me:

Thank you for a wonderful dinner last night. I hope to see more of you. –Henry

Would his charm never cease? I tried to remember the last time Peter had brought me flowers. Maybe our first Valentine's Day together over three years ago? Yes, there had been a bouquet of roses that day. Once we had started dating seriously though, his practicality had kicked in; flowers no longer made any sense because they just died, so he had bought books or clothes. One Christmas he had even bought a vacuum cleaner. That had not gone over well. I missed the flowers.

The coffee finished brewing, and I poured myself a mug, bringing it and the vase to my small kitchen table. As I admired the flowers, I thought back to the previous night. There must be something wrong with Henry; he was too nice, too charming to still be single. Though interested, I'd have to keep an eye out for whatever his fault was. I finished my coffee, a smile still on my face, before dressing for work.

I arrived at work just a few minutes before shift; Raquel stood in front of her locker, already dressed in her scrubs.

"Well, you look happy," she said closing the door.

"I do?" I tilted my head and smiled. "Well it might have to do with the fact that I received flowers on my doorstep this morning."

Raquel's eyes lit up, and she clapped her hands together. "Ooh do tell."

I laughed, "Not much to tell yet. I was making coffee, and I heard a knock at my door. When I opened it, a bouquet of pink carnations and white daisies lay on my doorstep. A card from Henry said he had a nice time and he hoped to get together again soon."

"He likes you," Raquel teased, "I knew he did. You could tell just from the way he looked at you."

A blush colored my face. "It's still early; I think he was just being nice."

Raquel raised an eyebrow. "Uh huh, sure nice. I don't think Philip has even bought me flowers yet."

"What? That's terrible."

"Eh, he's handsome and rich, so flowers aren't that big of a deal." Raquel flicked her hand in dismissal. "Oh, we better get going," she said, glancing at her watch.

I finished shoving my purse inside and closed my locker door. As I followed Raquel out, I couldn't help wondering if money was really more important to her than simple gestures?

When I returned to the apartment that evening, Henry's brown leather jacket greeted me at the door. Though I enjoyed having it in my apartment, he probably wanted it back. My watch showed 7 pm, surely it would be okay to bring it back to him now. After approving my reflection in the mirror, I grabbed the jacket, locked the door, and headed the few doors down to 2B.

As I stood outside his door, my stomach knotted. *Will he consider me too bold coming over here? Surely not; he sent me flowers after all.* I wiped my sweaty palm on my pants, took a deep breath, and then brought my knuckles down on his door. Waiting, I held my breath until the click of the lock sounded. The door swung inward, and Henry smiled from the other side. His blue shirt complemented his skin tone and hugged his muscular arms.

I swallowed, forcing my eyes to his face. "Here," – I pushed the jacket out to him – "I didn't mean to keep this last night."

His eyes danced back and forth, and a smile tugged at his lips as he reached for the jacket. "Thank you; I know you didn't. Would you like to come in for some tea?"

I bit my lip. I did want to come in; I wanted to know more about him, but should I go in? Even while the mental battle raged, I found my head nodding and my feet stepping forward.

His apartment was similar in layout to my own; we entered the living room first, which was decorated much more masculine in browns and blues. A kitchen was off to the right, and a hallway led out of the living room to the bathrooms and bedrooms. He was obviously neat as everything was in a place, but he was no minimalist. Three bookcases sat about the room, each teeming with books. A brown coffee table sat in the middle of the room and held a thick black book, a notebook, and a pen.

"Have a seat," he said, pointing to his tan couch. "I'll get the water going." As he crossed to the kitchen, I sat on the couch, taking the room in. A few nature paintings hung along the walls, but the most prominent art was a small wooden cross hanging over one of the bookcases. I don't know why it commanded my attention in the room; it wasn't even ornate, but I found my eyes drawn to it.

The sound of running water finally pulled my attention away from the wooden figure, and I glanced down to the coffee table and picked up the thick black book: The Holy Bible. I sighed, I should have known from him praying at dinner. Maybe this was why he was still single; he was one of those crazy religious nuts. Quickly glancing over my shoulder, I opened the book. I'd never really examined a Bible before, and the thinness of the pages surprised me, but not as much as the markings in the book. Yellow highlighter sprinkled across many verses and handwriting covered the blank spaces. I touched the thin paper; I'd never written in a book, and he had filled nearly every blank space.

"Do you read the Bible?"

I jumped at his voice over my shoulder and slammed the book shut. "I'm sorry," I mumbled, looking up at him, "I should have asked first. I was just curious."

He smiled. "I have nothing to hide in that book. You are welcome to look through it any time." The tea kettle whistled, and he turned back to the kitchen. A cupboard opened and dishes clanked. I opened the book again. I didn't know much about the Bible, but like the wooden cross, I felt an odd pull to the pages. My finger ran down the words and tingled. I wasn't even reading them, just skimming, but something felt different than other books.

"I was studying John," he said, sitting beside me and placing a tea cup on the coffee table for me. Steam curled above the brown mug. "Do you read the Bible?" he repeated.

I peered up at him. "I don't think I ever have. I mean I've never had a Bible so unless I read part of it somewhere else, I guess I haven't."

"Ah, well it's comprised of lots of books written by men inspired by God. John is one of the books that tells about Jesus coming down to earth to die for the sins of the world. Have you heard of Jesus?"

"A little, I think." I grasped the mug and let the warmth travel up my arms. "Wasn't he a nice person who did good deeds a long time ago?"

Henry nodded, "He was that, but also much more. He was perfect and sinless, and he performed miracles when he was on earth before he was killed. But there was something different about him. He rose from the dead after being crucified and ascended back into heaven three days later."

My head dropped forward, and I stared at him not sure I'd heard correctly. Alarm bells sounded in my head as my eyebrow shot up,

"You think he came back from the dead?"

"No," Henry shook his head and smiled, "I know he did. You see the Bible is God's word to us. It is a map of what happened and of what will happen. It tells me that Jesus died and rose from the dead three days later."

"Why did he have to die?" I took a sip of my tea and peeked at him, trying to decide if he was delusional. The story seemed crazy, but also a little interesting.

"Well, God used to allow sacrificial lambs to cover the sins of his people, but he knew that humans aren't perfect, and he wanted to offer a sacrifice that would last forever. He sent his son, Jesus, to be a sacrifice for all of us so that when we get to heaven, we will be able to stand clean in God's presence."

"So then everyone goes to heaven?"

Henry shook his head and studied his cup. His lips twisted to one side, and his voice took a more serious tone. "No, I'm afraid not. God gives everyone free will. He wants us all to go to heaven, but he also wants us to choose him, and sadly, not everyone will."

"Why would people not choose God?" I didn't know much about God, but it seemed if choosing him was the way to heaven, then it was an easy choice. I cocked my head and waited for his answer.

"Some people don't want to give up control of their lives. They want to be able to do what they want when they want. You see when you believe in God, then you also believe Jesus died for your sins, so you first have to believe you sin; many people don't. Then, Jesus told his disciples he was leaving them with the Holy Spirit when he returned to heaven. The Holy Spirit dwells within each believer, and therefore we should not want to do anything that would grieve the Holy Spirit. A lot of people don't like that part because they might have to give up something they love, like premarital sex or cursing or a multitude of other sins. Of course, God knows we aren't perfect and allows us to ask for forgiveness but Jesus said, 'Go and sin no more,' so we have to try and stop the sinning. What these people don't understand is that while they may have to give up some things on earth the eternity spent with God will be so much better than anything here. It makes the sacrifices worth it."

Henry's words stirred my excitement, until the mention of premarital sex. A weight descended on my shoulders, and I dropped my eyes to the mug cooling in my hands. I not only had practiced that, but had been living with my boyfriend and had eliminated a baby conceived in it. If premarital sex grieved God, how much more would killing my baby? He certainly would never allow someone like me into heaven.

"Sandra? Are you okay?"

Henry was staring at me. Biting my lip, I tried to come up with something to tell him. I certainly couldn't tell him about my past; he'd never like me if I did. My eyes darted to the large wooden cross and quickly away as I conjured up an excuse. "Yes, sorry, I just remembered that I have something important to do." I placed the cup back on the table and stood. His face pulled at my heart strings; I didn't want him to think I didn't like him, but the sobering thought had stirred the desire for a drink. Plus, I needed clarity to decide what to do about the new knowledge of Henry's character. "I'd love to chat together again, though," I offered in hopes of soothing the situation.

His eyes brightened, and he led the way to the door. "I'd really like that, too."

As I walked back to my apartment, I wondered if my terrible deed and Henry's religious outlook could ever co-mingle. I didn't know much about God, but Henry made him sound wonderful. With so many huge mistakes though, would God ever accept me? And would Henry if he knew how damaged I really was? Henry had said God sent

Jesus to die for our sins, but would he forgive my biggest sin? I didn't even know if God was what made Henry so different, but if it was, I wanted a taste of what he seemed to have.

After locking the door behind me, I headed straight for the bedroom like a missile. I needed the clarity and peace that only the bottle could supply lately. A satisfying swig soothed my ruffled nerves, but the questions continued swirling about in my head.

8

The Lies We Tell

Work consumed my next few days, not leaving much time to think about Henry or God's acceptance. I had just shrugged off my coat when a knock sounded at the door behind me. Glancing at my watch, I wondered who could be knocking on my door at seven at night. I turned around and opened the door to see Henry on my stoop looking boyish and nervous.

"I was wondering if you might feel up to a walk?" His hands were jammed in the pockets of his tan pants, and he rocked back and forth on his heels.

A warm sensation trickled over me. "I'd like that, but I just got home, and I haven't eaten." My hand covered my stomach. "I'm starving."

"There's a little cafe about three blocks from here," he suggested, "We could get our walk and dinner." He raised an eyebrow, and hope danced in his eyes.

I smiled, opening the door wider. "That sounds great. Come on in; I just want to change into something more comfortable."

As he entered the apartment, his eyes surveyed the room. "You can have a seat there if you'd like." I pointed at the couch. "I'll be right back." I dashed into the bedroom and ripped off my scrubs. Donning a pair of jeans and a peach shirt, I checked my makeup and breath and then slipped on some tennis shoes before heading back to the living room.

Henry rose from the couch as I entered. "You look nice in that color," he said. "Are you ready?"

"Yes, and thank you," I replied and followed him out the front door.

As we walked, he talked about his family back in Louisiana and his short stint in the Air Force, which was how he ended up in Texas. "I wanted to be a pilot, but after they found out I was color blind, they said it was a no go. I tried some of the different jobs involving planes, but my passion was flying, so after I served my four years, I got out."

"What made you stay here?" I asked.

"I liked San Antonia, where I had trained, so I figured I'd see what else Texas had to offer, and I found a job in Dallas and stayed."

"Do you miss your family?"

His eyes clouded over, and he turned his head away. A flatness colored his voice when he spoke. "I do, but I try to see them once a year or so."

I sensed a bigger story there but didn't press the issue. "I'm an only child. My parents live in Houston, but I couldn't handle the heat. It's terrible on your hair," I smiled. "When I had a chance to go to nursing school in Dallas, I jumped at it."

"Do you like nursing?" he asked.

"Yeah, I think so, for now anyway." As the words tumbled out of my mouth, I realized I didn't enjoy nursing as much as I had before the "procedure." I didn't deal with babies much or pregnant women for that matter, but the hospital itself held some kind of memory, and it just hadn't been the same. Plus, there was always the chance of running into Peter and Sheila.

We arrived at the quaint cafe then, and a waitress led us to a table. The cafe had an eclectic feel with brightly colored walls and healthy sandwiches. Large potted plants sat in the corners, and music played softly through the restaurant. The single sheet menus resided inside plastic casings, and after ordering, we engaged in more small talk.

When the food came, Henry once again prayed over it before he ate. I took the opportunity to really focus on him while his eyes were closed. He really was a handsome man, but even more than that was his demeanor. I wondered again if this God of his had something to do with that.

After dinner, we sauntered back to the apartments. The setting sun created a romantic painting of pinks and yellows in the sky, and Henry's hand found mine. My lips curled into a smile at the touch and the fact that no nausea accompanied it. I laced my fingers in his and enjoyed the warmth that traveled up my arm, enflaming my body. *I wonder if he'll kiss me goodnight. Would his kiss be soft or passionate?* My face flamed at the thought, and I turned my head to hide the color.

When we reached my door, I paused, giving him the opportunity. I tilted my head up and licked my lips. Henry's brow furrowed as if he wanted to say something, but wasn't sure what. His mouth opened, and then closed. He took a deep breath, and I closed my eyes, awaiting the sensation. "I know this might sound kind of strange, but I really feel like God is telling me to invite you to church on Sunday, so will you go with me?"

My eyes popped open, "I'm sorry, but what did you say?" Surely, I had misheard him. He couldn't want me to go to church with him, but then again, he didn't know my secret.

He cleared his throat and brought his other hand up so that he was holding my hand in both of his. "I'm asking you to go to church with me on Sunday. The service starts at 9:30, so I could pick you up at 9 am. It isn't far from here, and I'd really like you to see why God is so important to me. Will you come?"

His eyes pleaded with me, and my mind drew a blank on excuses. The only one I had, I couldn't tell him about. I blinked and nodded, unable to actually form the word yes on my lips. His eyes lit up as he squeezed my hand.

"Thank you again for accompanying me to dinner, and I'll see you soon." He dropped my hand and walked to his apartment. I stared after him, missing the warmth of his touch, but also a little in shock.

Unlocking my own door, I stumbled inside and locked it behind me before ambling numbly to my bedroom. *Why did I say yes? What if God strikes me down at the church door? Does he do things like that? Would everyone in church be able to see I didn't belong and my past sins?* The questions circled over and over like a hamster on a wheel as I changed into pajamas and brushed my teeth. Even after I climbed into bed, they plagued my mind, keeping sleep at bay.

At lunch the next day, I picked at my salad, contemplating what I could say to Henry to get out of church on Sunday but not scare him off. A metal dray dropped beside me, and I jumped. Raquel's bright green eyes met my gaze when I peered up.

"Guess what?" she squealed as she pulled out a chair and plunked down. "I'm getting married. Philip proposed last night." She held out her left hand where a large diamond ring adorned her fourth finger.

"Wow, isn't that kind of fast?" The words escaped before I could stop them, and I immediately felt bad when Raquel's face dropped.

"I'm sorry; I mean that's great."

Raquel tilted her nose up and away. Her feathers were definitely ruffled. "It may be fast, but when you know, you just know."

"You're right," I agreed, hoping to appease my friend. "Let me see it."

Raquel held her hand closer, and I oohed over the ostentatious ornament.

"Now, tell me how are things with Henry?" Raquel's voice lilted in a sing song manner, and she raised her eyebrows in a teasing gesture.

I sighed, *back to the question of the day*, "It was going great, and then he invited me to church."

Raquel shrugged and plucked a grape off her tray, popping it in her mouth, "So what? Go to church with him. It's probably not a serious thing. I know a lot of people who go to church on Sundays just to atone for their Saturdays if you get my drift." She nudged me with her elbow and winked.

"I don't know," – I shook my head, ignoring her insinuation – "God seems really important to him, but what if he hates me?"

"Who? Henry?"

"No, God."

Raquel leaned forward, her eyebrows arched. "Why would God hate you? You're amazing."

I bit my lip and lowered my voice, "Because of the 'procedure.'" I glanced around quickly, making sure no one had heard.

She sat back and picked up another grape, "Look, *if* there's a God, I'm sure he understands that you just did what was best for you. Isn't that what people always say, God wants the best for you?"

"I don't know if that's what they mean," I shook my head. I certainly was no expert on God, but that didn't sound like the same one Henry described.

"Well, I've been in a church since mine, and I am fine. I'm sure lots of other women have, too. Besides, Henry is worth it. He's a catch." She smiled and winked at me.

I nodded, letting Raquel's words sink in. They churned around in my stomach, but they carried a seed of confidence. Maybe I could go to church. Maybe it wouldn't be so bad.

When Sunday rolled around, I woke before the alarm clock. Doubt gnawed on my insides.

After showering, I stood in the closet, surveying the contents. What did people even wear to church? I'd only ever seen TV shows about it, and they always appeared dressy. I pulled on a simple peach dress and checked the mirror. Dressy but not overly, pretty but not too sexy. I swallowed the seed of fear that was steadily growing and entered the kitchen to start the coffee.

The rich aroma invigorated my senses, and I tapped my finger to the drip, drip, dripping. When the coffee pot finished, I sat down on the couch, with a steaming mug, trying to calm the nerves roiling in my stomach. At 9 am on the dot, a knock sounded at the door. Henry stood on the other side looking very dapper in a charcoal suit and blue shirt.

"You look very nice," he said and held out his hand.

I stared at his outstretched hand and ran my hands down the peach dress, smoothing out imaginary wrinkles. Swallowing the lump in my throat, I took his hand and shut the door, locking it behind me. He squeezed my hand as we began walking. The serenity he emitted traveled up my arm, and my heart returned to a normal rhythm. What was this calming presence he had?

"We're not driving?" I asked as we exited the parking lot on foot.

His smile stretched across his face. "Not when God made it so beautiful outside. It's not a long walk anyway." We continued in silence down the cracked sidewalk. Redbud trees lined the sides, and the sun warmed my skin. As I glanced down at our entwined fingers, images of

Henry and I together at other events flooded my mind. A smile tugged at my lips, and I bit the inside of my cheek to keep from grinning like a loon.

We turned the corner a few blocks down, and a white clapboard church came into view. A few trees dotted its yard, and a solitary cross sat atop its steeple. Groups of people milled outside chatting, and as we approached, a few waved at Henry. He returned the wave but didn't stop to chat. Relief flooded my body like a gently lapping wave. I didn't know these people from Adam, and I didn't want to try and have small talk as nervous as I was.

He led me into the small sanctuary where rows of pews with red velvet seats lined the left and right of an open center aisle. As I followed him to a pew on the right, in about the middle of the church, I gazed up at the beautiful stained glass windows that adorned the church. Each one depicted a different scene, but they made no sense to me. I'd have to remember to ask Henry about them later.

The velvet on the seats caressed the skin on my legs and clashed with the hardness of the wood meeting my back. On the back of the pew in front of us, a brown shelf held books.

"What are these?" I picked one up and began turning the pages. It was similar to the Bible, though not as big and with thicker pages.

He smiled. "Have you never been to a church before?"

I shook my head as I focused on the pages. Music bars stared back at me.

"That's a hymnal, so you can read the words if you aren't familiar with the songs, and that other book is the Bible in case you don't have your own."

I nodded and continued turning the pages as the church filled around us.

A few people came over and shook Henry's hand. He made introductions each time, and I would smile, but I wished people would stop coming over; I just wanted to listen to the service. Finally, a choir clad in black robes took the stage. One man stepped up to the mic.

"If you'll open your hymnal to page 584, you'll be able to follow along as we sing 'At the Old Rugged Cross.'"

I flipped the pages until I found the correct number. People began to stand all around me, including Henry, so I rose to my feet as well. I didn't know the song, but not wanting that fact to be obvious, I mouthed the words and enjoyed the deep sound of Henry's voice beside me.

The song was slow, but the words held a power. Different emotions played across people's faces: mostly joy, some sadness, and a few of indifference. I couldn't understand those people. I didn't even know what I was doing here, but I certainly felt a power. As the music shifted to a faster song, I gasped as people raised their hands and danced in the aisles.

"Do they always do that?" I whispered to Henry.

He smiled. "Only on the fast ones."

When the song ended, a black man in a light blue suit took the stage and began to preach.

I tried to listen to the words, though the "amen" from those around me were often distracting. I found myself turning to spot the shouter every time. I'd had no idea church was so lively. Church had always had the connotation of being formal and stiff.

As the preacher closed, the choir stood up and sang one last song before the service was over. When the music stopped, Henry stood, and I followed him out of the aisle and out the front entrance of the church. Again people waved, and Henry returned the waves and smiled, but he didn't stay to chat.

"What did you think?" Henry asked as we made our way back to the apartment complex.

I tilted my head and pursed my lips. "I think I liked it. I definitely enjoyed the music, and the sermon was nice, too."

His smile lit up his features. "I'm glad. Would you like to come again?"

As much as I had enjoyed the service, a small seed of doubt still remained. I squished the seed and returned the smile as a warmth enveloped me. "Yes, I think I would. Also, I think I'd like a Bible to read. Do you know where I could get one?"

"Any bookstore would have one for sale, but I bet the library at our apartment complex has one you could check out."

I sucked in my breath, hope bubbling inside, "Really? Will you go with me to check?"

The rather small apartment library consisted of two bookshelves in the corner of the main lobby. They held mostly trashy romance novels with a few classics sprinkled in, but at the very bottom of the first bookshelf, I struck gold. A black leather book with "The Holy Bible" embossed in gold down the spine called out to me.

"You were right," I said handing the book to him. He smiled as he ran his hand over the cover. I signed the book checkout log sheet, and we walked back to my apartment, the Bible tucked to my chest like a Christmas gift.

"I'd really like to take you to a movie," Henry said outside my apartment door. "Are you free Friday night?"

"I'll have to check my schedule, but I think I can make that happen."

After parting, I entered my apartment, Bible cradled against my chest, and sat down on the couch. I opened the book to the first chapter. Genesis 1:1 "In the beginning God created the heavens and the earth." *Hmm, that wasn't what I learned in school, but I always did have a problem buying the whole evolving from a monkey thing because monkeys are still around.* I continued reading.

"How was church?" Raquel asked as we ate lunch the following day.

I smiled as I pictured it again. "It was actually pretty fun. There was lots of music, and the message was good, too."

Raquel wrinkled her nose in distaste. "I can't imagine church being fun. I've gone a few times, and you're right; the music was good, but the sermon . . . ugh." She shook her head and then flicked her eyebrows up and down. "Philip and I spent the morning in bed, much more fun I think."

I chewed a bite of salad as I thought. "I don't know; the people I saw yesterday all seemed pretty happy. I started reading the Bible as well. Some of it is hard to understand, but it was fascinating."

Raquel's head dropped forward as her eyes widened. "You aren't going to go all religious on me, are you?"

A small laugh escaped my lips. I certainly didn't know enough to be considered religious, besides – the realization sunk in again – God probably wouldn't accept me anyway. "No, I guess not," I sighed.

"You say that like it's a bad thing." Raquel picked up her tray. "I think you're being smart. Get to know his interests, but don't get sucked into the crazy."

I nodded as I followed her out of the cafeteria, but it didn't seem all that crazy. In fact, it seemed rather nice.

When Friday evening rolled around, I sat in my apartment drumming my fingers on the couch arm and waiting for the knock on the door. I was really looking forward to spending the evening with Henry. Seeking the peace he seemed to have, I had been perusing the Bible nightly, but couldn't find the answers I sought. Perhaps tonight I would be brave enough to ask him about it.

At 6:45 on the nose, the knock sounded. The man was definitely punctual. I jumped up from the couch and smoothed my pale yellow dress. As I opened the door, I smiled at Henry on the other side dressed in khaki slacks and a light blue button down shirt, holding a red rose.

He bowed and held the flower out to me, “For you, pretty lady.”

My heart skipped a beat, and a blush heated my face. “Thank you.” Pulling the apartment door shut behind us, I followed him to his car.

“How was your week?” he asked after shutting my door and climbing in on the driver’s side.

“It was okay. Oh hey, did you hear Philip and Raquel are getting married?” His eyebrows furrowed as he started the car and pulled out. “What?” I pressed, “I thought you liked Philip.”

He sighed. “I do; it’s just he doesn’t seem like the marrying type.”

Concern bubbled up for my friend. “What do you mean?”

He shook his head. “Nothing, it’s just Raquel is the fifth girl he’s dated since I’ve known him, just over a year, but maybe she’s the one.”

I bit my lip and my own retort. As much as I loved Raquel, she was quite the player herself. I would just have to be extra vigilant to make sure she didn’t get hurt. The conversation stalled, and I mentally kicked myself, wishing I’d chosen a lighter topic so I could bring up my questions.

When we arrived at the theater, Henry purchased the tickets and held the door open for me as we stepped inside. We waited in line to get popcorn and drinks and then filed into the theater. I wanted to ask him about his peace, but the right words wouldn’t form.

He picked seats in the middle of the theater, and we munched on the popcorn as we waited for the movie to start. Warmth spread up my arm every time our fingertips touched. The lights dimmed as the movie began.

When the popcorn was finished, Henry set the bucket down and grasped my hand. The tingling warmth ran up my arm and spilled over onto the rest of my body. Though I tried not to react when the characters in the movie kissed, I couldn’t help wondering what kissing

Henry would be like, and I was glad the theater was dark because I knew every time the thought popped in my head that a red blush covered my face.

After the movie ended, we exited the theater still hand-in-hand. The outside warmth had gone away with the sun, and I shivered when the cool air hit my exposed skin. Henry wrapped his arm around me, pulling me close, and I smiled into his chest.

As we reached the car, his posture stiffened. Looking up to see the cause, I followed his gaze to a red BMW with fogged windows. "Isn't that Philip's car?" I asked. I knew nothing about cars, but his license plate 1CHIRO had stuck in my mind. Henry nodded, his lips pinched. "Should we go say hi?" I pressed, wondering at his silence.

He shook his head. "No, he looks busy."

I couldn't figure out why was he so upset by the sight. Had he never steamed up car windows? Henry opened my car door, but remained quiet on the drive back. When we returned to the apartment complex, he still seemed distracted.

"Is everything okay?" I asked.

He shook his head and smiled, but it didn't quite reach his eyes. "Yes, I'm sorry. I had a great time tonight."

"Me too." I placed my hands on his chest and tilted my head up to him. He took a deep breath and squeezed my arms.

"So, I'll see you Sunday for church?"

I blinked; I had been expecting a kiss. "Um, yes, I'd like that."

"Great, I'll see you then." He squeezed my arms again and then walked away.

"Okay," I said slowly to myself as I watched him walk back to his apartment. I shook my head and then entered my own apartment and changed for bed. As I lay in bed staring at the white ceiling, I realized I still hadn't asked him about his peace.

The ringing of the phone jolted me awake the next morning. Blinking my eyes, I glanced at the clock before grabbing my phone. 10 am? I rarely slept that late. "Hello?"

"Sandra? Were you still sleeping?" Raquel asked on the other end.

I rubbed my eyes and yawned. "Yeah, I guess I was tired from last night. I'm surprised you're awake; you were out later than I was."

"What are you talking about?" Raquel asked. "I stayed home last night and caught up on soaps."

Ice flooded my veins, and I was instantly awake. I pushed myself into a sitting position. "You weren't with Philip last night?"

"No, Philip's sister was in town, so he took her out," Raquel said. "Wait, why did you think I was out late last night?"

I swallowed and bit my lip. I'd really stepped in it this time; should I till Raquel the truth? I traced the seam on my bedspread. "Um, no reason. I just thought I saw Philip's car when we were leaving the theater, but I must have been mistaken."

There was a long pause and when Raquel's voice came across the phone again, it dripped deadly icicles. "What did you see?"

I cringed. "Um, we saw his car at the theater with the windows all fogged up. We thought it was you, or I did. Maybe that explains why Henry was acting so weird after," I trailed off, realizing the last part was more for my benefit than for Raquel's.

"I'm going to kill him," Raquel screamed into the phone. "I'll call you later." The phone went dead in my hand before I could even respond. Grimacing, I replaced the phone on the cradle and kicked off the covers. I would not want to be Philip today. Actually, Henry had some explaining to do as well.

After showering and dressing, I squared my shoulders and marched over to Henry's door. I rapped three times and leaned back, crossing my arms.

"Well, hello," he said with a smile as he opened the door.

"You knew, didn't you?" I poked my finger in his face.

He blinked and took a step back, "Knew what?"

"About Philip, last night, you knew he wasn't with Raquel, and that's why you acted so weird."

His face fell, and his shoulders slumped. "I wasn't sure. I thought I saw blond hair before the windows fogged up, but I wasn't completely sure, and I was hoping I was wrong. I wasn't though, was I?"

The sadness in his voice calmed my ire, and I unfolded my arms. "No, Raquel just called me and said she was at home last night because Philip was taking his sister out. I don't have a brother, but I doubt I'd be steaming up a car with him if I did."

"I'm so sorry." Henry gathered me into his arms. "I was hoping I was wrong about him, and that maybe Raquel was the one he would finally settle down with."

Tears filled my eyes as I raised them to meet his. "What can I say to Raquel? I feel so bad for her."

He brushed a tear from my cheek. "We can pray for her and for wisdom to know what to say," he said softly. His finger continued down my cheek to my lips and traced them. My breath caught in my throat, and my lips parted. *Please kiss me.* His eyes stared deep into mine, and as he lowered his head, I closed my eyes, savoring the soft velvety feel of his lips as they met mine. It lasted only a moment, but it left me breathless. "Come on," his voice was husky with emotion, "Let's go pray for Raquel."

I followed him inside and to the couch. He held my hands in his as we sat down. Then he closed his eyes and opened his mouth. "Lord, we bring our friend Raquel to you. We know she is hurting at this time, and we pray for peace for her. Though it's hard now, we pray for her to see the benefit in finding out before she married Philip. We also pray for the words to say to her. Help us be examples of you and show her your love as she grieves. Lord, I also want to thank you for bringing Sandra into my life. Please bless this relationship, and help us grow it in a way that would be pleasing to you. Amen." He opened his eyes and smiled at me. "I hope that last part was okay. It kind of just slipped out."

"It was perfect," I said.

Henry squeezed my hands and then leaned in to kiss me again. My heart skipped double time in my chest, and I wrapped my arms around his neck, pulling him closer. The familiar tingling ran down my spine, and my breath grew labored. Then he pulled back.

"What's the matter?" I asked, snapping my eyes open.

He ran a hand over his face and took a deep breath. "I just needed to take a break before we did something we might regret."

I regarded him, trying to decide if I was flattered or insulted, but he seemed genuine. His words about the Holy Spirit flew into my mind, and it made sense. "Oh right," I agreed. "Better to take it slow."

His face lit up. "I'm so glad you understand." Then he sighed, "I have to get to work anyway, but you'll still come to church tomorrow right?"

"Of course," I agreed, "I want to do some reading today anyway." Though my mind understood Henry's reluctance to go further, my body still fumed. A fire raged within. As I curled up on my couch and opened the Bible, the fire slowly simmered and died out. The words themselves had a calming effect, and I found myself relaxing into the story.

Raquel looked terrible when I entered work Monday morning. Her puffy red eyes competed with her splotchy face. Even her lustrous raven hair was piled lazily in a disheveled ponytail.

"I guess it wasn't good," I whispered to her as we filled out charts at the front desk.

"No, he denied it at first, but when I told him you guys saw his car, he fessed up. I guess he had been seeing his assistant, Tiffany," – her voice dripped with disdain as she said the other woman's name – "the whole time we were together. I really thought he was different." She sniffed and discreetly ran a hand across her eyes.

"You know I saw a lot of single men at Henry's church yesterday. Not that you would go there for that reason, but maybe they would treat you better. Henry seems to, at least."

She stiffened slightly and drew her shoulders back. "No offense, but I don't think that's my cup of tea."

I smiled. "I didn't either, but it's kind of growing on me."

"Heads up ladies," Nurse Hatchet roared behind us, "We've got a trauma coming in."

We dropped our charts and turned to the incoming door.

I sighed as I collapsed into bed that night. While I loved working in the ER, excessive traumas always wore me out. Today had been no different. A ten car pile-up on the Interstate had sent thirty or so people into the ER. There hadn't been time for a lunch or even a break, and I had scarfed down dinner when I finally got home before soaking in the tub.

Spying the Bible on the nightstand, I picked it up and began reading where I had left off. Though I still didn't think God would accept me, and I hadn't asked him to, I found peace in reading the Bible and discussing it with Henry.

The dreams had lessened, although I wasn't entirely sure if that was a good thing or a bad thing. Sometimes I missed seeing and holding the boy, even if he wasn't real.

Most evenings I spent with Henry, having dinner and discussing our respective days. I continued going to church with him and even made some new friends, but I still didn't feel "good enough" for God. Raquel started seeing another rich doctor, and was already sharing her apartment with him on weekends.

When the year anniversary of my "procedure" rolled around, my heart grew heavy again. The dreams returned with a vengeance, and though I thought I had accepted them, they began to take a toll on my concentration. I found myself turning to the bottle to sleep at night again, and every baby seemed to pull on my heartstrings.

"What's the matter?" Henry asked as we sat at dinner in a crowded restaurant.

My head popped up. "What do you mean? Why would something be the matter?"

He grasped my hand and stared into my eyes. "You've flinched at every cry from that baby over there, and you physically turned away when a toddler walked past you. Now, if you hate babies, we might need to have a talk because I really care for you, but I want children in my future."

My jaw dropped along with my heart. "Hate babies? I don't hate babies." *I just killed my own a year ago, but I can't tell you that.* What could I tell him though? I had to give him some reason; maybe a half truth? "It's just that," – I bit the inside of my lip as the words formed in my head – "It's just that I lost a baby a year ago." It wasn't the complete truth, but it was close.

His brow furrowed, and he sat back, letting go of my hand. "I don't understand. I didn't know you were married."

"I wasn't, but I was living with my boyfriend . . ." I trailed off as his face fell. Maybe this hadn't been a good idea. The memory of him saying premarital sex was a sin crashed into my brain. Was that why he hadn't made a move beyond kissing? "I'm sorry, is that a deal breaker for you?"

He took a deep breath and tapped his finger to his lips. My heart beat like a jackhammer. Please don't say yes repeated over and over in my mind. He opened his mouth and then closed it. Ba-bam, Ba-bam, the deafening sound pounded in my head. *Just say something.*

Finally, he leaned forward again. "It's not a deal breaker for me, but I'm a little disappointed. I always hoped that was something I could share for the first time with my wife on our wedding night."

My mind raced as I blinked repeatedly at him. *Does he mean to say he's a virgin*?

"You also have to know that I don't condone living with someone or being intimate outside of marriage, and I won't do that, but I do believe Jesus forgives, and it's not my place to judge your past. I am sorry about your baby, though."

I barely heard the words that fell out of his mouth. "I'm sorry; do you mean to tell me you've never been intimate with a previous girlfriend?"

Henry smiled. "No, I haven't. I'm saving myself for marriage because that's what Jesus would want me to do. You see God made marriage between one man and one woman. He never meant for us to be intimate with everyone we date. That's why the Bible says the man will leave his family and become one with his wife. God only meant for us to become one with one person."

I couldn't wrap my mind around a man who didn't crave sex. "But don't you want to? I mean haven't you in the past?" My face heated up at the scenario I was implying.

"Yes, my flesh has often wanted the intimacy both with you and with past relationships, but I have chosen not to give in to the flesh. You see when I accepted Jesus as my savior, and the Holy Spirit indwelled in me, I didn't want to do anything that would grieve him. I'm not perfect by any means, but I try my best to avoid temptation that would lead to sin. It keeps me from having to make hard choices I might regret later."

My breath caught at those words. Had he decoded my lie or was he just speaking in generalizations? Then the words sank in; I could have avoided that terrible choice if I had chosen the path that Henry had. Why hadn't I ever heard about saving myself? The TV shows always showed people being intimate, sometimes even on the first date, and even in school, we had discussed how sex was normal – if not expected – and we'd been handed birth control and condoms. We'd even spent a class period learning how to put them on bananas. But no one had ever said you didn't have to have sex. No one had said there was power and respect in waiting. Would I have listened if they had? Probably not, once the imprint of "do it; it feels good" was there, it would have been hard to listen to anything else, but I was listening now.

"I wish I had waited. What you're saying makes a lot of sense, and it would have saved me a lot of grief."

Henry squeezed my hand. "Whatever grief you are experiencing, God can help you overcome it, if you put your trust in Him."

"I want to," I began, "but I don't think he'd want someone like me." Tears welled up in my eyes, threatening to spill over. I blinked and wiped them away.

"Hey, God meets you where you are and changes you from there. You don't have to be perfect to meet Him."

I nodded, but I didn't really believe him. I wanted to, but it was such a terrible thing to have done. I just couldn't give it all away.

That night as I lay in bed, Henry's words ran through my mind again. Could God forgive even the sin of killing my own child? I wanted it to be true, but how could he? I had thrown away the gift he sent me.

I woke to the feeling of something on my face. Startled, I snapped my eyes open to see a toddler. His tiny hand touched my face again, and he smiled.

"Mama," he said and flashed a grin with only four teeth. He stood on the floor beside my bed, holding onto the side and bouncing up and down. "Mama," he said again and clapped his hands.

I tried to smile, even though a part of me knew he wasn't real. I had taken his life a year ago. He was so beautiful, though. "Hi baby," – I whispered as a tear rolled down my cheek – "Mama is so sorry. I'm so sorry I never gave you the chance to live."

The boy's smile faded, and his small hand touched my wet cheek. I grabbed his little hand and kissed it. If only I could go back. If only. I closed my eyes as I thought of how to make it up to him, but when I opened them again, he was gone.

"Even if God could forgive me, I don't think I'll ever forgive myself." Saying the words out loud solidified them in my mind. Sleep did not return that night.

"Woah, what happened to you?" Raquel said as I clocked in the next morning.

I glared at her. The dream and the lack of sleep had left me grouchy. "You don't remember?"

Raquel cocked her head and shot one eyebrow up. "No, should I?"

"It's been a year," I slammed the locker door and sank onto the bench in front of the lockers. "I thought it was getting better, but I had another dream last night."

"Oh, the procedure," Raquel said, sitting beside me.

I dropped my head in my hands. "And I lied to Henry about it. I was acting weird at dinner and he wanted to know why, so I told him I lost a baby."

Raquel shrugged, "That's mostly true."

I whipped my head up, daggers in my eyes. "It's not true at all. I killed my baby. I thought it would be easy and I'd forget, and some days I seem to, but then he comes to me in my dreams and breaks my heart again. And things are going great with Henry, but I don't think he'd support my decision, and now I've lied. How do I build a relationship on a lie?"

Raquel touched my arm. "Okay, first you need to calm down. While I agree lying isn't the best thing to do in a relationship, it happened before you knew Henry, and you only stretched the truth a little. You seem really happy with him, so I'd try to come up with a way to forget . . ." – I narrowed my eyes at her – "Or at least accept your stretching of the truth," Raquel continued. "Maybe it was a mistake, but you can't take it back, so perhaps if you accept it, it will get easier."

I sighed, but she was right. If I told Henry, I might lose him forever, and that thought scared me to death. I was falling in love with him and didn't want to be without him. "I guess you're right. There is nothing I can do now, so I'll just try to make better choices from here on out."

"That's the ticket," Raquel smiled. "Now come on, let's go save some lives."

I decided the best way to convince myself I could move on from the past was to be the best person I could be from then on. I joined Henry's church and the choir. Together we joined a Bible study that met weekly, and I even began memorizing verses. On the outside, I tried to live as righteously as I could, hoping eventually it would change the inside to match.

As Christmas rolled around, my joy grew, and I whistled as I decorated the apartment. This would be my second Christmas with Henry, and I had bought him the perfect gift. It was now sitting under the tree, begging to be opened, and he was due any minute. Raquel and her latest fling, Greg, were also coming. I hung up the stockings and had just finished lighting a candle when a knock sounded at the door.

Henry stood on the other side dressed in a green shirt and khakis. Warmth flooded my body as he held up a piece of mistletoe and kissed me. When we parted, I grabbed his hand, pulling him into the apartment.

"I come bearing gifts," he smiled and held up a small square box wrapped in red paper.

"Ooh, I can't wait to see what it is," I squealed as I took the box. "Can I shake it?"

He laughed, "Go ahead; it's not breakable."

I held the box to my ear and shook it back and forth, but no sound came forth; it tightly held its secret.

"Knock knock," Raquel said as she pushed open the door that had been left ajar. "Merry Christmas."

I rushed to my friend, enveloping her in a hug. "Merry Christmas to you, too. Here let me take your coats." I hung up Greg and Raquel's coat and led them to the tree to deposit their packages. "Who wants egg nog?"

"I'll help," Raquel offered, following me into the kitchen.

I pulled four festively colored mugs down from the cabinet and filled them each with the creamy liquid. Handing two to Raquel, I picked up the other two, and we returned to the living room where we chatted idly as Christmas music played in the background. Finally, I could contain my joy and curiosity no longer.

"Okay, who's ready for gifts?" I clapped my hands and surveyed my friends. They smiled and nodded, and I handed out a gift for each person. I picked up the little red box from Henry for myself, holding it in my lap like a cherished toy. "Open yours first," I nudged him.

He smiled and unwrapped the gift I had chosen for him. As he pulled out the book he had wanted, his smile deepened. "You remembered."

"Of course I remembered," I swatted him playfully on the arm. "You didn't already buy it for yourself, did you?"

"No, I was hoping my very attentive girlfriend would cover that base," he laughed and kissed my nose. "Okay, now you." He stared at me as I began to unwrap the little box.

Beneath the red paper was a small black jewelry box. A lump formed in my throat, and I turned silent eyes on him.

"Go ahead," he teased. "Open it."

I took a deep breath and eased the lid open, anticipating the sparkle of a diamond ring. My heart stopped; I blinked in confusion. "It's empty."

Henry rose from the couch and knelt on one knee before me. He clasped my hand with his left as he reached for his pocket with his right. "Sandra, I know it's been just over a year, but I can't imagine my life without you in it. Will you do me the honor of becoming my wife?" His right hand pulled out a simple gold band with a small diamond. It wasn't much, but it filled my heart with joy.

I threw my arms around his neck. "Of course I'll marry you," I whispered and met his lips with my own.

"Hey get a room," Raquel teased from the love seat across from us.

I blushed and pulled back. Henry slid the ring on my finger and swung me around. We finished opening the gifts, but I couldn't help staring at the simple flash on my left hand.

As the evening came to a close, Raquel pulled me aside. "I'm so happy for you."

I smiled as I looked down at the ring again. "I kind of can't believe it."

"You deserve it," Raquel said.

The words were meant to congratulate me, but they hit my weak spot instead. I didn't deserve Henry; I had lied to him. A rock settled in my stomach, and I tried to swallow the guilt away. Flashing a hesitant smile, I walked my friend to the door and bade her and Greg good-bye. As the door closed, Henry enveloped me in his arms.

"What's wrong?" He asked into my hair, "You seem a little off."

I turned my head up to kiss him. "No, I'm fine," I lied, "I'm just so happy."

"Well, it's late, and I should retire and let you get some sleep." Henry cupped my face, "Can I come see you tomorrow?"

"Of course," I smiled. He placed his lips on mine one final time before leaving.

After the door closed behind him, I shuffled to my bedroom. I sat on the edge of the bed and examined the ring. I wanted to marry him more than anything, but would he want to marry me if he knew my past? Would it be right not to tell him? My stomach churned at the thought of starting our marriage out in a lie, but I had worked so hard to be different. I couldn't lose him. I just couldn't. I pushed the thought aside. It wouldn't be important. What was important was us starting new. That was all that mattered.

9

Too Good to Be True?

The days wore on in much the same fashion: work, evenings with Henry, planning the wedding with Bride magazine in my room late at night, and church on Sundays.

It was around Valentine's Day that Raquel announced her engagement as well, with a ring three times the size of mine. I tried not to be jealous, but it was awfully hard to ignore the sparkle on Raquel's hand. That being said, there's nothing like sharing ideas for your wedding with your best friend, and I was elated to share the experience with her and gather her advice.

"We should go look at dresses," Raquel said one afternoon as we were clocking out.

I shrugged. "Sure, I'm not seeing Henry tonight. He had to work late. Do you think any stores are still open?"

"One way to find out." Raquel slung her purse over her shoulder and led the way to the parking lot. Deciding to just take one car to conserve gasoline, we climbed into her BMW.

A few minutes later we arrived at a shopping center. A bridal store sat prominently in the center, but it oozed the definition of expensive. Its sign alone was bigger than the other stores' signs put together. I bit my lip as I exited the car. Though I wouldn't be able to afford anything in here, it couldn't hurt to look. I just had to remind myself not to get excited.

As we entered the store, a woman in an immaculate blue suit with her hair pulled back in a bun greeted us. She clasped her hands in front of her chest and tilted her nose upward. "Welcome to Bonita, who's getting married?" Her eyes darted from Raquel to myself, but they returned and fixed on Raquel.

"Actually we both are," Raquel smiled, "but I think her wedding will be first." She pointed to me, and a blush burned across my face as the woman turned her attention to me.

"Yes, I'm getting married in six months," I stammered.

"Well, that should give us time." She unclasped her hands and pursed her lips. "What are you looking for?"

"Oh, something simple, white, maybe some lace," I said as I ground my toe into the ground.

The woman cocked her head, and her eyes traveled from my feet up to my head. "You're an eight or a ten?"

"Umm, a ten usually."

"Right; follow me, and we'll see what we have."

"Oh, this is going to be so much fun," Raquel squealed.

I smiled half-heartedly and followed the woman, but I didn't really see the fun in trying on dresses I could never afford. As we traversed the sea of dresses, I glimpsed a tag and nearly laughed out loud. $4000. I'd never be able to afford even half that much.

The woman led us to the changing rooms at the back of the store. To the left was a raised platform, carpeted in pink and surrounded by three full length mirrors.

"Take the middle one," – the lady pointed – "and I'll bring you some dresses."

I obliged and waited until the first dress appeared over the top of the changing door. It was a beautiful white satin dress with a long train covered in lace and beads. Finding the tag near the zipper, I turned it over and sighed. $6000. I almost didn't want to try it on in case I loved it, but I knew Raquel would never let me go without trying something.

It fit perfectly. As I opened the door, Raquel gasped and clapped. I blushed but continued to the raised platform. The dress was a dream come true, if not a little showy, but I forced myself to focus on the negative so that I wouldn't get excited, knowing I'd never be able to afford it.

"What do you think?" the sales lady asked.

"It's beautiful," I said, "but a little out of my price range. Even if I could clock a lot of overtime, I'd never afford this."

The woman's lips flattened and her nose rose in the air. "I see. Well, I'll check to see what we have on the sales rack." She spun around and marched off.

"I don't think she liked that," Raquel whispered smiling.

"I don't either, but I can't afford six thousand dollars."

Raquel whistled. "Yeah that is a pretty penny, even for me. It is beautiful, though."

The woman returned a few minutes later with another few dresses. I took one and returned to the dressing room. After carefully removing the first dress so as not to harm any piece of it, I then slipped the new dress on. It was much simpler: no beads, but still plenty of lace. The price was better – only $3000 – but still way out of my league. I rolled my eyes, but opened the door to show it off.

"Oh, that's nice too," Raquel said as I stepped on the platform for the second time.

"How's the price on that one?" the woman asked with disdain.

I blushed. "Um, better, but still more than I can afford."

The woman flipped through the tags of the other dresses she had brought over. She pulled out a dress near the bottom and held it up. "$1000 is the cheapest one I have." The contempt in her voice was nearly palpable.

"Well, it's very nice; they all are, but I'm afraid I can't afford it either." The woman scowled – probably feeling that we had wasted her time – so I quickly added, "Maybe Raquel should try some on now since she can afford more than I can."

The woman's face brightened at that prospect. "Yes, let's do that. What are you, a six?"

Raquel nodded, and I returned to the dressing room to change back into my clothes. If $1000 was the cheapest dress, I'd either have to find a way to earn the money or find a store that sold cheaper dresses. After putting my street clothes back on and hanging up the dress, I returned to the platform area to watch Raquel try on dresses.

Raquel was much flashier than I, and her dresses matched her taste. With plunging necklines and long trains, each one sported more beads than the last. The final dress she tried on was off the shoulder, had a bodice bedecked in beads, and a six-foot long train. "This is perfect," Raquel sighed, running her hands down her waist.

"It's one of my favorites," the woman agreed smiling. "Shall I put it on hold for you?"

"Oh, I'd love that," Raquel smiled back, "but do you have a temporary hold? I'd like my mother to see it before I decide to buy it."

"Of course; we can hold it for seven days, but then we'll have to put it back on the floor."

"That's fine," Raquel winked at me and returned to the dressing room to change. Afterwards, we followed the woman to the front where Raquel filled out some paperwork.

"Are you really going to buy that dress?" I whispered as we pushed open the door of the shop and walked into the parking lot.

"Doubtful," Raquel said, knitting her eyebrows together, "That dress was $10000. That's even out of my league."

My jaw dropped. "But you asked her to hold it."

She waved her hand in the air. "Of course I did; the sales people are always nicer if they think you'll come back. I didn't give accurate information though."

Shaking my head, I climbed into Raquel's car. I'd never understand rich people.

Raquel slid into her seat and tapped her fingers on the steering wheel. Her brow furrowed and she twitched her lips to one side. Then she snapped her fingers, and her eyes sparkled. "Aha, I've got it. Do you feel up to going to one more place?"

I shrugged. "As long as it has dresses under a thousand dollars please."

"Yeah, I think this place will be perfect. I can't believe I didn't think of it first." She pointed the car north, and fifteen minutes later, we pulled into another shopping center.

I scanned the store names but nothing appeared very bride like. "Where is it?"

"There," Raquel pointed. At the very end of the strip mall was a small shop. If there was a sign, it was so tiny that I couldn't even read it from where we were. Raquel parked the car, and we walked up to the door. LE BRIDE was stenciled in white lettering across the glass door. Raising an eyebrow, I swallowed my apprehension and followed Raquel into the shop.

A short plump woman greeted us immediately. She wasn't dressed in an immaculate suit, but she exuded an air of friendliness. "Welcome to Le Bride. How can I help the two of you today?"

The knot of apprehension immediately fizzled as the woman spoke. She looked like an older version of Mrs. Butterworth, though with gray hair and the name of Helen on her name badge. "I'm getting married in six months," I said. "I need something white and affordable."

Helen smiled. "I have just the thing. Come with me."

She moseyed toward the back, and we followed her. Helen flicked through a few racks, clicking her tongue and grabbing a few dresses as she went.

"Here we are dearie; try these on." She folded the bundle over my arm, and I stepped into the small dressing room, hanging the dresses up on the supplied hook. I inspected the first dress, but with its overzealous beading pattern, it didn't fit my style. Moving it to the side, I gasped as my eyes landed on the second dress. It was simple, but elegant. Lace covered the bodice and part of the back. The satin rippled like a sea of milk. I slid the dress on before even looking for a tag and sighed. My hands ran down the sides; it was a perfect fit. The white offset my darker skin, making me appear to glow. I twirled in front of the full length mirror in the room, enjoying the vision from all sides.

I opened the door and smiled as Raquel gasped. "Right?" I asked. "I think it's perfect."

"I agree. You look like an angel."

The woman appeared and pulled a pencil from somewhere in her gray hair. "Ah, yes, I knew this would be lovely. It is absolutely perfect on you, my dear."

I bit my lip; I just hoped it was affordable. "Can I ask how much?" Butterflies fluttered in my stomach as I waited for the woman's answer.

"It's on sale this week for $300."

My heart fluttered. It was expensive, but not unaffordable. "I'll take it." I turned back to the mirror and beamed at my reflection. This was really happening.

After paying the bill, I carried the new dress, wrapped in a beautiful gold lame box with a white bow, out to Raquel's car. "Now, I just have to make sure Henry doesn't find it, and I don't gain a ton of weight."

"I'll make sure of the latter, but the former is up to you," Raquel smiled.

A few weeks later, Henry and I met up to taste cakes for the wedding.

"Are you sure about this place?" I asked, raising my eyebrows at the small brick building that seemed out of place amidst the taller, newer buildings.

He smiled. "Don't worry, she's a client of mine. I know it doesn't look like much, but she's the best baker around." He opened the front door, and we stepped inside the little shop.

Three small silver tables dotted the room. Each table sported two white chairs, the backs of which curled up to form a heart. A glass cabinet housed a variety of tasty-looking treats, and a small sign – The Sweet Spot – hung behind it. Pink and silver striped wallpaper adorned the walls, creating a sweet, cozy feel. I had to admit the shop inside did look much better than the outside. A bell above the door announced our entrance, and a petite blond woman emerged from a door at the back, wiping her hands on her flour covered apron. A stray smudge covered her right cheek.

"Henry," she smiled, and her eyes lit up, "It's not Thursday; what brings you here today?"

"Hi Cassie. This is my fiancé Sandra. I told her you were the best baker around, and I'm hoping you have some cakes we can taste today. I'd love to have you do the cake for our wedding."

She clapped her hands together and danced back and forth on her feet. "I'd love to do that. I'm so happy for you." She turned her attention to me as she tucked a stray hair back behind her ear. "You've got a good man here. He's one of the best."

I gazed at Henry and smiled back. "I think so too."

"Okay, well, have a seat, and I'll bring you some cakes to taste." She turned and disappeared into the back again, and we chose the table nearest the small storefront window.

"She seems to know you well," I stated, trying not to sound as jealous as I felt. Images of Peter and Sheila briefly flashed in my mind.

Henry's eyes twinkled. "Don't be jealous. I helped her write a great insurance policy when everyone else was trying to get her to close shop so they could take over her lot. That's why she likes me. Plus, I come nearly every Thursday for her fruit tarts. They are amazing."

"I wasn't jealous," I wrinkled my brow at him. "Just curious."

Cassie appeared a moment later with four small white plates. Each held a different slice of cake. "We have classic white cake with a lemon filling, classic chocolate cake with a strawberry filling, a German Chocolate cake, and a marble cake with raspberry filling." She placed two forks on the table. "I'll let you taste, and I'll be back in a moment."

I picked up the dainty silver fork and eyed the tasty desserts. "Which one shall we start with?"

"Whichever one you like; I'll let you decide because I'll probably love them all."

"Hmm, I think the white cake first." I pushed the fork through the soft cake and brought the bite to my mouth. The tart lemon flavor lit up my taste buds. "Mm, that's good."

Henry took a bite and smiled back. "Pretty good, and I'm not even much of a lemon fan."

After a drink of water to clear the taste, I decided on the marble cake next, which was even more delicious. The tart raspberry perfectly complemented the sweet cake. Then I sampled the chocolate cake, simply to-die-for. The chocolate and strawberry swirled together on my tongue, and I sighed. Finally, I took a bite of the German chocolate cake. Though delicious, it didn't scream wedding cake fare to me. It seemed a little heavy with the thick glaze and the dusting of coconut. "Okay, so which do you like?" *Please say chocolate.*

He twisted his lips and narrowed his eyes in thought. "I think . . . I think I like the German chocolate cake the best."

I wrinkled my nose and blinked. "Are you sure? I mean it is delicious, but don't you think it's kind of odd for a wedding cake?"

"I like being different," he said. "Why? Which one is your favorite?"

"The chocolate one, but really they were all good." I thought for a moment. "I'll tell you what, you can have the German chocolate cake, but you have to give me something in return."

He tilted his head back. "Like what?"

I tapped a finger to my lips. What might be something he would fight me on? An idea popped in my mind, and I smiled. "I get to choose the wedding colors."

Henry cocked his head. I could almost see wheels turning in his head as if trying to decide if this was a good choice or not. "Okay, deal."

"Shake on it," I demanded, thrusting out my hand.

He grasped it and pumped twice. "Cassie? We've decided."

Cassie re-entered the small room carrying a notepad and pen. "Okay, what's it going to be?"

"We're going to do the German chocolate cake," Henry said as he stood up and crossed to the counter.

Her eyes widened slightly, "Really?" She turned her eyes to me,

"You agree?"

I joined Henry at the counter. "I traded. Cake for colors."

Cassie nodded knowingly. "Ah, smart girl."

"Why do I get the feeling I just got played?" Henry glanced from Cassie to I and back again.

"Oh, I'm sure it will be fine," Cassie winked. "Now, do you know how many people you need to feed?"

Henry's brow furrowed. "We haven't really discussed that yet." He looked at me and shrugged. "Maybe fifty?"

I scratched my head as I ran a brief mental tally of my friends and family. "Um, I'd have to sit down and make an actual list, but I probably have close to fifty myself."

Henry's eyes widened. "Really? Okay, well then I guess we better make it one hundred servings."

Cassie's pencil scribbled on the notepad. "And do we have a date picked out yet?"

"Yes, September 14th at 2 pm," I said.

"Okay, well I'll log this in, and if I have any more questions, I'll contact you. Will that work?"

"That's perfect, Cassie, and thank you," Henry said.

"No, thank you for the business," she replied.

We exited the little shop and returned to his car. "Thanks for bringing me here; she's amazing," I said buckling my seatbelt. "We'll have to come back to try her other desserts."

"I already have," he laughed as he started the car. "Okay, where to next?" Henry put the car in drive and headed out of the parking lot.

"Let's go look at a tux for you."

"Uh oh, what is that mischievous look about?"

I smiled but said nothing.

A few minutes later we pulled into a tuxedo rental shop, The

Penguin Shoppe. Henry opened my car door, as usual, and took my hand as we walked in. Dark suits and bright vests covered busts around the small shop. A cluttered desk sat in the middle.

A short balding man with a mustache that covered most of his face glanced up from the desk and greeted us. "Welcome to The Penguin Shoppe. What can I do for you today?"

"We need to look at a tux for him," I smiled, squeezing Henry's hand.

"Okay, come with me." The man turned and waddled towards the back where three mirrors were set up for viewing. He really was like a little penguin. The man whipped out a measuring tape – seemingly from thin air – and began taking Henry's measurements. "Mmhmm, okay, yes, that's perfect," he mumbled as he wrote numbers down on a little white pad.

Henry raised his eyebrows at me, and I smiled in return.

"Wait here, and I'll be right back." The man disappeared into a side room and returned with a sharp black tux. "Let's make sure this fits." He slipped the jacket on, and it was indeed a perfect fit.

"It's perfect," I sighed, and my pulse quickened at the sight of Henry in the suit jacket. There was something about a man in a suit.

"So, what else do you need? Vest, tie, cummerbund?"

"No cummerbund," I said, "but definitely vest and tie. Do you have a color chart?"

The man nodded and produced a white board with color swatches lined four across and four down. The colors ranged from deep purples and blues to bright reds and oranges. I touched the color swatches and pursed my lips. Sneaking a glance at Henry, I smiled. "I like this color for the groomsmen," – I pointed at a dark blue – "and this one for Henry."

Henry leaned over my shoulder. "Purple?" he asked.

"Magenta," I smiled.

"Um, why can't I wear the blue?"

"Because you got German chocolate cake," I teased, "and I got to pick the colors. Besides the magenta will look great on you." I held the board up to his face. "Wouldn't you agree?" The salesman tugged on the side of his mustache and nodded.

Henry pleaded with his eyes, but I remained resolute. Finally, a smile tugged at the corner of his mouth. "Okay, you win."

As the planning continued, invitations were ordered, the caterer and photographer were hired, and, of course, the pastor of our church was asked to officiate.

Summer burned through Mesquite and the school year ended. Children of all ages ran around the apartment complex and splashed in the pool. Though the sight and sounds of children still rubbed the wound, it was less. Planning the wedding kept my mind off of the past, and I convinced myself that I was healing, that once I got married the dreams would end and the guilt would go away, that if I could just make it to September the past could be forgotten.

The scorching heat faded into the beginning of muggy fall. The leaves on the few trees turned brown and began their descent from the limbs. Children returned to school, and quiet resumed during the day at the apartment complex. I sat at my small kitchen table addressing invitations and enjoying the blissful silence on a day off. A stack of white envelopes lay on one side of the table and a stack of invitations on the other. I stuffed the invitation in the envelope and licked it, but as I pressed the seal down, a sound reached my ears and froze my heart.

I stopped, hoping it would go away. Sucking in a breath, I closed my eyes and listened. "Mama? Mama, why?" The voice was faint, but it was there. I squeezed my eyes tighter, willing the sound to disappear. I hadn't been visited by the baby recently, and I had hoped it would stay that way. I had almost convinced myself that I had really miscarried instead of what I had actually done.

"Mama?" The voice was closer this time and then the soft pitter patter of tiny feet hitting the floor joined the voice. *Oh please*, I clenched my hands at my side, *please go away*. "Mama, why didn't you want me?" The words broke my heart, and my shoulders heaved. The lies and the walls I had built so carefully began to crumble, and I began to shake. Then a tug came at my pant leg, and I couldn't keep my eyes closed. My eyes snapped open; a toddler, clad in blue overalls and a red shirt, stood beside me. His chubby hand tugged again on my pants, and his wide brown eyes spoke sadness. "Why did you let them take me, mama?" His mouth turned down as a solitary tear spilled out of his eye and rolled slowly down his cheek. I longed to touch his soft brown curls and breathe his scent, but I glued my hands to my thighs. If I could just get through this, maybe they would stop.

I had thought once that maybe I could live with the visions, but the child seemed to grow every time. I was seeing what my son would have been, and it broke my heart every time.

"You're not real," I whispered, but it didn't ease the ache in my heart. "I'm so sorry. I wish I could take it back. I'm trying to do it right this time."

"But what about me?" he asked.

"I didn't know." My vision blurred with tears. Unchecked, they tumbled down my cheeks, one after the other. "I didn't know," I repeated. "I thought I couldn't handle it. I was selfish. I'm so sorry." Through my blurry vision, I saw the boy hang his head, and his shoulders slump. The vice on my heart squeezed ever tighter. Closing my eyes and wrapping my arms around my chest, I let the sobs take control. I don't know how long I cried, but when I opened my eyes, the boy was gone.

Isaac. The name blazed in my head. *Is that what I would have called him or is that what God named him when he got to Heaven?* I hoped he was in Heaven. I'd never had the courage to ask Henry or anyone else because I was too afraid of the answer, but in my reading I had convinced myself that all babies went to Heaven because Jesus found them so precious, and it had helped. But these visions did not help. They made me ever more unsure about lying to Henry.

I rose from the table and wandered into the bedroom. I hadn't had a drink in a long time, but my nerves were on edge. I needed the calming sensation.

The nightstand was empty; I had never replaced the last bottle. Dropping to my knees, I peered under the bed. A lone bottle remained. When I had retrieved it, I held it up to the light. Only a bit of liquid sloshed in the bottom. Hoping it would be enough, I screwed off the lid and downed the fire.

As I sat in the last pre-marital counseling session with Henry later that evening, I wanted to tell him about my visit, about my past, but fear convinced me to keep my mouth shut.

My finger ran up and down the seam of the leather couch as the events of the afternoon paraded through my mind again. The drink had helped a little, enough that I had returned to the kitchen and finished the envelopes, but not without turning on music first and situating my chair so that my back was to the wall.

"What do you think Sandra?"

I whipped my head up at the sound of my name. "I'm sorry, what?"

"I was asking you about joint accounts. Do you plan on combining your accounts when you get married?" the pastor repeated.

"Um, sure, I guess, I mean why wouldn't we?" I stammered.

Henry shot me a concerned look, and I plastered a smile on to reassure him.

"I think it's a good idea," the pastor said, tapping his fingertips together. "If you are truly going to join together, then it ought to be with everything. Well, unless there's something else," – he leaned forward, hand on his knees, expression serious – "that's all I have."

Out of the corner of my eye. I saw Henry shift in his chair and cough into his hand. "No, I think we're good. Right, Sandra?"

My head nodded. "Yep, feeling good. Ready to be married."

The pastor narrowed his eyes at the forced statements, but said nothing. He rose from his chair and held out his hand. "Alright, I'll see you in two weeks for the ceremony then."

We both shook the proffered hand and then left the office. As soon as the door clicked behind us, Henry whirled on me. "What was going on? You seemed really out of it in there."

I sighed. "It was just a long day is all. I'm sorry. I really am excited to be marrying you."

He stared at me as if deciding if that really was all and then nodded and continued walking. I couldn't help but think that he was hiding his own secret.

10

When Opposites Collide

Though the wedding planning kept my mind busy and the dreams mostly away, a new worry replaced the dreams. My parents were flying in today to help finish the final details and attend the rehearsal dinner. I was pretty sure my mother would like Henry; she was a traditionalist – though with a flair for fashion – but I wasn't sure about my father. Ex-military and very strict, his distaste for Peter had been obvious, but whether that was because of Peter or because we were living together, I wasn't entirely sure.

Even more nerve wracking was the fact that Henry's family was flying in soon after. He rarely spoke of them, so I had no idea what to expect. What if they hated me? What if I hated them? They did live back in Louisiana, so it wasn't like we'd see them all the time, but still it unnerved me. I wish I knew more about them.

I pulled into the Dallas-Love Field airport and found a parking spot. I hated coming into the city, but hopefully I wouldn't be here long. After locking the car door, I trekked into the airport, trying to calm my nerves. What would I do if they didn't like Henry?

I scanned the big TV screens to find their flight and then made my way to their gate. Suddenly my mother's flashy garb caught my eye; she always did dress larger than life. Today she sported a bright red and gold dress. My straight-laced father in his black button up suit stood next to her.

"Sandra." My mother bobbed up and down, pumping her hand. I blushed at the shout, but smiled and stepped in that direction. A moment later, she enveloped me in a giant hug.

"Hi mom," I said into her shoulder.

"My baby," she cried, "I can't believe my baby's getting married."

"Mom, I'm twenty-seven. I'm not a baby anymore," I sighed.

My mother waved my hand in dismissal. "You'll always be my baby."

I rolled my eyes and turned to my father, the antithesis of my mother. He stuck out his hand in lieu of a hug, and I shook it. Though I had always hoped he would show more affection, it seemed some things never changed. I led them through the busy airport to the baggage claim.

"So, when do we get to meet the man?" My mother asked as we waited for the baggage carousel to start up.

"Um, well we can probably meet up for dinner," I replied, keeping my eyes on the carousel, "but his family isn't here yet."

"When are they coming?"

"Tomorrow, I think." The conveyor belt roared to life, and we moved forward to watch for luggage.

"There," my father pointed as a hard grey suitcase came into view. I elbowed my way closer and hefted it off the belt.

"Are there more?"

"No, just that one."

He took the handle, and I led the way back to the car.

"Where is your Mustang?" my father asked when I stopped at the Taurus. I bit my lip. I had gotten so used to this car that I had forgotten all about the Mustang.

"Um, it was economics really. This car gets much better gas mileage, and when Peter moved out, I needed to cut finances somewhere." I hoped this would satisfy his practicality.

"Well, I hope you at least got a good deal," he said.

I convinced him I had as we loaded in. My mother spent most of the ride complaining about the lack of humidity, but my father remained quiet, true to his nature.

When we arrived at my apartment, I took the suitcase to my spare room. My mother followed, still prattling on.

"Ugh, you need to do something with this place. It's so . . . bland." Her nose wrinkled as she waved her hand at the white room.

I rolled my eyes at the familiar criticism. Though I loved my mother, she always pointed out the negatives first. "Mom, it's a guest room. It's not supposed to be exciting."

"I'm just suggesting a dab of color. Everything is so white."

"Mary, it's fine," my father spoke up. "We're only here for a week."

I shot my father a thankful glance and hefted the suitcase onto the queen bed. "I'll go make some tea and let you guys unpack."

"Do you have chamomile?" my mother's voice reached my ears as I shut the door behind me.

Sighing, I squared my shoulders and sauntered into the kitchen. It was going to be a long week.

Henry showed up that evening at 6 pm, handsome as always in his casual attire.

"Thank goodness you're here." I hugged him and then stood on my tiptoes so my mouth would be right beside his ear. "My parents are too."

He nodded against me as he returned the hug. "Don't worry, I'm good with parents," he whispered back with a wink and followed me into the apartment.

"Mom, Dad, this is Henry. Henry this is my mom, Mary, and my father, Bruce."

My parents rose from the couch where they had been sitting. Extending his hand, my father nodded curtly, "Henry."

"It's nice to meet you, sir," Henry replied, shaking the outstretched hand.

I watched the exchange intently, biting my thumbnail. My father was measuring Henry with this handshake. An initial opinion would be formed based on this one simple greeting. He nodded again, and I smiled inwardly that he seemed pleased with the strength of Henry's grip.

Henry turned to my mother, prepared to shake her hand as well, but she engulfed him in a hug instead. His eyes widened in surprise though he recovered nicely and returned the hug.

"You'll have to forgive my mother," I said, pulling her back. "She forgets not everyone is as into hugs as she is."

"It's no problem," Henry replied as he smoothed his shirt.

"Well, aren't you just a tall drink of lemonade," Mary smiled, and her eyes roved up and down Henry in appreciation.

"Mom," I hissed as Henry's face colored, "Why don't you come help me in the kitchen?"

She threw a wink at Henry, but acquiesced and followed. As soon as we rounded the corner and were out of sight of the men, I whirled on my mother, hands akimbo.

"What?" my mother asked holding out her hands defensively. "I was just saying he's handsome."

"You don't have to say it so loud or with those words. You're embarrassing me."

"Oh, I'm sure a man like that is used to hearing it."

She waved her hand in dismissal again, and sighing, I turned to the cupboard and pulled several plates down. "Here make yourself useful." I placed the plates in her hands and pointed to the table.

My mother rolled her eyes, but took the stack and began setting the table as I finished the last minute preparations. When everything was ready, I called the men in, and we all sat down around the small table.

Dinner was polite, though reserved. My father grilled Henry on his job, his plans for the future, and his past. Henry, to his credit, answered each question as it arose, and his answers seemed to satisfy the ex-army man, though both Mary and Bruce seemed surprised about Henry's religious views.

After dinner, the men retired back to the living room while my mother and I cleared the table and put the dishes in the sink. Leaving them to be washed later, we then joined the men. I was surprised to hear my father discussing religion with Henry as I had no idea he had an interest.

When my mother began stifling her yawns, I suggested we call it a night.

Henry rose, and I followed him out, promising to be right back. Though dusk, the air held a warmth, and it lay like a light shawl on my skin.

"Thank you for being so amazing," I touched his arm. "I know my parents are rather quirky."

Henry smiled and took my hand. "I thought they were sweet. Besides," – his eyes clouded over – "my family has some quirks too."

"Do you want to talk about it?" I asked hesitantly.

He stiffened, displaying his answer before he voiced it. "No, we'll talk about it later."

I nodded, curious, but deciding to let it go for now. "Are they arriving tomorrow?"

"They are. Shall we meet for dinner again?"

"We might as well," I agreed, "they have to meet sometime."

We kissed goodnight, and I re-entered my apartment.

My mother stood waiting to pounce on me. "He seems lovely."

"He is," I agreed. I curled up on the couch with my mother beside me. I regaled her the story of how Henry and I met, minus the breakdown and the abortion. Those taboo topics I kept to myself.

The next day, I took my parents around the town. There wasn't a lot to see in Mesquite, but we found some antique shops my mother loved, and some trails that kept my dad's interest for a time. A local barbeque place served as a late lunch before we returned to the apartment.

Once inside, my parents each brought out a book to read, while I went to shower and freshen up. As I pulled on a soft yellow dress, my throat grew dry at the prospect of meeting Henry's family. Because he rarely spoke of them, all sorts of images played in my imagination.

Promptly at 6pm, the doorbell rang. I gave myself one last glance and then shuffled to the door. Henry stood looking uncharacteristically stiff in a blue button down shirt. Behind him was an older man, clearly his father, as the resemblance ran deep. He was also dressed smartly in a blue dress shirt and slacks. Henry's brother, a younger version of himself, stood to the left of his father, but it was the woman who stood out to me. With her short hair, suit, and severe expression she seemed such a contrast to Henry.

"Come in," I smiled, opening the door wide to allow passage. The group shuffled in, and I wiped my sweaty palms down my dress as I shut the door behind them. Introductions were made around the room, and then a tense silence descended. Sylvia, Henry's mother, checked her watch, while David, his father, and Anthony, his brother, dug their shoes into the carpet. My eyes darted to Henry for some clue as to what to do.

"Well, I'm hungry," Henry said, breaking the tension. "Who's hungry and wants to join me?"

"I'm famished," my mother spoke up.

"I'd offer to make something, but my kitchen table barely seats four, and I don't have extra chairs, so . . . out?" I suggested.

Everyone agreed, and since neither of us had a car large enough to hold seven people, we decided to take two cars to the restaurant. Henry and his family piled in his car, while my mother and father came with me.

We drove in silence and then pulled into the parking lot of a fairly upscale restaurant. I wrinkled my forehead hoping Henry knew what he was doing because I didn't have the money to afford dinner here.

Henry spoke to the hostess, and after a short wait, we were shown to a table. Henry held out my chair as normal, but before I could sit down, his mother spoke up.

"Stop doing that. Is she broken? She can get her own chair."

All conversation stopped as a silence fell on the group. Henry's father stared down at his feet. I glanced up at Henry in surprise, but he mirrored his father's embarrassment. My own father stiffened, the strain of holding his tongue evident on his face. My mother put a hand on his arm, and he relaxed, but his eyes remained on me for my reaction.

"It's fine, ma'am. I actually like it," I smiled.

Henry's mother scowled. "It's women like you who will set us back years."

"I'm sorry?" My eyebrows raised at the tone. How dare this

woman, who didn't even know me, attack me.

"Equal rights. You know women get paid less than men. We have to prove we are equal and not pulling out your own chair shows weakness." Sylvia pulled her own chair out and sat down, not even glancing at her husband.

My face flamed, and a fire licked up my belly. I splayed my palms on the table to control their shaking. "I happen to think that it was just a nice gesture. I don't think Henry was trying to say I was weaker. I thought," – I said pointedly – "that he learned such manners from you."

Sylvia scoffed. "Not from me, my dear. I never let him do such things for me. I tried my best to instill in my children that men and women are equal and deserve the same rights."

"Yeah, and look what that got us," Anthony spoke up softly.

Henry shot him a look, and Anthony dropped his eyes to the table. I considered one brother then the next; what did that mean?

Another tense silence descended. Whatever implication Anthony's words held had at least quieted Sylvia. She surveyed her menu, silently, as did Henry's father. Henry sat down next to me, and I turned questioning eyes on him. He shook his head slightly to indicate that now was not the time.

"Well, I think I'll be having the steak," my mother spoke up, trying to change the mood.

"Yes, me too," my father added, and the topic lightened to food and drink, but the damage was done. Sylvia and I shared a terse silence the rest of the evening. When I wasn't deciding if I wanted this woman to like me, I was trying to decipher what secret the brothers were sharing and if it would impact our wedding and our future.

When dinner ended, the waiter brought the check. "Will one check be fine or would you like me to split it up?" he asked, looking at each of the men.

"Actually, I'll take that," Sylvia said, snatching the bill. While I was grateful – as I didn't have the money to cover it – I wasn't sure if Sylvia was doing it to show off her money or her "equality." Regardless, I was relieved I wouldn't have to return in the same car with her. After hugging Henry goodnight and promising to meet up later, I got in the car with my parents.

"Well, they seem lovely," my mother said with a fake brightness. My father and I both whirled to face her.

"Sylvia seems horrible," I sighed. "What am I marrying into?"

"Perhaps you should have found out more about them before accepting the proposal," my father suggested softly.

I opened my mouth to reply, but before I could, my mother interrupted, "The thing to remember is that you are marrying Henry and not his mother."

"But she's bound to be a part of our life." I backed the car up and began the short drive home.

"I'm curious how Henry turned out so chivalrous," my father murmured, "Did he serve in the military?"

"Yes, a short stint in the Air Force," I replied, "but I think a lot of his behavior has to do with God. I've been attending church with him, and most men there are very respectful of women, just like Henry."

"Tell us more," my father said, and my excitement built as I rattled on about the church and all that I had learned. I still didn't believe God would forgive me, but maybe if I enlightened my parents, they could be saved. Telling them about Jesus gave me a sense of peace as well, and by the time we reached the apartment, I had almost forgotten the tense evening.

11

The Joining of Two Lives

The next few days flew by, filled with so much last minute preparation that I forgot to ask Henry about the secret with his brother. The rehearsal dinner proved a little stressful as Sylvia tried to assert her opinion, but Raquel was a force to be reckoned with and kept it running smoothly. Before I knew it, the morning of my wedding day dawned.

I woke with butterflies zooming around my stomach. After showering and dressing, I wandered into the kitchen for a cup of coffee.

"Are you ready?" my mother asked, turning from the coffee pot and holding a mug out to me.

I took a deep breath. "I'm more nervous than I thought I'd be."

"Don't worry, I was too." She sat down at the table, and I took a seat across from her and listened as she replayed her wedding day. It helped to hear her fears. I just wanted some consolation that I wasn't crazy; that butterflies were okay; and that I wasn't making a mistake.

My father entered the kitchen a few minutes later, but after pouring his cup and staring at me briefly, he left the room.

"What's up with him?" I asked my mother.

"He thinks he's losing a daughter," she smiled and took a sip of her drink, "and it's hit him kind of hard. You're his baby," she continued. "Though he hasn't always shown it, he really loves you."

"Huh, I never would have thought." I sat back in the chair and crossed my arms. My father had never shown much emotion, so I certainly hadn't expected my impending nuptials to affect him. My mother tossed me a wink, and we finished our coffee in silence.

As we pulled into the church parking lot, my heart fluttered ever faster. I grabbed the bouquets as my mother pulled the dresses and other supplies out of the trunk. My father grabbed his suit and then pulled me in for a fierce hug. I patted his back awkwardly; I couldn't remember the last time my father had hugged me.

"I'll see you soon," he said, emotion clouding his voice. He sniffed loudly, drew his shoulders back, and walked off to join the other men getting ready on the other side of the church.

My mother and I entered the church through the closest side door. The small hallway held only a few doors. One, a white door on the left, sported a handwritten sign: "Bride's Room" and we entered. A few chairs, a small table, a full length mirror, and a clothing rack filled the tiny room. I hung the wedding dress on the rack and set my shoes down in a chair near the mirror. As I arranged the bouquets on the table, the door flew open and Raquel rushed in.

"Sorry I'm late," she said as she threw her purse in the corner. "Greg decided he had to do some last minute rounds. He does this all the time; I don't know if we're going to make it. He's always working so long." She began unzipping her garment bag, seemingly unaware of my mother and I staring at her. "What?" she asked when she finally noticed the silence in the room. Suddenly her face shifted, and she clasped her hand to her mouth, "Oh, I'm so sorry. I didn't mean to jinx you. You guys will be wonderful together."

I pushed my shoes to the floor and sunk down on the chair, dropping my head in my hands. "What if I'm wrong? What if I shouldn't be marrying him?"

Raquel scurried over and touched my shoulder, "Hey, from the time you guys met, you have seemed perfect together. He treats you like a princess. I can't imagine anyone better for you."

I stared up at my friend who evenly returned the gaze. Her serious expression calmed my nerves. "Okay, you're right," I said, pushing myself up. "Let's get ready for a wedding."

Raquel smiled and hugged me, and then she turned to slip her dark blue dress on. My mother also changed into a dark blue dress with a maroon flower pinned on. I pulled out the white satin dress and took a deep breath. This was really happening. After removing my street clothes, I slipped on the milky satin and then sat to apply my makeup. Raquel came over and helped pull my hair up and attach the veil.

After the makeup was completed and the hair was in place, I stood to admire the final look in the mirror. Though simple, the white of the dress stood out against my caramel skin. The butterflies began another looping around my stomach, and my heart pounded a double step in my chest.

"Are you ready?" my mother asked, lightly touching my shoulder.

I nodded. "Ready as I'll ever be, I guess." I picked up the bouquets and handed Raquel's to her. While there weren't very many blue flowers, we had added what we could and then filled the bouquets with the deepest red roses and whitest baby's breath we could find. Ribbons of sapphire blue and maroon wrapped around the stems and curled over our hands.

We exited the room and turned right towards the small sanctuary.

My father stood outside the closed doors, picking lint from his tux and shifting his weight from side to side. He pulled me in for another hug and sniffled in my ear. I returned his hug, though it felt strange, not sure what else to do for a man who had never shown much emotion. The doors opened slightly, and Greg and Anthony slipped out.

"Are you ready ma'am?" Greg asked, holding his arm out to my mother. She nodded and squeezed my hand before placing it on Greg's arm. My father and I stepped to the side, out of sight, and Greg opened the door and walked my mother down the aisle. The music from the sanctuary hit home again how real this was, and my throat dried up. A minute later, Anthony took Raquel's arm, and they disappeared inside as well. The music changed, and I signaled to my father that it was our turn.

"You look beautiful," my father said in a shaky voice, "and I'm sorry I didn't tell you that enough."

His words brought tears to my eyes, which I quickly brushed away. "Thank you, daddy. Are you ready?"

He nodded, and I hooked my right arm in his. As we stepped onto the maroon carpet, my eyes sought Henry who stood at the front with Anthony and the pastor. I barely registered the friends sitting on either side of the aisle as my heart sped up in my chest. The room grew quiet, but the sound of the beating of my heart thundered in my ears. My feet pushed forward with a mind of their own.

"You look like a princess," Henry whispered, taking my hand as I stopped next to him at the end of the aisle in the small Baptist church.

I fidgeted, touching the simple white dress, "It's not much, but I didn't want to start our marriage in debt."

"Better than this maroon tie," he winked, leaning his head in close to mine.

"It looks handsome on you, and besides it was the compromise for German chocolate cake, remember?"

The pastor cleared his throat to get our attention. Heat flamed up my neck and ears. Henry's face colored as well. We turned to face the pastor.

"Dearly beloved," he began, "We are gathered here today to celebrate the union of Henry Dobbs and Sandra Baker. They have made a commitment to each other and stand before us today to publicly declare that commitment. Henry James Dobbs, do you take Sandra Elaine Baker as your wife, to love and to cherish, to have and to hold, through sickness and in health, till death do you part?"

"I do," he said and squeezed my hand.

"Sandra Elaine Baker, do you take Henry James Dobbs as your husband, to love and to cherish, to have and to hold, through sickness and in health, till death do you part?"

"I do," I breathed softly.

"Do you have the rings?"

Anthony pulled the rings from his tuxedo pocket and handed them to Henry.

"Repeat after me, Henry. With this ring, I thee wed."

Henry repeated the words and slid the ring on my finger. Then he handed the other ring to me. I too repeated the words and slid the ring on his finger.

"I now pronounce you husband and wife. You may kiss the bride."

Henry leaned in and touched my lips with his own. It felt different this time, more real, more serious, and my arms wound around his neck. I had completely forgotten about the people in the room until applause and cheering erupted. My face flamed as I pulled back. Henry must have felt the same pull of desire I did because the need was visible in his eyes. I smiled softly and took a calming breath. We turned to face the crowd, and then, hand-in-hand, we rushed down the aisle and out of the sanctuary.

I pulled him towards the room I had changed in. As the door shut behind us, Henry pushed me against the wall. Passion enflamed his kisses, and his hands roved up the sides of my waist. My breath grew ragged as desire flooded my body. Heat radiated through me, and then a coldness descended. I opened my eyes to see Henry pulled back, panting.

"We should wait until after the reception," he said in a halting cadence.

My body screamed "no" but then the thought of all our guests waiting for us flooded my mind. Even if we were quick, we would be longer than normal, and everyone would know what we had been doing. The dampening effect was immediate. Though the desire remained, the intense need lessened, and I nodded.

"Besides," he added, "I don't want my first time rushed and in a church."

A blush crawled across my face at the thought. "You're right." I smoothed my dress as Henry readjusted his tux, and we exited the room. Holding hands, we walked down the hall to the kitchen area where the reception had been set up.

A small kitchen attached to a large open room, where tables had been set up and covered with maroon and blue table cloths. As we entered the room, a cheer erupted. Friends gathered around us to issue congratulations. After a plethora of hugs and handshakes, we finally made our way to the center table where a buffet had been set up with sandwiches and fruit. Though I was hungry, I could barely eat.

As I sat at the table, nibbling on a sandwich, I examined the room and smiled. Beautiful flower arrangements in reds, blues, and whites sat atop the tables, and white Christmas lights hung from the ceiling, creating a soft, romantic glow. I couldn't believe the transformation. A glance at Henry sent another blush searing across my face. The thought of what was coming after the reception kept jumping to my mind.

When most of the guests had finished eating, the music began. Henry took my hand and led me to the floor. As I gazed into his eyes, the rest of the room faded from sight, and for a moment, it was just the two of us. When that song ended, my father stepped up and took my hand. His eyes were still red and watery, and I wished I knew the words to say to him. He smiled down at me as we swayed to the music. Across the floor, Henry danced with his mother, who, for the moment at least, appeared happy. When the song ended, I headed back to the table, but Anthony met me before I got there and asked for a turn. I agreed, returning to the floor with him.

"You've really made Henry happy," he said. "I haven't seen him this happy since Camilla died."

I turned my head up at him, my brow wrinkled, "Who's Camilla?"

"Our sister. Didn't Henry tell you?"

I shook my head and sneaked a glance at Henry. "What happened?"

He sucked in his breath and looked away. "I'm not sure I should say if Henry didn't tell you, but she died five years ago. Henry took it hard. That's when he moved away and found religion. I guess it helped him heal."

"So the rest of your family aren't believers?" I asked.

Anthony shook his head. "I doubt mom ever would; she considers it a weakness, but I've thought about it, and I think dad has. It sure seems to give Henry something, a peace or something, you know?"

I nodded; I knew exactly about that peace as I had seen it in him myself. Unsure of what to say next, I pondered how Henry could have failed to tell me about his sister. Was that why his demeanor changed whenever he discussed his family? The music ended, and after thanking Anthony, I returned to Henry, more questions than ever coursing through my mind. Time seemed to crawl from that point on, but finally the end of the reception neared.

"It's time for the bouquet toss," the DJ announced into the microphone. Blushing, I grabbed the bouquet and headed to the middle of the floor where a chair was set up. Stepping onto the chair, I surveyed the small crowd of single women. Then I turned the opposite direction and tossed the bouquet into the air.

"I got it," Raquel's voice called, and I smiled. I figured she would be marrying soon whether she caught the bouquet or not, but I had hoped it would land in her hand.

Raquel and Greg carried the gifts outside to our car, and I approached my parents, handing them my spare keys. "Please enjoy the apartment. You can leave the keys on the table when you go, but don't forget to lock the door."

"It was so good to see you baby. Don't forget to come visit," my mother cried, hugging me as tears streamed down her face.

"Mom, why are you crying?" I asked, shaking my head.

"Because my baby is married," she sniffled into a tissue.

"Good grief, mother. I'm not going anywhere. You're just gaining a son."

My mother nodded and embraced Henry. "Take care of my baby."

Henry nodded, promising he would. Then he turned and shook my father's hand. Sylvia and David came over next and hugged Henry. David hugged me as well, but Sylvia could only muster a tepid handshake. I wondered if I would ever have a relationship with my mother-in-law. Raquel and Greg returned with the keys to our car and Raquel pulled me in for a fierce hug.

"Have a great time," she whispered in my ear, and my face flamed again.

"Well, shall we?" Henry held out his hand.

The guests had formed a line, and as we made our way to the car, tiny grains of rice pummeled us. I laughed, ducking my head and running faster as Henry tugged my hand.

When we reached the decorated car, the ball of nerves began to tangle in my stomach. The weight of Henry never having been intimate settled on my shoulders. What if it wasn't good and he hated it or felt cheated? What if he wished he'd never married me?

"What's wrong?" Henry asked, touching my arm and causing me to jump.

"Oh, nothing," I blushed, but decided to be honest anyway, "I just don't want you to be disappointed."

"Hey," – he folded me in an embrace and kissed my forehead – "I followed Jesus' commandments. He will bless our union, so I am not worried."

I nodded again, but the ball of nerves continued to tangle.

During the quiet drive to the hotel, the ball wound tighter. During the awkward check-in, it wound tighter still. When Henry took the hotel key, and we walked silently down the hall, I thought the nerves might tumble out of my stomach in a heaving mess. Henry inserted the key and turned the lock.

The door swung open, and he flicked the light on. A king size bed filled my view, and the nerves clamored up my throat. I swallowed to diffuse the sickening sensation.

This would be my first intimate encounter since "the procedure," and I had no idea if I'd be able to participate. The nausea had never surfaced with Henry, but what if it did in the middle of the act? I had never been able to be intimate with Peter again, but was that because it was Peter or because I was ruined for life?

Fear glued my feet to the floor, and Henry turned to see why I hadn't entered. His eyes roamed my face, and then he smiled and stretched out his hand. My arm wouldn't move at first, even though my heart wanted to go inside. I closed my eyes and took a deep breath; finally, my hand ventured up. The touch of his hand jolted my feet, and I crossed the threshold. The door clicked shut behind me.

On autopilot, I followed Henry to the bed, flanked on either side by a small brown dresser. The flowered pattern of the bedspread filled my vision as Henry laid me back. His lips moved down my neck, and as desire welled up inside me, I held my breath, hoping the nausea would not flare up.

An hour later, I lay smiling in his arms. As I traced a pattern on his chest with my finger, I felt a little lighter, as if one brick of the wall I had built over the last couple of years was finally crumbling. Sighing, I listened to the sound of his even breathing. I couldn't remember the last time I had felt such peace, and then I stiffened as another thought filled my head. What if I had a dream of the baby tonight? How would I ever explain them? The thought dimmed my good mood. I'd become so accustomed to sleeping alone that I hadn't thought about sharing the night with Henry.

Suddenly the urge for a drink blanketed me, and I licked my lips. I hadn't noticed a mini-bar in the room, and I didn't want to chance waking Henry by leaving the room, so I sent up a prayer for peace. Though not really expecting an answer, the desire ebbed, and my eyes grew heavy.

The next morning, Henry and I drove to the airport. I knew Henry didn't have much money to spend either, so I was surprised when the ticket he handed me said Hawaii. I peered up at him, questions in my eyes.

He smiled. "My mother has made quite a fortune," he said, "she bought us these tickets before she knew you weren't her kind of feminist, but she decided to let us use them anyway."

I laughed, and we headed to the terminal. After passing through security, we hurried to the gate and onto the plane. Having never been out of the continental United States, excitement and nervousness battled within me at the same time.

During the long flight, excitement won out, as the view shifted each time through my window. When we exited the plane, a woman handed us a lei. After grabbing our luggage, we took a shuttle to the hotel Henry's mother had booked.

The hotel sat right on the beach, and after dropping our bags in our room, we decided to take a walk down the sandy beach.

As we walked, I glanced at our entwined hands, happiness flooding my body. I smiled as I thought that maybe, just maybe, life was going to be okay now.

12

The Calm Before the Storm

After a wonderful week in Hawaii, we returned to the real world. As we pulled into the parking lot of our apartment complex, I laughed out loud.

"What is it?" Henry asked.

"Well, I guess we better decide whose apartment we are going to live in. It makes no sense to keep both."

He smiled. "Actually, I thought we'd look for a house."

"Really?" Immediately an image of a wrap-around front porch and a white picket fence jumped into my mind.

"Of course, apartments aren't great for kids. I want to have a big yard, so the kids will have lots of room to run. And maybe a pool." His eyes lit up as he was speaking, and I smiled back, hoping it would come true. Somewhere in the back of my mind though, I worried that I had ruined my chance of having kids. I knew, from attending church, that God did not condone abortion. What if my punishment was to never get pregnant again?

"That sounds lovely. I can't wait."

"For now, let's stay in yours. I have fewer clothes I would have to move," he laughed.

We each grabbed a stack of presents and carried them inside. After setting them on the table, Henry went back out for the rest of the gifts and our suitcases, and I took the moment to glance around the apartment. I didn't have any bottles still lying out, did I? I was pretty sure I had thrown away the last bottle when I had finished it.

Henry returned, and we stared at the mountain of gifts flowing off the table.

"I guess we better get started," I said, grabbing a notepad to keep a list of what was given by whom so I could send thank you notes later. We sat on the couch and took turns opening the gifts. Most of them were things we could use like towels and matching plates, but a few oddball gifts made their way into the stack.

"Does anybody actually use these?" I asked, holding up an ugly gravy boat with a weird blue symbol on the side.

"No one ever did in my house," he agreed, smiling, "but then again, we didn't eat a lot of gravy."

After finishing the gifts, we retired for the night. The jet lag was kicking in, and we both had work in the morning.

As I curled into Henry's arms in bed that night, I thought again about how perfect everything seemed.

Rising for work, after being off for a week, proved no easy task the next morning. After several eye rubs and two large cups of coffee, I made it out the door.

Raquel cornered me as soon as I entered the hospital to let me know she had set a date. I plastered a smile on my face and congratulated her, but I wondered if Greg would end up like Philip and so many other guys she had dated.

I invited her to church with us again, but, like always, she declined. I wasn't sure how much I should push her, especially since I wasn't sure of my own "status" with God, so I let the topic go and just enjoyed her company for the rest of the day, but I was really looking forward to going back home to Henry's arms.

I had always loved intimacy, until the "procedure" anyway, but there was something so much more special about being intimate with a spouse. No fear existed of him seeing someone else another night. No worry loomed about picking up some unknown disease or getting pregnant out of wedlock. In fact, I wrestled with the desire of wanting a baby now. On one hand, I really wanted children with Henry. I wanted them to fill the yard we didn't have yet and hear them laughing, but then I would remember how I threw my first child's life away, and I would wonder if I really deserved more children. How could I love them when I couldn't love that first baby enough to fight for him?

When I arrived home that evening, Henry stood waiting just inside the door, keys in hand.

"Are you ready?" he asked.

My forehead wrinkled, and I tilted my head, "Ready for what exactly?" I stifled a yawn; I was definitely ready to crawl into bed.

His eyes gleamed as a steady smile spread across his face. "Ready to see a house? I spoke with an agent today, and it sounds like everything we want. It just came on the market, and he can meet us in fifteen minutes. Want to go?"

I had never seen him so excited; he was nearly bouncing up and down. His exhilaration radiated off of him, sending my exhaustion to the back of my mind.

"Let me just change clothes," I said and hurried to the bedroom to pull on some jeans.

"So where is this house?" I asked as we drove.

"You'll see." Henry tapped his fingers on the steering wheel and hummed. A contagious smile stretched across his face from ear-to-ear. I found myself smiling and singing along with the music too.

The drive wasn't far, just twenty minutes or so to the edge of Mesquite. As he pulled into a driveway, I sucked in my breath. It was like he had read my mind. A white picket fence gated the blue and white house, and a huge wrap-around porch encircled it. A wooden rocking chair even sat on the porch, completing the mental picture I had formed in my imagination.

He parked next to what I assumed was the agent's car, and we got out. The gate squeaked just a little as he pushed it open, and then we walked up the gravel path to the front porch. As we reached the door, it swung open, and a man I vaguely recognized from church stood on the other side.

"Henry, Sandra, you made it. Welcome."

"Thank you James for letting me know about this." Henry stuck out his hand, and the men shook hands.

"You bet. Come on in. So, this house is 2100 square feet. Four bedrooms and three bathrooms."

Immediately dollar signs filled my head, and I flashed back to the first wedding dress shopping fiasco. Was I going to fall in love with the house only to find out we couldn't afford it? "That's way more house than we need," I said, imagining the payment and trying not to get my hopes up.

"Not if we plan to fill it with children," Henry teased and squeezed my hand. My face flushed hot, and James laughed.

"Well, this is, of course, the living room," James continued. The beige carpet in the spacious room appeared in decent shape, but the floral patterned wallpaper would definitely have to go. "And here's the kitchen," James led us into a charming beige and blue kitchen with white appliances.

"Plenty of room for a large dining table," Henry said, holding his hands in a square as if picturing it.

"And back here is a guest room or an office."

"Or a playroom for all the kids," Henry teased.

"And a bathroom," James continued. The bathroom was small – just a toilet and sink – but its soft rose color helped offset the size. "And upstairs we have the bedrooms, if you'll follow me." The staircase had an ornate brown rail, and as my hand trailed up it, I could almost see children sliding down it in the future.

The landing opened up to another beige carpeted hallway. The three bedrooms were all about the same size and shared the guest bathroom on one end. The master bedroom was situated at the other end, and as James opened the door, my jaw fell. The huge room gaped with space; plenty of room for a king-sized bed, a dresser, and even a desk and chair if we wanted. To the left, another door opened into a large walk-in closet and a large bathroom with both a shower and a soaking tub.

"Here's the best part." James brought us back into the room and led us to the large window. When he pulled back the curtain, a small balcony that oversaw the backyard appeared. A small swing set and slide were set up, but plenty of open grass remained for kids to run around in.

"It's perfect," I sighed, "but it has to be more than we can afford. It's so much house."

"Why don't we go back downstairs, and we can talk price," James suggested.

We followed him back to the kitchen, and he laid out some papers on the bar. “Okay, now, generally speaking this house would go for $120,000, but the owner is a friend of mine, and she specifically said if I found the right family for this house that she would take $100,000. I know you don’t have children yet, but Henry told me about your dream house and his dream of a house full of kids, and I think you guys are that family.”

“I can’t do that math in my head; what does that come out to each month?” I held my breath, hoping the answer would be low enough for us to afford.

“It’s about $500 a month, depending on taxes and your credit, of course.”

My heart stopped; he couldn’t be serious. A smile broke out across Henry’s face.

“We can do that,” he whispered. “We can do that.”

I nodded and squeezed his hand. “What do you think?”

He gazed into my eyes, and together we turned to face James. “We’ll take it.”

It took a few weeks for all the paperwork to go through, but soon we were moving into our new house. I convinced Henry to take down the hideous wall paper in the living room, and though he grumbled, he agreed the final result was worth it. We did a few other minor touchups, but the house had been pretty move-in ready.

Raquel, Greg, and a few other friends from church showed up to help us move. The men did most of the heavy lifting, while Raquel and I began unpacking. She rattled on about her upcoming wedding as I put away clothes in the dresser.

“Did you hear me?” she asked.

“I’m sorry, what?” I turned to face her.

“I said, I think I’m pregnant.”

My heart froze. I knew Raquel well enough to know she probably still wasn't ready to be a mom, but I couldn't believe she would have another abortion and tell me about it, knowing how terrible my experience was. "What are you going to do?" My voice came out barely more than a whisper, and I twisted the shirt I was holding into a knot.

"I don't know," she sighed, "I'm not sure I'm ready to be a mom yet, and besides I would never fit in my dress." My jaw dropped at her. Was that all she could care about? "But," – she continued, seeing my face – "though I didn't have the bad experience you did, I'm not sure I want to have another abortion either. It certainly wasn't the best thing I ever went through, and it can't be good on your body. I don't even know why I'm telling you; I guess I just needed to say it out loud. I haven't told Greg yet."

I pursed my lips, trying to think of the right words. Raquel was my friend, and I loved her, but I could no longer condone an abortion, and I wasn't sure if I would be able to be around her if she chose another one.

"I'm sorry. I shouldn't have said anything," she said. "Maybe I'm wrong anyway. It's only been a few days."

"If you're not wrong," I said, "please don't have an abortion. Give the baby up for adoption if you guys can't raise him or her, but please don't kill the baby. Henry would probably even want to raise the baby, if you can't."

Her eyes grew wide at the serious tone in my voice. "Okay, I'll think about it," she agreed, and a tense silence fell on us as we went back to our tasks.

I could think of nothing else the rest of the evening, and as I lay in bed with Henry that night struggling to focus on our devotional, he touched my arm.

"Hey, what's the matter? You've been acting weird all day."

I sighed. "I'm not sure if I should say anything; it isn't about me, really."

He picked up my hand and caressed the top. "I'm your husband. You can tell me anything, and I promise to keep your secret."

His brown eyes radiated sincerity, and I decided to trust him, at least with part of it. "Raquel thinks she might be pregnant, and she isn't sure she's ready."

His finger stopped its circling pattern on my hand. "I see. Are you jealous because she might beat us, or is there something else?" His voice sounded slightly off, and I glanced up at him. A hardness burned back in his eyes.

I had never seen this side of him. "Are you okay?"

He stared at the ceiling and took a deep breath. "Do you remember the night you met my parents?"

"How could I forget?" I scoffed. When he didn't laugh with me, I knew something serious was on his mind.

"Do you remember what my brother said?"

I thought back to the night a few months ago, and the scene replayed in my head. Suddenly, I remembered I had wanted to ask him what the cryptic exchange had been about, but I'd gotten so busy that I'd forgotten. Then my mind jumped to the wedding and Anthony telling me about the death of their sister.

"What happened to Camilla?" I asked. Henry's head snapped my direction. His eyes widened and filled with questions. "Anthony mentioned her at the wedding," I held my hand up as his eyes sparked. "He didn't know I didn't know."

He sighed and rubbed his forehead. "I should have told you a long time ago, but I guess I was ashamed."

"Of your sister dying?" I asked.

He shook his head. "Of the way she died." He took a deep breath. "Five years ago, my sister – who was a lot like my mom if you get my meaning – had too much to drink at a college party and ended up getting pregnant. I don't know if she wanted an abortion, but my mom convinced her to have one. For a while everything seemed okay, but then one night I went to surprise her with a pizza and . . ." his voice faltered as tears fell from his face. I squeezed his hand and waited. He wiped the tears and continued, "I got to her room and found her in bed. An empty bottle of pills lay on her nightstand. I called the ambulance, and they rushed her to the hospital, but it was too late." He ran a hand over his face, "When I went back to the dorm room to help pack up her stuff, I found the note she had written under her bed. She took the pills because she was so depressed from the abortion. We never even knew."

My heart fell as I thought about my own past. I could never tell Henry the full truth now. He would surely hate me forever.

"My mother refused to believe she was depressed over the abortion, and that's when I knew I had to get out of there. I moved out the very next day. In fact, I hadn't seen my mother face to face until she showed up for the wedding."

"Oh Henry, I'm so sorry. And I don't want Raquel to make the same mistake, but what can we do?"

"We can pray," he said, and he grabbed both of my hands. Together we prayed for Raquel, for God's will and his wisdom, for the life of the unborn child that might be growing in her belly at the very moment, and for healing for Henry. I silently added a prayer for myself, my past, Raquel's past, and the future with Henry. Though our subject was heavy, both of us felt lighter after giving the worry over to God. "Now, what do you say we work on making our own baby," he said, and I curled into him.

13

The Secret That Won't Go Away

"So, is there any word yet?" Henry asked, looking up from his plate as we ate dinner one night. Though he tried to be casual, I could sense the urgency in his voice.

I pushed the green beans around on my own plate, avoiding his gaze. "It was negative again."

"Hey, it's okay." He cupped his hand over mine. "It's only been six months. I'm sure we'll get pregnant soon."

I nodded, but the old doubt resurfaced. Peter and I had gotten pregnant the first time we didn't use protection, so why wasn't I getting pregnant with Henry? Now, when I was finally ready for a baby.

Even worse, I couldn't understand why Raquel was pregnant and I wasn't. She had had an abortion too and considered a second. Thankfully when she had told Greg, he had convinced her to choose life. It turned out, he really wanted to be a father. They had married, but it had been a rushed wedding before she began putting on weight. Henry and I had done it the right way, and I was remorseful of my procedure. So why was she pregnant and not me?

Henry switched the subject then – pulling my mind back to our situation – and began discussing his day. I nodded in all the right places, but my mind processed none of his words.

As I lay in bed that night, trying to read a book, the words blurred together as my vision filled with tears. Henry was being so supportive, but what if he wanted a divorce since we couldn't have kids? Here we had bought this huge house for kids, and we couldn't have any to fill it. I folded the book on my lap and closed my eyes.

"Lord," I whispered, "I know you probably don't listen to prayers from people like me, but please help us to have kids, for Henry's sake. I promise this time I won't squander the life you give."

My lips had uttered the same prayer nearly every night for the last few months, but every month the answer had been the same: a negative pregnancy test. As more tears fell down my cheek, I put the book away. There would be no reading tonight. I clicked off the light on the bedside, thankful that Henry was still watching news in the other room, and darkness descended.

The creak of the bed woke me some time later. I rolled over, expecting it to be Henry coming to bed, but a toddler in blue train pajamas bounced on Henry's side of the bed.

"Mama!" Pure joy lit up his face, and he toddled across the bed to me. My throat swelled as I blinked back the tears threatening to flow again.

"Baby," I reached out to him. The baby jumped into my arms, and I squeezed the boy tightly. The fresh clean scent of soap radiated from him. He put both of his chubby little hands on my face and peered into my eyes.

"Mama, why didn't you want me?"

The tears broke the dam, spilling down my cheeks. "Oh, baby, I'm so sorry. I didn't know you'd be so beautiful."

The boy cocked his head. "So if I were ugly, it would be okay?"

"No, I just . . ." I had no words. How did I explain to this little boy how selfish I had been? How did I tell him how much I wished I had made a different decision? "I'm just sorry. I wish I could take it back."

"Me too, mommy. I miss you." He sighed as he laid his little head on my chest, but it was the three words that broke my heart the most. I squeezed him even tighter and cried into his dark hair.

"I miss you too," I said over and over.

"Sandra, wake up." I opened my eyes to see Henry above me, hand on my shoulder. "What's wrong, Sandra?" He wiped a tear from my cheek, and I bit my lip, deciding how much to tell him.

Pushing myself into a sitting position, I asked hesitantly, "Do you remember when I told you I lost a baby?"

He nodded.

"Well, I have dreams of the baby sometimes. This time the baby was almost four, and he told me he missed me. I'm sorry if I woke you." *And I'm sorry I can't tell you the whole truth.*

"It's okay. I have dreams like that about my sister sometimes."

I nodded, "I can understand that. I'm sorry I didn't tell you about my dreams. They haven't come recently, and I thought they were over, but I guess not."

"Losing a child is hard."

I bit my lip. He had no idea. I lay back down and curled into Henry, but sleep didn't return for a long time. Losing a child was even harder when you were the reason they were gone.

Three months later, I stared down at Raquel's beautiful baby girl, Alyssa. Dark brown hair covered her head just like her mother's. She was perfect, and my heart ached as I held her. I so wanted a child of my own.

"You were right," Raquel said when it was just her and I in the room.

I glanced up from Alyssa's face, "Right about what?"

"How wrong we were. The moment I saw the first ultrasound I knew. She was a living being even then, and then I felt her move," she broke down in tears. "I've felt so guilty for months." Her shoulders heaved, and the tears poured down her cheeks.

Unsure of what to do, I rose from the chair and, cradling Alyssa in one hand, I placed another on Raquel's arm.

She grabbed my hand. "How did I not know? Why didn't we have ultrasounds then? Maybe it would have stopped me."

I sighed, "I don't know, I didn't get the feeling that they cared about me when I was there. Maybe it's just about the money to them. If it were really about choice, I would think they would want to give us all the options."

"How do I go on?" Her voice teetered on insanity. "How do I forgive myself?"

I squeezed her arm, "I don't have all those answers, but I know that you have to try. You have a beautiful daughter now, and she needs you. You can't just leave her."

Raquel sniffled, but a calmness returned to her eyes. "I know. I would never do anything to hurt her, but I can't stop thinking about the other baby now."

"I know. That's how it's been for me from the beginning, but hopefully you can move on now. We can't even get pregnant, and I'm starting to think something's wrong." It was the first time I had voiced my suspicion aloud, and ice trickled through my veins at the thought.

Raquel gasped, and her eyes widened, "Oh, Sandra, I'm so sorry, and here I was going on. Do you know for sure?"

I shook my head. "No, I've been too scared to check. I'm going to give it a little longer. I keep hoping it's just stress or something else, but I'm so afraid." Tears spilled down my cheeks.

Raquel squeezed my arm back, and together we cried over our past mistakes.

Six months after that, I sat on the floor of my living room playing with Alyssa. Raquel sat nearby reading my Bible. After our discussion in the hospital, she had started coming to church with us, and like myself, she had found comfort in the words of God. Unlike myself, she seemed to have been able to forgive herself and move on, not that she still didn't have bad days where she cried for the baby she had killed, but she seemed more like Henry, more complete. I wondered if I couldn't get there because I couldn't get pregnant. Would I be able to forgive myself easier if I had a new life to look after?

Alyssa cooed, and I smiled down at her. Raquel had asked me to be her godmother, and I had gladly accepted, but even all the time I spent with her couldn't take away the desire to have my own child.

"You know what's odd?" Raquel spoke up from the couch. "I can't actually find anything about abortion in the Bible. Why do you think God didn't put a specific commandment in there? Do you think he didn't know how far we would fall?"

"I don't know about that. I've heard people at the church say that God knows everything we will ever do, so I guess he would have had to see this coming. And there is a commandment about killing: Thou Shall Not Kill, but I think more importantly, and what people forget, is that God believes life begins at conception. There are many verses that talk about women being "with child" and God breathing life into their wombs. I've heard a lot of times that Jesus spoke in parables to make sure those who read them really wanted to know, and I think some of the other big questions are like that too. God didn't want someone to just be able to open the Bible and pick out a specific verse; he wanted us to gain knowledge from reading and letting the Holy Spirit talk to us."

Raquel regarded me with wide eyes.

"What?" I asked, shrugging. "I listen when they speak. Just because I have a hard time believing God could forgive me doesn't mean I wasn't paying attention."

"You know he will forgive you if you ask," Raquel said quietly. "He forgave me, and you are no guiltier."

"What if I ask, and I still can't get pregnant?" I asked. "What will I do then?"

Raquel sighed and shrugged her shoulders. Here we were, two people who didn't really understand God or his word completely, trying to help each other and failing miserably.

Alyssa took that moment to move forward just an inch on the carpet, and the discussion was forgotten. "You did it," I scooped her up, planting a kiss on her delicate porcelain cheek. She smiled in return and babbled at me. I hugged her close, relishing the smell of baby lotion and milk, and she slapped her hands on my face. My mind wandered back to the last dream of the boy touching my face in the same way. The dreams had been surprisingly absent, and I wasn't sure whether that was a good thing or a bad thing.

The front door opened, and Henry entered laden with bags. I handed Alyssa to Raquel and hurried to see if he needed help.

"What is all this?" I smiled as he set down the bags.

"Well, I thought maybe we could use some positive vibes, so I bought paint, and I'm going to paint the nursery. Maybe if we get it ready, the baby will come."

Hope glistened in his eyes, and a stone fell in my stomach. I pasted on a smile, though. "That is awesome. Do you want some help?"

"No, I've got it. Hi, Raquel." He waved to her before planting a kiss on my cheek and then took a bag in each hand up the stairs.

"You have to get checked," Raquel whispered as I sat beside her on the couch.

I dropped my head in my hands, "I know, but I'm so scared."

I sat in the doctor's office biting my nail. After nearly two years of trying, Raquel had finally convinced me to at least get checked out. When the exam ended, the doctor had showed me to her office while she went to view the tests and gather the paperwork. As terrible as the thought was, I hoped it was a problem on Henry's side. It would be awful having to tell him, but we could look at other options, but if it was my fault . . . what would I tell him?

The door opened, and Dr. Warren entered with paperwork in her hand. Her blond hair was pulled back in a ponytail and her horn-rimmed glasses sat on her nose, but it was the expression on her face that enlarged the lump of fear in my stomach. Normally a pleasant serene woman, the serious expression appeared out of place on her face. Dr. Warren sat at her mahogany desk across from me and pushed her small grey glasses up her nose. She cleared her throat and clasped her hands. Her eyes still focused on the papers on her desk.

She shuffled some of them around before looking up at me. "Um, I have to ask you, Sandra. You said in your history that you lost a child; was that a natural loss?"

My blood ran cold, and my throat tightened. I dropped my eyes to my lap. "What . . . what do you mean?"

When I peeked up, steely gray eyes met my gaze. "I mean that you have scarring in your uterus as if you had a pregnancy terminated. Did you have a pregnancy terminated?"

The lump clawed its way up my stomach and lodged in my throat. "I did," I whispered. "Five years ago. Is it bad?"

The gray eyes softened, and Dr. Warren sighed, "I'm sorry, Sandra, the scarring is so bad that you'll never be able to have children again."

The world grew silent around me, and my hands clenched into balls in my lap. "No, there must be something we can do," I shook my head, willing her to be wrong.

"There isn't. The damage is too extensive. I'm sorry."

"But . . . but they told me it was safe. It was supposed to be easy." I tried to grapple with the knowledge, but my brain refused to accept the words coming out of the doctor's mouth.

"I'm afraid there is a risk with any surgery." She leaned forward in her chair. "Are you saying they never went over any risks with you?"

I shook my head. "I don't remember any."

"Well, that is unfortunate. They should at least inform you of all the risks. You might be able to take some legal action if you can prove it. Take as long as you need, and again I'm really sorry, Sandra." Dr. Warren stood and picked up the papers. She paused for a minute, as if unsure if she should say more, but then turned and exited the room.

I stared at my hands. What was I going to tell Henry? He'd be devastated. He had made no secret of the fact that he wanted a big family. He had even painted two of the rooms, one pink and one blue, so we'd be prepared either way. Worse yet, I'd have to tell him about the abortion. Embarrassment compounded on the grief, and my long forgotten loathing of Peter and myself bubbled back to the surface.

Why had I ever let him convince me to have an abortion? It had not only ruined our relationship, but now my chance to have children, and he was probably married to Sheila by now with kids of his own. The anger boiled inside of me, and I grabbed my purse and stalked out of the office.

As I drove home, the anger turned to despair as I practiced ways to tell Henry the bad news. Nothing sounded right.

The white picket fence came into view, and sweat broke out on my palms. What was I going to do? I pulled into the driveway and took a deep calming breath. I'd just wait until the time was right. That would be the best way. Thankfully Henry was still at work, and I hadn't told him about the appointment, so I wouldn't have to tell him right away.

I set my purse down and wandered into the living room. The wedding picture of us called to me from the coffee table. I picked it up and touched Henry's face. Happiness was written on both of our faces. Could we continue that happiness now that we couldn't have kids? Would Henry forgive me and look at adoption? Or would he want to leave me as he'd wanted to leave his mother when she convinced his sister to have one?

Henry's key sounded in the lock. "Sandra," he hollered.

I put the picture frame down and met him in the front entrance. "What is it?" I asked, hoping my face wouldn't give me away.

"I just wrote a huge policy. We should go celebrate. Let's go out to dinner." He picked me up and twirled me around.

His enthusiasm was contagious, and I found myself smiling in spite of my news. "Okay, let me go change."

"Yes, something special. Let's go somewhere nice."

I headed into the bedroom and picked out a nice black dress. Henry entered behind me and changed his shirt, adding a tie. Within thirty minutes, we were both ready and locking the door behind us.

Henry drove to an upscale steak restaurant, and after a short wait, we were seated at a table near the back. The dimmed lights created a romantic glow. I nibbled on a slice of bread as Henry regaled his day. If only I had good news to share with him as well; instead I had the ball of lies roiling around in my stomach. I took a drink of water, but it did nothing to douse the acidic flame churning inside.

The waiter came, took our order, and left. Henry continued to share the details of his policy, and I tried to listen and nod in all the right places. Dinner came, and I forced the food into my mouth, even though my appetite had disappeared as the churning grew. Henry chatted on between his bites, unaware of my lack of conversation. He even ordered dessert, and we shared a warm chocolate brownie topped with ice cream. Then the check came; Henry paid; and we arose from the table.

Fall was approaching, and the air held just a bit of chill as we exited the restaurant. Henry wrapped his arm around my shoulders as we walked to the car, and the guilt grew. As he opened my door, I thought for just a second that maybe we could just go on like this, just the two of us, or that he'd be open to adoption. Maybe, everything would be okay. Maybe, I could just never tell him and continue to pretend not to know why we couldn't get pregnant. Henry started the car and turned on the heater. The warm air conflicted with the icy turmoil inside me, and beads of sweat broke out on my forehead.

"This policy will pay for college for the kids, I think," he said pulling onto the street. "And maybe we can look into in vitro fertilization. I know it's expensive and still relatively new, but there must be some reason we aren't getting pregnant, and maybe that can help. If I can just write a few more policies like the one today, then we could probably afford it. . ."

My guilt grew as he continued talking. I bit my nail and stared out the window.

"... Maybe they'll let us do a payment plan. Then we could really look into it."

And finally it bubbled over, and I burst out, "I can't have kids."

He turned to look at me, "What do you mean you can't have kids? I thought you said you lost a child five years ago. You got pregnant then; why couldn't you get pregnant now?"

I took a deep breath. Now was as good as time as any. "About that, I haven't been completely honest with you." His face had turned back to the road, but his eyes glanced over at me. I twisted my hands in my lap. "I told you I lost a child about five years ago, but the truth is I had an abortion." He sucked in his breath and his knuckles, gripping the steering wheel, turned white. I hurried to spit the rest out before I lost my nerve. "Evidently they botched the procedure, and it scarred my uterus. The doctor told me today I would never be able to get pregnant again." His head whipped to stare at me, and I shrank back from the anger in his eyes. I had never seen him angry. "I'm sorry," I repeated and clutched my hands together. His mouth opened, but no sound came out, and then a horn blared.

I turned as lights filled my vision. "Henry," I yelled. He yanked the steering wheel to the right, narrowly avoiding the oncoming car, but the car over-corrected and hit the gravel on the side of the road, spinning out of control. "Lookout!" Henry tried to turn the steering wheel, and the squeal of tires braking hit my ears, but it didn't keep us from slamming into the big oak tree. My head slammed forward hitting the glove compartment and everything went dark.

The sound of scraping metal woke me. The air was metallic and cold. I tried to turn my head, but the pain was too great. Out of the corner of my left eye, I could see Henry's face against the steering wheel, blood poured down his forehead. "Henry," I called, "Henry, talk to me."

"This one's alive." A male voice reached my ears, and the scraping of metal grew louder. I wanted to plug my ears, but my hands wouldn't move either. The scraping stopped, and the man spoke again. "We're working to get you out ma'am. Just hang on. What's your name?"

"Sandra," I replied, "How's my husband, Henry?"

"I'm not sure, but we're working on getting you both out. Try to hold still now."

The scraping grew louder again, and then cooler air hit my skin. How long had we been in the car?

"My name is Brad. We're going to get you out. Does anything hurt?"

I closed my eyes to focus. "My head, and I can't move my arms or legs."

"Okay, just hold on." Hands reached in and cut the seatbelt off. Then more hands pulled me from the car, and I found myself leaning back on something hard. The stars were out.

"What time is it?" I asked.

"It's two am." Kind brown eyes filled my vision. "Do you know what time you crashed?"

"Um," – I closed my eyes trying to remember – "we left dinner at eight-thirty so between then and nine, I guess."

"Okay, that's good."

Blocks appeared and were placed on either side of my head. Straps closed across my middle and my forehead. The bright flashing lights of the ambulance blinded me. I blinked and tried to look around for Henry.

Brad laid a hand on my arm. "Hold still."

"My husband, Henry. Where is he?"

The gurney was hoisted up, and the ceiling of the ambulance came into view. The light was bright, but I had to know. The kind brown eyes glanced at the other EMT in the back of the ambulance as the doors slammed, and it started moving. "I think they're still working on him. We'll know more when we get to the hospital. Try to relax."

I closed my eyes and sent up a small prayer for safety for Henry and for myself. The ride to the hospital felt long and bumpy. The EMT set up an IV, but I barely felt the poke in my arm. The loud siren squealing in my ears deepened the pounding in my head, and the lights were too bright, even behind my closed eyelids.

Then the ambulance stopped, and the door opened. The gurney was pulled out, and the cool night air chilled me again. I heard the whoosh of the hospital doors, and a bevy of doctors appeared on all sides. The EMT rattled off medical jargon that should have made sense to me – if my head hadn't been so fuzzy – and then the doctors took over. Hands unstrapped my head, my torso, my feet. *My feet had been strapped?* One doctor held my head as the others rolled me slightly to remove the wooden board. Then I was on my back again.

A Hispanic woman with dark curly hair came into view. "I'm Dr. Torrez. We're going to take you for an x-ray to see what we need to do, okay?"

"Okay," I whispered as I still couldn't move my head to nod. The tiles of the ceiling flashed by as I was wheeled down the hall. How different the view was this way! I had walked this hospital a million times, but it appeared so odd being wheeled down the familiar hallways. We turned left into a darker room with a large x-ray machine. A team of nurses hefted the gurney onto the x-ray machine.

"Ma'am?" Dr. Torrez's face appeared in my vision again. "We're about to do the x-ray. Is there any chance you're pregnant?"

Tears welled up in my eyes again. "No, no chance at all."

The woman squeezed my hand and departed. The whir of the machine was the only sound in the room. When it was finished, the team came back in and hefted me back on the rolling gurney. Then I was wheeled back down the hallway and into a room in the emergency room.

"I'll be back as soon as I have the x-rays," Dr. Torrez said.

"Wait, can you tell me about my husband, Henry?" I asked before the doctor left the room.

"I'll check for you."

The silence descended as the door closed. Pity crept in and blanketed me. This "easy" procedure five years ago had already taken a relationship, my chance to have children, and now caused an accident. What else was it going to rob from me? I bit my lip as worry for Henry crawled in as well. No one seemed to know what had happened to him, but he hadn't looked good in the car.

I could hear the bustle of doctors and nurses outside and a hum of some kind of equipment in the room. Finally, Dr. Torrez re-entered the room.

"How are you doing, Sandra?" the doctor asked.

"I'm nervous. I still can't feel my feet, and no one has told me about Henry. Do you have some news?"

Dr. Torrez's eyes shifted quickly to the right, and she took a deep breath. "I have some news about you, but I still haven't heard anything about Henry."

"What is it?" I asked as a sinking sensation swam down my throat.

"I'm afraid you've injured your T4 and T5 vertebrae."

"What does that mean?" Even though I had studied anatomy, the words refused to form a conclusion in my brain. The room began to close in on me.

"I'm afraid it means that you are paralyzed from the waist down."

The words tumbled in my foggy head. "So, I'll never walk again?"

"No, but you have full use of your arms, and you should be able to drive a modified car if you need to."

"Are you sure? Maybe if I exercise enough? Or Therapy? Surely, there's some surgery . . ."

Dr. Torrez shook her head. "I'm sorry, Sandra; your injury was extensive. I don't see walking in your future."

As the words began to sink in, tears pooled in my eyes again. "I see. Can you check on Henry for me?"

"I can. Do you want me to call anyone for you?"

I bit my lip thinking. I didn't want to tell my parents yet. Was there anyone else? "Yes, can you call my friend Raquel Miller? She works here."

"Of course," Dr. Torrez nodded. "I'll have the nurses come make you more comfortable. We'll want to keep you a while for observation and some therapy." She turned and left the room, leaving me in silence once again.

I tried vainly to wiggle my toes, but I could feel nothing. Still, I wasn't entirely sure I trusted the doctor's opinion. Perhaps a second opinion would yield different results.

A few minutes later, two nurses entered the room. One was tall and muscular with short brown hair, and the other was shorter and blond.

"Hi, I'm Jennifer and this is Alex. We'll be your nurses tonight till six am. We're going to get you in something more comfortable, okay?"

I nodded at the taller one speaking. I didn't trust my voice to say much.

Jennifer pulled out a hospital gown and a pair of scissors. She cut the dress, which was already ripped in several areas, and the two of them helped me sit up. Then Alex helped me slip my arms in the purple flowered gown, and they tied it in back and laid me back down, pulling the black dress out from underneath me. Jennifer pulled the sheet up over my legs. "I'm going to go get you some water, but is there anything else we can do for you right now?"

I shook my head.

"Okay, well here's the remote if you want to watch some TV." She handed me a white remote. "We'll be in to check on you every hour or so. There's a call button here if you need us before then." Jennifer pointed to a button in the rail of the bed.

"Thank you," I managed, and the two women left the room. I glanced at the ceiling as tears slid down my cheeks. "Is this my punishment, God?" I whispered. "It took this long, but finally I'm being punished? I'm so sorry. I'm sorry I ever had the abortion. Please forgive me."

Though I had been attending church with Henry for years, I had never truly asked for forgiveness because I had thought God would not forgive me and because I could not forgive myself, but now as I lay on the bed, fairly certain I would never walk again, I realized I had nothing to hold on to but hope. So for the first time in five years, I truly gave it over to God, hoping that he would help Henry and myself. A tiny sliver of peace formed in my heart.

A knock sounded at the door and Dr. Torrez poked her head in. "Hey, Sandra, how are you doing?"

"I guess as good as I can be. Do you have news about Henry?"

Dr. Torrez shuffled in, shutting the door behind her. "I do. I'm afraid it's not good. They worked really hard to get Henry out, but when they were finally able to, they found the impact had fractured his skull. I'm afraid there was nothing they could do."

My heart froze. "What . . . what does that mean?"

Dr. Torrez stepped closer and took my hand. "I'm afraid he was killed on impact. He's not coming back, Sandra."

"No," I shook my head, "No, you have to be wrong. He can't be gone. He can't."

"I'm so sorry, Sandra." Dr. Torrez pulled up a stool and sat beside me. "Can I get someone to come and talk with you until your friend arrives?"

"Um," I searched my mind. Was there anyone who could help me? Maybe not, but I did have questions, and only one person would be able to answer those. "Is there a pastor or chaplain on site?"

Dr. Torrez blinked. "Uh yeah, I think so. Shall I call him for you?"

"Please."

Dr. Torrez nodded and squeezed my hand. "I'll have him check in soon with you."

"Have you called Henry's family? His parents and his brother?"

"Yes, I believe they've called them. Would you like me to tell them to come see you when they get here?"

"Yes, I need to talk with them."

"Do you want me to call your family?"

I thought about my mother, how excited she had been the last time we had seen her and told her we were trying to have kids. I pictured my father, who once again had hugged me tight when we left their place, and I just didn't have the heart to tell them right away. Still they would be mad if they found out the news from someone else. "Yes, please call my parents. They'll have to take a flight in."

The doctor nodded and left the room again. The peace I had felt just moments earlier was ebbing away, and I desperately wanted it back. "Lord? Are you there, Lord? I don't know how to go on without Henry. Please Jesus, show me what to do. Help me. Please help me." The little kernel of peace began to grow again, shrouded as it was in sadness.

Sometime later, a knock sounded again. A short balding man with gray hair stepped in the room. "Sandra? I'm pastor Clive. The doctor said you wanted to see me?"

"I did. I need help." I poured out my story from sordid beginning to sad present. Pastor Clive sat by the bedside holding my hand.

"My dear, I am so sorry for your loss. Have you talked to his family?" he asked.

I shook my head. "They aren't here yet. I don't know what to say to them. I knew he hated abortion after what happened to his sister; I don't know why I told him in the car."

"Some things are not for us to know. Now, let me ask you daughter, you said your husband was religious. Do you know God as your father and savior?"

"I don't know. I've been attending church and reading the Bible, but I never thought God could accept me because of the abortion, you know?"

He patted my hand. "That is a grave sin, you are right, but God can forgive even that if your heart is in the right place, and you confess that it was a sin."

"It was the worst thing I've ever done, but I want to move on. I want to know God the way my husband did; how do I do that?"

He led me in a prayer of confession, and amid my despair, a peace like I'd never felt before trickled down my spine. However, it didn't erase the sadness and confusion raging through my body.

Though I feared his answer, I had to know. "Did God take Henry because I didn't ask for forgiveness a long time ago?"

He shook his head. "That isn't how God works. Unfortunately, this world is imperfect and sinful, and bad things happen. You need to ask forgiveness from Henry's family, and then ask God how to use you now. It won't be easy, but God will be there for you."

Pastor Clive shared some verses from the Bible with me, and we prayed again before he left.

Raquel arrived shortly after the pastor left, dressed to the nines in a form-fitting black dress. "Oh honey, I'm so sorry. They told me what happened at the front desk." She hugged me, and the tears I thought were gone started anew.

"What am I going to do, Raquel?"

"I don't know, but we'll find a way to work through this together. We'll pray, and we'll figure something out."

She pulled up the stool beside me and grabbed my hand.

"Where's Alyssa?" I asked.

"She's still with the babysitter. Greg and I were having a nightcap out. He went home to be with her, and I canceled my shift for tomorrow, so I have a little time with you."

I nodded and poured out the entire story to Raquel, who cried along with me, dabbing her eyes every few minutes. When there was nothing left to say, we sat in silence until my lids grew heavy.

Sylvia, David, and Anthony arrived the next day. I had just finished lunch when the knock sounded on my door. As the door opened, I hit the button to raise the bed, so I could sit up to talk to them.

They entered slowly, and I swallowed. Sending up a quick prayer for the words to say to them, I started with, "I'm so sorry."

David and Anthony crossed to either side of the bed, but Sylvia held back.

"Can you tell us what happened?" David asked quietly. His face was more haggard than I remembered, as if he'd aged ten years in the last two.

I bit my lip and glanced from one man to the other. "Well, Henry and I were trying to have children. After nearly two years with no positive results, I went to the doctor." I took a deep breath. "Five years ago, I was with another man, and we got pregnant. He wasn't ready to be a father, and he convinced me to have an abortion." They all noticeably stiffened, but I continued. "The procedure caused scarring and left me unable to have children. I didn't mean to tell Henry in the car, but he kept talking about our future kids, and it just spilled out. He took his eyes off the road, and we veered into traffic. Then he overcorrected, and we hit a tree. I'm so sorry." I had thought I had no more tears left, but after telling the story again, they made their way down my cheeks like soldiers in formation.

"It's my fault," Sylvia moaned behind us as she sank to the floor. "It's all my fault. If I had never pushed Camilla to have an abortion, she wouldn't have died, and Henry wouldn't have left and had the reaction he did. I didn't want the shame of a pregnant daughter who was not married, and I told Camilla the abortion was empowering as a woman, but I was wrong. It's horrible, and now it's taken two of my children." David went to his wife and put an arm around her as sobs racked her body.

I stared at Anthony, unsure of what to say. He squeezed my hand, telling me that he, at least, didn't blame me for the accident. It also gave me the courage for the words that poured out of my mouth. "I don't know if you know God like Henry did, but I just truly found him yesterday. Can I pray for all of us?"

The family nodded, and I led a prayer, feeling closer to them than I had in the last two years. We shared tears before they left to deal with the funeral preparations.

My parents arrived later that afternoon. My mother entered the room, frazzled, an unusual look for her. She rushed to my side and enveloped me in a hug. My father hung back at the door. Thankfully Raquel had filled them in on the story when she picked them up at the airport, so I didn't have to go over it again. I returned my mother's hug and then motioned for my father to come closer. As he stepped to the bed, I realized he was struggling to contain his emotions. His red and puffy eyes betrayed the fact that he had recently been crying.

"It's okay dad. I don't know how, but I know God is going to take care of me."

He nodded and clasped my other hand, but he didn't seem convinced.

"We're going to stay until you get out. Maybe a little longer. Your dad's going to work on adapting the house for you," my mother's words tumbled out in a rush.

"You don't have to do that," I said.

"Yes we do," my father added, "and we aren't taking no for an answer."

I nodded, and my eyes filled with moisture. I guessed some help would be necessary to get reacquainted with my new life.

Though I wasn't set to be released for another two weeks, the doctors allowed me to attend Henry's funeral as long as a nurse went with me. I'd never been so thankful that Raquel was a nurse. She showed up the morning of the funeral – Alyssa strapped to her chest – with a bag for me. My mother and father entered behind her.

After setting Alyssa down to let her crawl around, she and my mother helped me get into the simple black dress and into the wheelchair. Though I had been working with therapy, there were still so many things I couldn't do. I wondered sometimes how I was going to survive on my own. They helped me wheel into the bathroom, so I could brush my teeth and apply makeup. When I was finished, Raquel set Alyssa on my lap and pushed me out of the hospital with my parents following close behind.

I hugged Alyssa, but a new tug pulled at my heart. The possibilities of ever having my own children were definitely gone now. If I could barely take care of myself, I wouldn't be able to adopt. A seed of jealousy stirred in my heart. Why had Raquel been given a second chance when I hadn't? Alyssa patted my face, and I smiled, swallowing the sadness and pity that had been building up and squelching the jealousy, for now.

Raquel had borrowed a van that could load a wheelchair, and after we were secured, she headed to Potter's cemetery. A large crowd had assembled at the gravesite, but they broke apart as we approached, letting us make our way to the front. The pastor spoke first, and then it was my turn. I rolled to the front and turned to face the crowd. *Lord, please give me the words to say.* Closing my eyes, I took a deep breath before beginning.

"Henry was the best man I've ever known. He loved God, and he loved me. He took me to church when I wasn't a believer, and he was patient with me. I don't know why bad things sometimes happen to good people, but I know Henry is in heaven watching down, and I know I will see him again one day."

Other friends stepped forward and shared their stories of Henry, and then it was over. I threw a rose in on Henry's casket and hugged the friends and family good-bye. Alyssa had fallen asleep on Raquel's lap, and she handed her to me as we wheeled back to the van.

The quiet ride back to the hospital allowed the reality of my life to encroach on me. How was I going to manage? What was I going to do for a job? I could no longer be a nurse, so what would I do now?

"I wish I could stay longer," Raquel said as she dropped me off, "but I really need to get Alyssa back."

"And we need to finish getting the house ready for you," my mother added.

I nodded and assured them I would be fine, but in my heart I wondered if I really would be.

14

The Light at The End of the Tunnel

After two weeks of extensive therapy, the hospital finally released me. Raquel helped set me up with a modified van, and I was able to drive myself home, but Raquel followed to make sure everything was set up at the house.

As I pulled up to the house, the sadness set in again. Though the house appeared the same on the outside, except for the ramp my father had erected over the stairs, I knew the empty inside loomed. There would be no Henry waiting for me, and there would be no Henry coming home.

I rolled up the ramp, and opened the door. A cold chill descended. And silence. No children would ever slide down the banister. The swings would remain motionless in the backyard. There would never again be a husband to come home to. Before I could stop it, a giant sob escaped, and I began crying uncontrollably.

Raquel dropped the bag she was carrying and rushed to my side, "Are you okay? Are you hurt?"

"It's gone," I said, "It's all gone."

"Oh, Sandra, it will be okay. We're here for you. I'll bring Alyssa to come play, and it will be okay."

I nodded, but that seed of jealousy flared inside me again, and all I really wanted was her gone. Why had I been unable to have kids while she had Alyssa? Why had my husband died when hers was at home waiting for her? "Can you go and get some clothes from the bedroom upstairs so I don't have to? I'll sleep on the couch for now."

"Of course," she hurried up the stairs, and my mind wandered to alcohol. I hadn't had a drink in years, but suddenly I wanted nothing more. Though my parents weren't at the house now, they would be back soon. How was I going to get a drink? I couldn't ask Raquel, could I? Maybe if I had just the right excuse. She came back down the stairs, arms laden with clothes. "I wasn't sure what all you might need, so I grabbed some pajamas, underthings, casual clothes, and socks. Oh and your toothbrush and toothpaste."

"Thank you, that will be perfect." I paused, searching for the right words. "Could I trouble you for one more thing?"

"Sure, anything."

"I'm not sure where my parents are or when they might be back. Could you get me a bottle of wine? I just need a little to calm my nerves. It will be my first night in the house alone without Henry." It wasn't my usual fare, but I figured if I could drink most of the bottle, then it might do the trick, and I certainly couldn't ask her to buy me vodka. She'd never agree to that. I hoped my puppy dog eyes would convince her.

She cocked her head at me, narrowing her eyes, but finally agreed, and an hour later I was alone with my bottle. Turning on the TV, and foregoing a glass, I upended the bottle and chugged. It didn't have the burn I so enjoyed, but after the third or fourth chug, the world finally grew hazy. I set the bottle on the floor beside me and closed my eyes.

"Mama, mama wake up." A hand tugged at my sleeve. As I opened my eyes, I found myself staring into a pair of brown eyes on a young boy's face.

"Isaac?" It had been so long since the dreams had come.

"Hi mama," he smiled.

"Go away." I closed my eyes, hoping he would just disappear. "I wouldn't be in this situation if it hadn't been for you."

"That's not fair mama; it was your choice remember?"

Choice. I hated the word now. It wasn't my choice to become sterile or to lose my husband or my ability to walk. It was one decision, one stupid wrong decision. "Go away," I repeated.

"Mama, look at me." Little hands touched my face, and I opened my eyes. A little boy still stood before me, but there was something about him. Something different. "You are not done yet. You have to help the others."

"What others?"

"The other women, the other babies. Tell your story so that others may live."

And then he was gone. My story? How was I supposed to tell my story? Sighing, I picked up the bottle and finished it. I had just closed my eyes again when I heard the key in the front door. For a second, my heart sped up, hoping it was Henry, but then reality set in again as I heard my parents' voices.

"Ssh, it looks like she's sleeping." My mother's voice met my ears. Then silence until the slight squeaking of the stairs which meant they had headed upstairs to either our room or the guest room. I sighed, letting sleep overtake me.

I woke the next morning to the sound of my mother making

breakfast in the kitchen. After climbing into the wheelchair, I rolled into the kitchen. My mother stood at the stove, frying some eggs. She turned when I entered.

"Hi honey, how are you? I'm sorry we weren't here for you yesterday. We thought you were getting home today."

"It's fine mom; Raquel was with me." I rolled to the pantry and opened the door, surprised to see everything on the bottom few shelves within easy reaching distance. I grabbed the coffee and a filter and rolled over to the coffee pot. It was just out of reach.

"Here, let me help you," my mother said coming over. She took the coffee and filters and set the coffee up brewing.

Sighing, I rolled to the table, dropping my head in my hands. "This is going to be harder than I thought. I can't even make my own coffee."

"Don't worry honey." My mother placed a plate of eggs and bacon in front of me. "Your father is working on ways to make it work, and we'll stay until it's done. I can definitely move everything a little closer for you."

"Thanks." I ate the food in front of me, but tasted nothing. The last thing I wanted was my parents waiting on me hand and foot.

My father entered a few minutes later and joined me at the table. He handed me a mug of coffee and sipped his own. "I've finished the ramp at the front of the house and a ramp in the bathroom to reach the sink," he said. "I'm going to build you a lower table in here, so we can move all the electronics you need to it. Is there anything else you think you will need?"

"I just need my dresser brought down or one down here. I can't make it up the stairs, so for now I'll be staying on the couch."

"Okay, we'll take care of that for you today." My mother joined us at the table.

I finished eating and excused myself to get ready for work. Raquel showed up a few minutes later to go with me. Though I had no idea what I was supposed to do when I got there, they had promised they would have something for me.

When we arrived at work, everyone rushed over with condolences. Although I knew they were trying to be nice, all it did was grind the pain in more. Nurse Hatchett even tried to hug me before sending me to human resources to find out what my new job would be.

"Ah, Sandra, I'm so sorry for your loss," Doug, the human resource manager, said as I entered the office.

"Thank you." The response automatically tumbled out now.

"Well, ah, we are looking to see if there's an area we can modify for you, but until that happens, I have chart entry that you can do." He pointed to a stack of Manilla folders on the corner of his desk and a computer in the back corner.

Pasting a smile on my face, I hefted the stack onto my lap and wheeled back to the computer. I didn't mind data entry, but this was not what I trained for, and I couldn't imagine doing it long term.

On my way home that evening, I stopped at a liquor store and bought three bottles of vodka. I told myself I would only drink a little. I lied. After my parents had gone to sleep for the night, I drank half of the first bottle before falling asleep.

The next morning, I woke to my mother shaking my shoulder. "Sandra, you're late for work."

I couldn't remember a time I had been late, but the alcohol had knocked me out, and I had slept through the alarm. Thankfully, I had hidden the bottles before I had fallen asleep.

After quickly dressing and downing some breakfast, I hurried to work. Though Doug chided me, it seemed everyone was too "sorry" for me to really lay the hammer down. I sat at my desk – mindlessly inputting numbers – and thinking about my next drink.

"Are you coming to church?" Raquel asked me as we clocked out for the day.

We had both been attending a Bible study on Wednesday nights before my accident, but I hadn't been back since. I ran my hand over my neck and dropped my eyes to avoid her gaze. "Uh, no, I'm tired tonight, and my parents are leaving in the morning, but I'll try to make it Sunday." Raquel nodded, but she didn't believe me. I didn't either.

The next morning, my parents stood in the living room, concern all over their faces.

"Are you sure you're going to be alright?" my mother asked. She twisted her hands together and her forehead wrinkled. Her familiar gesture of worry touched me, but I couldn't live with my parents forever.

"Mom, I'll be fine. Dad adapted everything so I can reach it. It's just going to take time to adjust, but I'll be fine."

My mother bit her lip and looked to my father. "Okay, but please call us if you need anything. I just hate leaving you all alone here." I hugged them goodbye and watched them walk out of the door.

The silence set in immediately and closed over me. A distraction; I needed a distraction. After glancing around the room, I decided on a book. I hadn't read in ages, but it had once been a favorite past time. Plucking a random book off the shelf, I situated myself in the chair and opened the book. The black lines swam, and the silence grew deafening. When it became unbearable, I tossed the book aside and sought the safe refuge of the bottle.

When Sunday rolled around, I called Raquel with the excuse of a headache. I didn't even really know why I didn't want to go to church. Was it because it reminded me of Henry? Or was it because I had so quickly fallen from my connection with God?

It had seemed so real in the hospital, but then I had returned to an empty house. Henry hadn't been there, and my Bible had just sat on the table. I had tried to read it a few times, but even as the words entered my mind, it would wander to why Raquel and not me? So I had stopped reading. And I had stopped going to church. And I had stopped praying. Really, I had stopped living.

Six months later, I sat in my van nursing a vodka, surrounded by the last few things I owned.

My nursing badge hung from the rearview mirror where I had hung it after Doug fired me.

"Sandra, I'm sorry, but this is your third tardy this week. We all feel for your loss, but we can't keep paying you to not come to work."

I nodded, and after accepting the small box Doug offered, I packed the few things I kept at the hospital and left.

"What are you going to do?" Raquel asked me that evening. She'd come by as soon as she'd heard the news.

I shrugged; I couldn't muster the energy to care. "I don't know. I'm sure something will come up."

She shook her head. "Sandra, you need help. How much are you drinking?"

"Drinking?" I scoffed. "I'm not drinking."

"Don't lie to me." Her serious voice cut through my fog for a minute. "I can tell. Your eyes are too bloodshot, and this behavior isn't you."

My pity took control. "Maybe it's the new me. The new, crippled, childless, widowed me."

"Henry wouldn't want this."

"Henry's dead." The intensity of my voice startled me, but it affected Raquel deeply.

"I love you," – She rummaged in her purse before producing a white business card – "but I can't have you around Alyssa the way you are right now. Please call them, and get some help."

She held the card out, and when I rolled my eyes and turned my head, she laid it on the coffee table and left.

I hadn't seen her since, and the bank had come soon after and taken the house away; Henry's insurance money had only gone so far. Still I couldn't seem to care, so I had packed some clothes, some memorabilia, including the pictures of Henry and I, and I had taken to living in my van.

Though I had avoided church after my accident, I sought out church parking lots now that I was homeless. I was still mad at God for taking everything I loved, but the people at the churches generally left me alone and sometimes let me use the bathroom to clean up a bit. Maybe, if I was honest, I parked at churches for the connection. The last time I remembered being truly happy was when I was with Henry in church.

Mesquite View church was one of my favorite places. The green manicured yard reminded me of spring and the tall, old trees gave shade to my van. Plus, the staff always let me in to use the bathroom.

When the bottle was empty, I grabbed my pillow, propping it against the window in hopes of catching a quick nap.

A rapping at the window startles me awake. The sun hadn't set, but the lack of cars in the parking lot signaled the passing of time. A young man and woman with dark hair stood outside the window, motioning for me to roll the window down. Fear formed as a lump in my throat. Surely the worst they could do was call the cops. Grasping the handle, I turned it clockwise just enough to be able to hear them. They seemed nice, but what if they were trying to mug me? It was evening and everyone seemed to have vacated the church for the day.

"Hi, what's your name?" the man asked.

"Sandra," I said cautiously.

"Hi, Sandra. I'm Tony, and this is my wife Margaret. Are you homeless?"

I bit back the rude reply that immediately came to mind, but what did spill out wasn't much nicer. "No, I just enjoy taking all my belongings with me every day." The two exchanged a glance, and I felt bad for my sarcasm. They seemed like nice enough people. "Yes, I'm homeless," I sighed.

"Well, Sandra, we'd like to invite you to our home for dinner and a shower. Would you do us that honor?"

My jaw dropped, and my eyes narrowed as I contemplated the offer. "Why would you want to do that?" she asked.

"I'm an associate pastor of this church," he said, pointing to the building. "We've noticed you here a few times, and God told us today that we should invite you to our home."

"But you don't even know me."

"No, but God does, dear," – the woman spoke up – "and that's good enough for us. I've got a roast in the oven, and it's more than Tony or I can eat by ourselves. You'd be doing us a huge favor if you'd join us."

My mouth watered at the mention of roast. I hadn't had a decent meal in weeks, and surely a pastor and his wife would mean me no harm. Taking a deep breath, I nodded. "Okay, I'd like that."

The woman's face lit up. "Wonderful. We're parked right over there," she pointed to the only other vehicle in the lot, "will you follow us then?"

After nodding, I watched the couple walk to their car hand-in-hand. As I started my engine, a seed of apprehension tumbled in my belly, but the thought of real food and a shower tamped it down. The ripe smell emanating off me bothered even my own nose. As I watched Tony open the door for his wife, my breath caught. All the times Henry had done the same thing for me flashed through my mind. I bit my lip to keep the tears at bay and put the van in drive, following them out of the parking lot.

A few minutes later, we pulled up to a modest single story home with tan siding and a darker brown trim. I turned off the van and hit the button for the ramp.

Margaret appeared at the van's side, "Can I help you?" she asked.

"Only if you don't have a ramp." I rolled the chair down the ramp attached to the van and hit the button to raise it back up and lock the doors.

"I'm afraid we don't have one, but I'm sure Tony could help you up the stairs." Margaret waved Tony over.

"Thank you," I replied.

A few minutes later, I entered their quaint living room. A few portraits of the two of them adorned the cream colored walls, and the small stains in the beige carpet gave the room a lived-in feel. A single dark brown couch and recliner sat around a glass-topped coffee table. No television was visible, but I assumed a second living room housed it somewhere else in the house. The smell from the roast filled the house, and my stomach rumbled audibly.

Margaret smiled. "The kitchen is just back this way. Follow me." She led the way through a doorway and into the country-themed kitchen. A small dining table and a counter that wrapped around in a u-shape filled the room. Margaret grabbed another plate and utensils and set them at the table. Then she moved one of the chairs aside, so I could roll my chair up to the table. "What would you like to drink?" she asked turning to the fridge. "We have water, lemonade, and iced tea."

"Iced tea is fine." I glanced at the kitchen sink, wanting to wash my hands, but the height was unmanageable in my wheelchair. "Do you have a lower sink or some wipes I could clean my hands with?"

"Oh yes, of course." Margaret opened a cabinet under the sink and produced a tub of wipes. "I'm afraid all the sinks are about his level, but we have these."

"These will be fine, thank you." I opened the wipes and took a few to vigorously clean my hands. When Margaret's back was turned, I also wiped it over my face, wanting to clear as much grime and odor as possible.

Pastor Tony entered the kitchen, gave his wife a quick peck, and asked if he could help in any way. She pointed to the glasses, and he took them to the table while she grabbed the roast and the bread.

I wheeled to the scratched dining table that had obviously seen some love. Tony took the chair on my left and Margaret the one on my right. They each reached for one of my hands. I furrowed my brow, "What are you doing?"

"Praying. We always thank God for our food," Tony said, and the two bowed their heads and closed their eyes. I followed suit, enjoying the familiar gesture Henry and I had once done over every meal together.

As we ate the delicious meal, Tony and Margaret asked questions of me, but not the deep probing kind, so I answered each one. When the last kernel of food disappeared off my plate, disappointment flooded my body. With no idea of when I might get such a meal again, I wished I had savored the bites a little longer.

Margaret excused herself from the table, but returned shortly with a hot apple pie for dessert. My mouth watered as she cut a large slice and placed it in front of me. I took my time with each bite.

"We'd like to offer our house to you tonight," Margaret began as she finished chewing her mouthful. "We have a guest room that is right next to the hall bathroom. You could shower and get a good night's rest."

I tipped my head to the side trying to decide if there was an ulterior motive. "Why are you being so nice to me?"

Margaret took my hand. "You have obviously had a tough time. We'd love to hear about it if you ever want to tell us, but we were put on this Earth to help people in need, and honestly" – she smiled at Tony – "it's a little quiet around here."

"Besides, as I said earlier," Tony added, "God called us to help you, and we'd like to honor his wishes."

I gazed into their sincere eyes and then dropped my head. "I don't know why God would want to help me. I've blamed him for everything, and I certainly haven't been a good Christian. Even when I had a chance, I was only strong for a few weeks, and then I drifted away."

"God loves you no matter what you've done," Tony said. "He understands our anger with him when things happen that we don't understand, but he still loves us. He waits patiently for us to come back to him, and when we do, he welcomes us with open arms. You may see brokenness, but God sees you mended and loved."

A glimmer of hope sparked in my chest. "Do you really believe that?"

"I know it to be true," he affirmed. "Not only because I've read it in his word, but because I lived it once. You see, just after I finished seminary school my father was diagnosed with cancer. I couldn't understand it because cancer didn't run in our family, but my dad was a fighter. I prayed every day for God to heal my father, and being a new pastor, I was cocksure that he would. After a year-long battle, my father passed away, and my anger burned at God. My father had been a wonderful father and a good Christian; I couldn't understand why God would take him and not the other people who seemed much worse in my eyes. I even gave up preaching for a time, but then my wife reminded me that not only was my father in Heaven and no longer in pain, but that God answers prayers in many ways. While I thought God wasn't answering my prayers, maybe his answer had been that extra year. Maybe he was supposed to die earlier, but God gave me more time. Also, she reminded me that God said we should all long to be in Heaven where it's perfect. I missed my father, but I knew he was no longer hurting and that I would get to see him again one day. Slowly, I turned back to God and to ministry, and God began to bless my ministry."

"I wish my story were that easy," I sighed.

"It wasn't always easy," Margaret said, "but it was always worth it. God is an amazing and loving God, and he only wants what's best for us. Now, how about that offer?"

Margaret's face held lines that showed her ability to laugh, and her eyes sparkled. A shower and one night couldn't hurt, so I nodded okay.

"Great. I'll show you to the room and the bathroom, and then after your shower you can join us for our nightly devotional if you'd like." Margaret rose and led the way out of the kitchen and down a short hallway. "Our room is the on the other side of the kitchen, so you'll really have this whole side to yourself." She opened the door to a smaller room with lavender walls, a full-sized bed, and a dresser. "Here's the bedroom. Right next door is the bathroom. I'll put a towel out for you. I have a pair of pajamas you could borrow if you'd like, or I could have Tony get some out of your car."

"No, that's fine," I said, "everything in the car probably needs a washing. I'll borrow what you have."

"I'll bring them back and lay them on the bed. We'll be reading in the living room if you want to join us after." She pulled some towels out of the hall closet, laid them in the bathroom, and then headed back to the kitchen.

What made these people so different? The world was a dangerous place, and not many people would invite a stranger in, feed them, and give them a room for the night, but Tony and Margaret seemed completely trusting. Did they really have that close of a hotline with God? What must that be like?

The tight squeeze in the bathroom required a little maneuvering, but I managed to get into the bathtub. As the warm water filled the tub, I sat back, letting the warmth flood my body. Thankfully, a low shelf held some shampoo and body wash, allowing the ability to wash my hair and myself.

I don't know how long I sat in the tub, certainly long enough for my fingers to prune and for some of the tension to ebb out of me. Of course, the sadness tiptoed in to fill the empty space. How had my life gotten so off track? Tears slid down my face and mixed with the bath water. When they were spent, I hoisted myself out of the tub and dried off. The beige towel shrouded my body like a cloud of soft cotton.

Back in the bedroom, a package of unopened underwear and a long pink flowered nightgown lay across the bed. Margaret had thought of everything. After changing, I wheeled back to the living room. I hadn't attended a Bible study in a long time and wasn't sure I was ready to give up my anger, but the curiosity of what made this couple so different won out.

"Hi, Sandra," Tony said as I entered the living room. "I'm glad you could join us. I don't know if you have your own Bible, but Margaret has one you can borrow for tonight."

Margaret held out a well-worn black leather Bible. "I do have one in the car," I clasped the Bible, the marbled cover familiar to my touch, "but thank you."

"We're studying Job," Margaret said, "I hope that's okay with you."

"Isn't Job the guy who had everything taken away from him?" I asked.

"He is," Tony nodded. "If you'd like, we can study another book tonight, but I think there might be some insight you can take away."

"No, it's fine," I hadn't read Job since my life had fallen apart, and I wondered if Tony would share something that might pertain to me.

"So, I think one of the biggest things I've taken from Job is that suffering isn't always deserved. I have so many people ask me what they did to deserve what they're going through, and if you look at Job, he did nothing. God allowed Satan to try and tempt Job to show his righteousness," Tony said.

"Why does he do that?" I asked.

"Sometimes it's to show his glory. Remember God made the world and all of us, and sometimes he has a bigger plan in mind. While Job suffered, he also blessed Job tremendously at the end. It's not always easy, but it's always worth keeping our faith in God."

"I know I always have trouble with God allowing Satan to tempt us," Margaret spoke up. "Sometimes it hard to reconcile that a loving God would allow us to be tempted, but again I think it speaks to what Tony was saying that God is blessed at the end if we are strong enough."

They shared a little longer back and forth, but the rest of the words landed on deaf ears. I had heard exactly what I needed to hear.

As I wheeled back to the bedroom that night, my head was reeling. Job had lost even more than I had, and he had still kept his faith in God. Why hadn't I been able to? More importantly, could I get it back?

The bed squeaked as I hefted myself into it, and again as I rolled over, but anything would be better than the car had been. After fluffing the pillow, I confronted the conflict in my mind. I hadn't talked to God in so long, would he still hear me? The words that spilled out were soft, paper-thin. "Lord, I know I turned from you, and I have made a mess of things. I don't even know what to do or where to go from here, but if you can still use me, please show me how." I waited for a whisper in return or a powerful feeling, but nothing came. I sighed and closed my eyes.

"Mama."

My eyes snapped open. Isaac, six now, sat on the bed next to me wearing blue jeans and a Sonic the Hedgehog t-shirt.

"Mama, you have to help the others."

"What does that mean?" I asked him.

"You have to tell your story to save others," he said. "Please mama, don't let it be for nothing." He touched my face with his little boy hands and planted a kiss on my cheek with his soft lips, and then he was gone.

I lay, staring at the ceiling, wondering what he meant. What I was supposed to do? The question plagued me until the early rays of dawn filtered in the lace covered windows.

The noise of someone stirring in the kitchen granted me the courage to get out of bed. Hopeful that it would be Tony, I formulated the thoughts careening in my head as I trekked down the hallway.

Tony sat at the table, his Bible open. He glanced up as I entered. "Good morning, Sandra, did you sleep well?"

"Not really, but I was hoping I could talk to you about it."

"Sure, would you like me to get Margaret? I think she's just getting dressed."

"No, that's fine. She can join when she comes in. I . . . um, I'm not sure where to start." I didn't know how much to tell him, but it seemed necessary for him to know the whole story in order to offer assistance, so I took a deep breath and dove in. "Five years ago, I had an abortion. It was the worst thing I could ever have done. When I met my husband Henry a year later, he brought me to church and introduced me to God, but I didn't totally accept him, and I never told Henry about the abortion. A few years into our marriage, I found out I could no longer have kids, and when I told Henry, he lost control of the car, and we crashed into a tree. It paralyzed me and killed Henry. I think I really found God after that, but then life got too hard without Henry, and I began drinking heavily. I lost my job, my home, my friends."

"I'm so sorry," he said. "I guess our reading of Job really did hit close to home."

I waved my hand in dismissal. Though it had felt close to home, it wasn't what was really bothering me. "It was my fault, my decision, but," – I leaned forward – "I keep having dreams of the baby. I had another one last night where he told me to tell my story to help others. I don't know how to do that. I was hoping maybe you could help me."

He folded his hands and regarded me for a moment, as if gathering his thoughts. "Have you told others about your experience?"

"Not many. I told Henry's family, my friend Raquel, and a Chaplin at the hospital."

"Well, it sounds like God may be asking you to share your story with more people. Sometimes he uses dreams to reach us. Have you thought about sharing your story in a church or writing about your experience?"

"I don't really belong to a church anymore," I said looking down at my hands.

"Well, we'd love to have you join us," Tony said.

Margaret entered the kitchen then, and I filled her in on my story. She poured us each a cup of coffee and sat down at the table across from Tony. "Have you ever thought" – she turned the mug in a slow circle – "about telling the women who go to the center your story?"

My eyebrows climbed my forehead. "You mean sit outside and talk to the women coming in?" The thought startled my heart into a galloping pace, and my eyes widened. I never wanted to see that place again.

Margaret touched my arm, "I know it would be hard," she said, "but imagine how many women are going in like you did, not really wanting an abortion but feeling pressured to. What if telling your story to them could help them make the choice to save their baby?"

A wave of emotion rolled over me. The very thought of going back there churned my stomach, but I didn't want any other women to end up where I had. What if I could make a difference? What if I could save a baby from the same fate mine had met and a woman from the awful guilt that plagued me? What if someone like me had been there that fateful day when I had gone? "I want to, but I don't know if I could."

"I know it's a big step, and maybe it's not something you can do right away, but I'll be happy to go with you if you ever do decide it's something you want to do."

"Why don't you try something in the meantime?" Tony suggested. I raised an eyebrow, waiting for him to continue. "Why don't you stay with us, get off the alcohol, let us help you get a job, and" – he rose from his chair and walked into the living room. A drawer opened and closed, and then he was back. – "become a prayer warrior." He handed me a brown leather journal.

The leather still smelled new, and the cover creaked as I opened it. I peeked up at Tony, questions in my eyes.

"It's to write down prayer requests. That way you can pray for people by name or by physical description if you don't know their name. You can put checks beside them when you've prayed for them, so you know who you've done each day. Sometimes praying for others is the best thing we can do for ourselves."

"Thank you." I ran my finger over the cover again. "I'd like that."

"Now, can we bring in some of your things?" Margaret said.

"Yes, but I'm afraid they probably all need to be washed." I cringed at the thought of them touching my dirty clothes.

"It's fine. Finish your coffee, and we'll get them."

"Can you also get the picture of Henry?" I asked. "He was my husband."

"Of course."

As they exited the kitchen, I picked up the journal again. The grace and hospitality they had shown me was unfathomable, but it sparked at desire to get my life back on track.

A month later, I sat at the table, checking my watch every few minutes.

"Would you like me to go with you?" Margaret asked.

I shook my head. "No, I need to do this alone."

After kicking the alcohol and returning to Jesus, the need for reconciliation with Raquel had emerged. Though dubious, she had agreed to meet at a coffee shop and at least hear me out.

"However, I think I'm ready to share my story at the clinic. Will you go with me tomorrow?"

"Of course, I'll be happy to."

As I arrived at the coffee shop, my apprehension grew. I took a deep breath and opened the door. In the empty store, Raquel was easy to spot at her table near the window. "Hi, Raquel."

She nodded at me, but there was reservation on her face. "Sandra."

"I know you probably don't want to see me, but I wanted to apologize. I made a mess of everything." She nodded again, and I continued, "I couldn't get past the pain of losing Henry, and I went back to drinking. I thought I could handle it like I did the first time. I never told you, but I drank a lot after the abortion too. Anyway, when I hit bottom, I found some people, Tony and Margaret, and they helped me up. I'm living with them until I can save enough to get an apartment again. I'm sober now, and I'm taking counseling classes. I'm going to look into becoming a counselor."

The ice slowly melted off Raquel's face. "That's great, Sandra, I'm really glad to see you getting back on your feet. I've missed you, and I know Alyssa has too."

"I've missed you both as well. I know I still have a lot to prove to you, and I'm going to work hard to do that, but I also wanted to ask you a question." I took a deep breath; the idea still scared me. "I'm going to start sitting at the center where I had my abortion and trying to tell women my story. I know you work a lot during the days, but I was wondering if on your next day off you might come with me."

She regarded her coffee cup, and I waited. While I wanted to know what she was thinking, I didn't want to pressure her. When she peered back up, tears glistened in her eyes. "I don't know if I'm strong enough," she whispered.

I squeezed her arm. "I know I'm not, but I'm counting on God to give me the words, and if we can save any of them from going through what we did, isn't it worth it?"

Slowly, she nodded. "I still wonder; you know? Would Alyssa have a brother or a sister? I don't even know. Some days it gets really bad, and I think I don't deserve to live, and then I look down at Alyssa and realize I have to. I'm sorry I wasn't there for you more; it must be even harder for you." She squeezed my hand, and tears rolled down both of our faces. "I'll be strong for you."

"I'll pray that God gives us both strength."

After sharing a few more tears for our past, she filled me in on her life the last few months and promised to meet me at the center on her next day off. Considering it a good start to my new life, I drove back to Tony and Margaret's, happily singing along to the radio.

Upon returning home, I sought out the prayer journal Tony had given me and opened it up to the first page. The smell of leather brought a smile to my face as I stared at the empty page. *Strength for Raquel and I,* I wrote and paused. It needed more. *Give me the words to say to reach women.* Filling the first line in the journal filled my heart with joy for the first time in a long time. Though it wasn't the same, and I knew there would still be days I missed Henry and Isaac and the other children we never got to have, the feeling that I was finally doing what God wanted me to do was pretty good. I felt almost complete.

15

A New Beginning with A New Purpose

Margaret, Tony, and I prayed together the next morning before Margaret and I headed out to the center. As Margaret drove, the nerves balled in my stomach and my hands shook. I hadn't been back to the center since the horrible day, and fear consumed me. What if I couldn't handle it? What if they yelled at us? What if I passed out like I had the day I was there last? I sent up a prayer for peace and slowly the questions dissipated from my mind.

Margaret pulled into a nearby lot, and we made our way to the center. My heart doubled its beat in my chest, and my throat tightened. A hand touched my shoulder; Margaret smiled down at me. I took a deep breath and nodded.

As we touched the path leading to the center, dread settled on my shoulders. The ordinary building seemed dark and foreboding. Death and destruction lingered here, and I shivered. How had I not felt this presence the first time I had been here?

A small bench sat out front of the center, and we parked there-Margaret on the bench and me in my wheelchair next to it. For a moment silence reigned. No cars, no birds, no talking. It was just us, God, and the menacing building. God's presence cut through the darkness, surrounding my shoulders like a comforting blanket. Minutes later a young woman, probably in her late twenties, came walking up the concrete path. Her tight bun complimented her immaculate blue suit. I doubted her reception to the words, but God told my heart to speak anyway.

"Please don't kill your baby," I said softly as she approached us.

She looked up, fear in her eyes. Although she appeared completely put-together in all other ways, her eyes told the real story.

"Please don't kill your baby," I repeated. "Can I tell you my story?"

"Leave me alone. It's my choice." And she hurried past us into the clinic.

I sighed, "I don't think that went well."

Margaret squeezed my arm. "We won't win them all, but when we can't reach them with our words, we pray for them." She closed her eyes and bowed her head; I followed suit. "Lord, we don't know the woman who just entered this center, but we saw the fear in her eyes. Please Lord, work on her heart and help her to see the error in her decision. Lord, protect the unborn child growing within her as only you can. Help us to have the right words to say to reach the women coming and going from this place. Amen."

We waited in silence. Soon another girl came walking up the pathway. Blond hair covered her downturned face which focused on the ground. Her hands clenched and unclenched at her side.

"You don't have to do this," I said to the girl. My voice came out louder this time.

Her head lifted to reveal a pale face with wild eyes, "I'm not doing anything." She had to be young, seventeen or eighteen.

"You're planning to have an abortion," I said, "and you don't have to. In fact, I don't think you even want to. You know it's a baby, and that God has a plan for that baby's life." The girl's eyes widened. I had no idea where the words had come from; they had just flowed out, but I could see that they affected this girl.

"I . . . I've messed it all up." Tears shimmered in the girl's eyes.

"No, you haven't. Not yet."

"You don't understand. My father's a pastor, and I slept with my boyfriend on prom night, and now I'm pregnant. This would ruin my father's reputation."

Margaret spoke up then. "Let me ask you this. Would your father be angrier that you had sex or that you killed your baby?"

The girl's eyes darted to the left, to the right, to the ground. She clasped her hands together. "I don't know."

"Well, I'm a pastor's wife, and I don't have children yet, but I can tell you that while I hope my daughter won't get pregnant out of marriage, I would never want her to have an abortion. People make mistakes, but God forgives, and our reputation is not worth a child's life."

A spark of hope flickered in the young girl's blue eyes. "Do you really think so?"

"I know so," Margaret said, "and if you'd like help talking to your parents, I'd be happy to be there with you."

The young girl sank to her knees on the sidewalk and put her hands on Margaret's lap. "Thank you. I've been praying for a sign not to do this, and I guess this is my answer. I'm so glad you were here. Will you go with me now before I lose my nerve again?"

Margaret glanced over at me, and I nodded.

"Of course," Margaret said. "Let's go talk to them now."

The two headed off, leaving me alone in the chair. I sent a prayer of thanks up to God, and also one requesting clarity. It seemed like having someone talk to these girls and tell them there was hope was good, but actually telling their families with them might be needed as well. Was that what I should be doing? A shout interrupted my prayer.

"Hey, you, you can't harass patients here."

I opened my eyes, and my heart froze. The woman, who had been my nurse six years ago, stood before me. More hardened than before, but it was her.

"I'm not harassing anyone. I'm simply telling them what you won't." My hand shook on my lap, and I tucked it under my leg to conceal it.

"What are you talking about? We give full disclosure here. We are strictly by the book."

I tilted my head and gazed evenly at her. "You don't remember me, do you?"

"No, why would I?" The woman flapped her arms in exasperation before crossing them across her chest.

"Because six years ago, I had an abortion here, and you were my nurse."

"You had an abortion and now you're trying to take the choice away from other women?"

"This center never told me of the risks. My abortion caused scarring on my uterus that prevented me from having a child when I was ready."

"There are always risks to surgery. It was on the form you filled out when you came in."

That gave me pause because she could have been right about that. I remembered filling the form out, but had no memory of what was on it. "I was young, and I was scared. The risks should have been told to me, so I truly had a choice. What you do here isn't choice. It's an assembly line butcher shop. I lost my ability to have kids, and I may not reach them all, but I will sit here and talk to as many women as I can to try and save them from what happened to me. You can't stop me from talking. I'm not blocking them from entering your building."

"I'm calling the police," she said, whirling around back to the building.

"Go ahead," I called after her, "the law is on my side." As the door closed behind her, I shook my head at the boldness that had come out of me. It had to be God, because inside I was shaking like a leaf.

The door opened again; the woman in the blue suit exited. It had been too fast; she couldn't have had the procedure that quickly. Maybe I was being given a second chance. When she saw me, she dropped her eyes and walked a little faster. Swallowing my fear and taking a breath to calm my heart, I spoke louder.

"I regret my abortion. Please don't make my mistake."

She stopped and slowly raised her face to look at me. "You had an abortion?" Her voice was barely a whisper.

I nodded, "It was the worst mistake of my life. I had it here, and they botched the procedure and scarred my uterus. I'll never be able to have kids. When I told my husband, we ended up in an accident, and that's how I ended up in this chair. I'd do anything to take mine back. Please don't make the same choice."

The woman sat down on the bench beside me. "I'm not ready for children though. I just started my career, and my husband just started at his firm. He's working long hours, and we can't afford a baby right now."

"What's your name?" I asked her.

"Melanie."

"Melanie, people always say they can't afford a baby, but God provides. He has given you a precious gift. I know it seems impossible right now, but if you ask him, God will show you how you can make it through a difficult time. Have you told your husband?" Melanie shook her head. "Well, I think he deserves to know. Maybe he'll surprise you and tell you he is ready for a child. Even if he doesn't, if there's even a chance that you could end up like me, are you really willing to take it?"

"I don't know," Melanie wrung her hands. "I don't know God; so why would he help me?"

"Because he loves you, and he loves that child growing inside of you right now. This is not what he wants for you. If you need help, there are churches and agencies who will help you throughout your pregnancy. I'd love to introduce you to my church if you want. Please, at least take a few days and think about it."

Melanie nodded slowly. "Okay, I will. Thank you."

As the woman walked away, I sent up another prayer for her.

Margaret arrived back a few hours later. "The parents were so understanding," Margaret said. "They were disappointed, naturally, but they told her that they still loved her and that they would love the baby whether she decided to keep the baby or put him/her up for adoption. I wish more kids knew their parents would be supportive."

"Maybe we can start a class at church, a communication class. We can teach parents how to communicate with their teens and teach teens that their parents will listen. Do you think people would come?" I asked.

She smiled at me. "I think that would be amazing, and yes I think people would come. There are so many issues that I think parents miss today. Opening communication between parents and their teens would be huge."

We stayed the whole day until the clinic closed. We didn't reach everyone, but the fact that we saved even one baby excited us.

That night after the devotional with Tony and Margaret, I lay in bed looking over the prayer journal. I had written down the name or description of every woman who had come into the clinic that day. As I ran my finger down the list, I prayed for each one again. Though it had been hard to be there and even harder to know we didn't save all the babies, just knowing that we had saved one gave me a new purpose for life.

The next day Margaret and I spent the morning at the center and the afternoon at church speaking with Tony and the other pastors about our idea for a communications class. Though most of the men, besides Tony, were all older, they agreed that a need definitely existed for a class.

"I also wanted to ask if we had or could set up an outreach program of sorts?" I spoke up. "There were a lot of women who seemed to want help telling their spouses or parents and others who needed help knowing how they would get through the nine months. Do we have something like that?"

The men exchanged glances. "We don't," Pastor Dan, the head pastor, said, "but how would you feel about starting one?"

My heart thudded. I didn't know the first thing about starting one, but if they believed I could, I would do it. "I don't know how, but I'd be honored to."

"In fact," Dan continued, "Tony's been telling us a lot about you, and we'd like to interview you as our ministry outreach person. It doesn't pay a whole lot, but it would be enough that you could get your own place again and live comfortably."

My hand flew to my heart as my eyes widened, "You want me?"

"You have a gift for talking to these women, and you've already discovered ways to help them. We think you'd be a natural. We'd even like you to continue your ministry at the clinic, so the position would be morning at the clinic and afternoons here allowing you to meet with women or hold classes.

"I'd like to pray about it," I said, trying to control the smile bursting on my face. Though I had no idea exactly what it would entail, this sounded like a dream job for me.

"We wouldn't have it any other way," he agreed, "and of course we need to do a formal interview."

Margaret squeezed my arm, and after shaking all the pastor's hands, she and I left. "Oh, Sandra, that's wonderful," she said when we reached the hall.

Emotion overwhelmed me, and I stared at her through watery eyes. "It's amazing, and it never would have happened without you and your husband. I can never thank you enough."

That night, as I lay in bed praying for clarity, a peace descended on me. I had no doubts whatsoever that this was what God was calling me to do, and I couldn't wait to tell Raquel the next morning when I saw her.

When I pulled into the parking lot, the fear fell on me again. While I knew what I was doing was right, it didn't stop the fear and disgust I felt for this place. I wondered if it would ever get easier.

The sun was shining today, and it seemed odd. Here was this black, soulless place in the middle of the warm sunshine. I shivered and brushed the thought away. A few minutes later, Raquel came walking up. She shivered too and wrapped her arms around her.

"Ugh," she said as she sat on the bench beside me, "it's like this place steals the heat away.

My eyes widened at her, "You feel it too? I thought it was just me because this was where I killed Isaac."

She shook her head, "No, it's not just you. I didn't have my procedure here, but it feels dark. I don't remember feeling like that when I went to the clinic for the procedure, do you think we feel it now because we know how wrong it is?"

"Maybe," A glance around revealed no ominous shadows lurking.

"So, what do we do now?" she asked changing the subject.

"First, we pray," I said and led us in a prayer for strength, wisdom, and the ability to reach the women who were undoubtedly coming. Then I filled her in on my interview later that day.

"Sandra, that's wonderful, and what a great idea. I'll ask at the hospital if there's anything we can do to help. Do you think we would like your church?"

"I thought you guys were happy at the old church?"

She smiled, "We are, but now that it appears I've got my friend back, I'd like to go to church with her, especially since I don't see her at work anymore."

A warmth flooded over me, and I returned her smile. "I'd love that."

At that moment, a dark haired woman came up the sidewalk. "Please don't kill your baby," I said to her.

She whipped around to glare at us. "It's my choice," she said, "I can do what I want, and it's none of your business."

"I thought it was my choice too, but it took my ability to ever have kids," I called to her, but she had hurried ahead and my words bounced off her back.

"Are they always like that?" Raquel asked as I pulled out my journal to write down the woman's description.

"No, sometimes they're worse, and sometimes they're better."

"What are you doing?" she asked.

"This is my prayer journal, and I write down every woman who comes by so I can pray for her."

"What if they have the procedure though? Not much to pray for then."

I tilted my head at her, "Do you think you and I don't need prayer?" Her face scrunched in confusion and then her hand found her mouth, and I knew she understood.

The morning was slow, which gave Raquel and I time to talk and catch up. Only five women came in while we were there, and while we didn't save the first one's baby, we saved one for sure and left the other three thinking. Raquel hugged me goodbye and wished me luck on the interview, promising to come to church on Sunday.

I should have been nervous on the drive to church, but God had granted me peace today. I knew this was where he wanted me right now, and I knew that unless I made some giant mistake that the job was mine.

The interview room was small and windowless. Two men and two women took turns asking me questions and writing down my responses. The words flowed without much thought. At the end, the four smiled, and the pastor in the middle offered me the job on the spot. I accepted, and one of the women showed me to what would be my office.

It wasn't much, a small room with a desk, two chairs, a bookshelf, and a window, but as I rolled behind the desk, I knew it was where I belonged.

That Sunday at church, Pastor Dan called me on stage to introduce me to the congregation. I took the mic he offered, apprehension fluttering inside.

"Hi, my name is Sandra," I began. The sea of faces stared back at me, and my mind went blank. As I scanned for a familiar face to calm my nerves, I saw a man smile at me from the back. I blinked; the man could have been Henry's twin. Suddenly the words flowed back into my mind. "I'm the new outreach minister here, and I'd like to tell you about my passion and some exciting things that are coming." I continued my prepared words, but my eyes remained fixed on the man in the back. I had to find out who he was. As I finished, I handed the mic back to Pastor Dan, taking my eyes off the man in back for a split second. When I looked again, the man was gone. Somehow I knew then that it hadn't been a doppelganger of Henry, but Henry himself. I smiled to myself as I rolled back to my seat.

16

A New Outlook on Life

A few weeks later, I was moving into my own apartment. It wasn't the house I had shared with Henry. There was no white picket fence, no backyard swing set, but it was mine.

"Are you sure you won't stay longer?" Margaret asked as we unloaded the last of my things.

"You and Tony need your house back," I said, "besides it looks like you'll be needing that room soon for your baby."

Margaret smiled as her hand covered her still very flat stomach. They had just found out they were pregnant. "You'll have to promise to come visit."

"I'll be over all the time," I smiled. "Besides, I needed to have a place where Alyssa can come and play without worrying that I'm bothering you." The chubby dark-haired, two-year-old played quietly in the corner with her doll.

"She's welcome anytime too," Margaret said and hugged Raquel. Then she turned and hugged me before leaving.

"Well, shall we unpack some?" Raquel asked looking around the small apartment.

It was just a small one bedroom, but plenty of room for me. We began unpacking the few books I still had in the lone bookshelf in the living room so we could keep an eye on Alyssa. Then we moved into the kitchen and finally the bedroom. After my meager belongings were unpacked, Raquel and Alyssa left, and I returned to the bedroom. I picked up the picture of Henry and I, touched his handsome face, and set it back on the nightstand.

After brushing my teeth in the lowered sink and pulling on pajamas, I sprawled out in bed. I picked up my Bible and read my devotional, and then I exchanged it for the brown leather journal. As I opened it up, I read down the list of names and descriptions again. I put a star by the women I knew had had the procedure because I felt like they needed a different prayer. Some, I didn't know if they had, like Melanie at the top. I hadn't seen her come back, but maybe she had come in the afternoon. I sent up another prayer for each woman listed then replaced my journal and turned out the light.

A noise caught my attention, and I opened my eyes. The room was still dark. I held my breath and listened. The bed squeaked again. I clicked the light on to find Isaac and Henry sitting on the bed beside me.

"Hi mama," Isaac smiled, "Look who I found." He turned and gazed up at Henry.

My heart swelled with love and sadness at the same time. "Hi baby, I'm so glad you did. Henry is such a good man, and he will look after you. Thank you Henry, and I'm so sorry."

Henry smiled back and squeezed my hand. "We'll be here waiting for you when it's your time."

"Keep telling your story mama," Isaac wrapped his little arms around me in a hug, and the tears broke free.

"Wait, are you going?" I wiped my face as they began to fade away.

"I can't come again," Henry said, "but Isaac will be back."

And then they were gone. My heart ached for them, and just for a minute I wanted a drink. Then a voice inside me whispered, "Your time is not yet daughter, but you'll see them again." Though it didn't erase the pain of missing them, it did soothe the immediate ache like aloe on a bee sting. I prayed for God to ease the rest of the ache and turned off the light once again.

A few days later, I sat in a room full of teenagers at church. We were having the first of what we hoped would be several communication meetings, and we had decided the best way to talk to them first would be to separate the adults and the teens. I really wanted to hear the teens' concerns in order to put together a great way for them to communicate and make it meaningful. Raquel and Margaret were also helping; they were with the adults in another room.

The teens fidgeted in their colorful plastic chairs, talking quietly amongst themselves as I gathered my thoughts and sent a prayer up for guidance. I cleared my throat, swallowing to ease the dryness. Talking to people was hard, but talking to teens seemed even harder.

"So today" – I began, trying to get their attention – "Today, I want to talk about the issues that are important to you guys and what you think your parents would never understand." The teens quieted down and turned to the front to face me. "I'd like it to stay organized, so if we can raise hands that would be helpful. Who would like to go first?" The teens glanced at each other, and the silence dragged on. I wanted to jump in with ideas, but I felt the need to wait.

An arm rose slowly in the second row. A girl with dark brown hair and bangs spoke up, "I don't think they understand the pressure on us today."

"Okay, what kind of pressure?"

"Um, well" – she dropped her eyes to her hands – "pressure to do well in school and also pressure to be accepted by people."

A few others nodded. "That's good, but let's get more specific," I urged her.

Her face flushed red. "Well, I'm not doing it, but I hear a lot about girls are having sex with their boyfriends, and for those of us who don't do that, sometimes we're made fun of." The girls in the room nodded their heads in agreement. Some of the boys shifted uncomfortably in their chairs.

"Okay, let's talk about sex. Have your parents talked about it with you?" A few of the kids nodded, but the majority shook their heads. My eyebrows raised slightly, and I tried to keep my face from showing any more emotion. "Alright, for those of you who have talked about it with your parents, what has the discussion been like?"

"Well, my parents just say it's only for a man and wife to do together, but if that's the case then why is it all over TV?" a blond haired boy spoke up.

"That's a great question. We all know that sex sells, but does that make it right?" This time there were a few head shakes but a lot of shoulder shrugging. "What does the Bible say about it?"

"The Bible says it's to be between a man and a wife, and it's mostly to have children."

"Right, and that's really important. See, while sex has this benefit of making you feel good, the main reason God created it was to populate the earth. It's the reason he meant for sex to be shared between a husband a wife. How many of you want to have a baby right now?" Their eyes widened and every head shook back and forth. "How many of you think your friends who are having sex right now are ready to have a baby?" Again they all shook their heads. "Okay, now how much does your health class stress that sex leads to babies?"

"Mine didn't say much. They talked about pregnancy a little bit, but then they discussed condoms, birth control, and even abortion." Other heads nodded in agreement.

"Okay, so we know that God really gave us sex to have children, and we know that we aren't ready to have children yet, but what if you slip up? How many of you think your parents would understand if you got pregnant?" Glances passed back and forth, but not a hand rose in the air. "Wow, you see that's how I felt too, but I was wrong. I was living with my boyfriend, but then I got pregnant. I didn't think my parents would understand my pregnancy, and so I had an abortion." Their eyes widened, and I held up my hand. "I don't tell you that to condone abortion. It was the worst thing I ever did. The guilt haunted me immediately and destroyed the relationship anyway. So girls, if you think having one will save you and your man, you're wrong. And boys if you pressure a girl into having one, it will tear you apart and probably her as well."

The teens nodded in rapt silence.

"Years later I found a wonderful man and got married, but we couldn't have kids. I found out the abortion had caused scarring, and I was unable to ever have kids. These are just a few of the risks that they never tell you about. The worst part is, I had the abortion because I thought my parents wouldn't support me, and I was wrong. My parents weren't even believers then, and they would have supported me. I don't know each of your parents, but the fact that they are believers and they know they were forgiven by Jesus tells me that they would forgive you too and be there for you. Now, this is not to say that you should be intimate before marriage because I truly believe it is wrong, but this is just one scenario to show that your parents will listen and will be there for you."

The teens exchanged glances with each other, trying to confirm if I was speaking the truth.

"What's another area you think your parents wouldn't understand?" I asked.

"Peer pressure to drink or smoke," another teen suggested.

I nodded, "Ah, yes, that one's been around a long time. Your parents probably had the same pressure, but it goes along with something else I wanted to say about being intimate. You guys have all accepted Jesus, right?" They nodded emphatically. "Okay, so you know when you accept Jesus that the Holy Spirit comes and lives in your heart right?" Again nods. "Well, do you think the Holy Spirit wants to drink or smoke?"

Eyes widened as if the teens had never thought about this.

"You can think about that when you think about being intimate too. Do you think the Holy Spirit wants to be intimate with everyone you are?" There were uncomfortable glances, but I could tell the point had hit home. "Look, it isn't always easy being a Christian, especially when the world tries to tell you that you are hateful or intolerant, but it is important, and the biggest thing I want to get across is this: Your parents care about you, and they will listen when you have a problem, so take it to them and give it to God. Remember he never gives you more than you can handle. So, that's a lot for today. I want to thank you guys for coming, and next time we'll tackles some more issues, okay?"

The teens nodded and began exiting in small groups, still discussing amongst themselves. I surveyed the note sheet I had been keeping. Some good issues jumped out at me.

"Excuse me." A petite blond girl stood in front of me.

"What can I do for you?"

"I was hoping maybe I could ask you a question." She twisted her toe in the carpet and dropped her eyes.

"Sure, honey, what's your name?"

"It's Sarah. I . . . um, I didn't get pregnant, but I was intimate with my boyfriend. After this meeting today, I want to stop and get right with God, but how do I tell my boyfriend? It seems like that's all he wants to do now." She peeked up at me through lowered lids.

"Sarah, I'm glad that you've decided to stop, but you're right; it won't be easy. I didn't talk about that, and maybe we should have, but once people try sex they want to keep doing it, so it gets much harder to stop. But you need to tell your boyfriend that you changed your mind, that you don't want to sin against Jesus or risk pregnancy. Is he a believer?"

The girl bit her lip. "I don't know. Is that terrible?"

I shook my head. "It's not terrible, Sarah, but God tells us we shouldn't be unequally yoked, meaning we shouldn't date non-believers. Do you know why that is?"

Her head moved slightly back and forth.

"Well, the reason is because they don't see sin the same way we do. Like sex for instance, they don't see it as a sin outside of marriage, so they push their partner to do it. This usually causes the Christian to stumble and fall into temptation. However, if you are with a believer, he should want you to follow Jesus and will try to make sure you don't sin. So, I think you need to have that discussion with him first. If he isn't a believer, you can tell him why you are and see if his heart is open to God. If it is, that's great news, and he should want to stop sinning right along with you. If he isn't, then I'm afraid it might be a relationship you will want to end."

She nodded thoughtfully, but she didn't seem convinced.

"One more thing," I continued. "If you do decide to stay in the relationship, you might consider telling your parents you want help staying pure and asking them to watch out for you, make sure you don't put yourself in situations where you might be tempted. Maybe that means you guys only date in groups, or you have a chaperone, whatever it takes. It won't be easy, but following God's commands aren't always easy. They are, however, always worth it."

"Thank you," she said, "and thank you for having this meeting. I don't think I ever would have told my mom, and then I might have ended up in your situation. No offense."

"None taken," I smiled. "I'm not proud of the path I chose, but if telling my story helps others like yourself then that is a burden I will carry."

She leaned in and gave me a hug, surprising me. I wrapped my arms around her and hugged her back. As she left, Raquel and Margaret walked in.

Margaret raised her eyebrow at me, "What was that about?"

I smiled, "Someone turning back to God. How did it go with the parents?"

Raquel and Margaret pulled up a chair and sat across from me. "It was good," Margaret said, "but we have a lot of work to do."

"The parents had no idea what schools are teaching their kids nowadays," Raquel jumped in, "and almost none of them had talked with their kids about sex."

"Yeah, I saw that here too. Very few kids had had any kind of talk, and the few who did, they basically were told just don't do it because. I think our next class should be just for the parents and focus on why it's important to have the conversation, and also that they should give reasons for waiting. These kids today are pressured to have sex more than ever, and I don't see it getting any better in the future."

"I agree," Margaret said, touching her belly. "I'm so afraid for this child and what the world will be like for him or her."

17

As Time Goes On

My job really began to take off. In the mornings, I sat at the clinic talking to women as they came in or left. In the afternoons, I met with women and helped them find resources they needed.

Margaret even helped set up a pregnancy pantry at the church. In it, we stocked diapers, wipes, blankets, clothing, and other items to help women get started. We also began partnering with the local food bank to help low income women get food assistance, so they could feel secure they could provide for their babies.

As the months wore on, Margaret grew increasingly bigger until she wasn't able to work at the church. Two weeks later, her son was born. She decided to take a lengthy maternity leave, but we kept in touch. A few months after that, Alyssa turned three.

"Are you guys going to have any more?" I asked Raquel as I helped her clean off the table after the birthday aftermath.

"I don't know," Raquel answered from the sink where she was washing dishes. "We want more, and it's not like we aren't trying, but we can't seem to get pregnant again."

My heart went out to her; I knew exactly what that felt like. "Well, maybe Alyssa is our angel, and we'll just have to enjoy her." I picked up the last paper plate and paused. "Do you think they would have been friends?"

"Who?" Raquel turned to face me as she dried her hands on the tan dishtowel.

"Isaac and Alyssa," I said softly.

"Oh, Sandra," Raquel rushed to my side, "Of course they would have been. I bet he would have been like her big brother."

I nodded and bit back the tears that threatened to overflow. Today had been so joyous; I didn't want to ruin it with tears.

"Do you still see him?" she asked, placing a hand on my arm.

"Sometimes, but never as clear. I can't seem to see his face anymore, it's more like a shadow or a feeling of him. He would have been nine this year, can you imagine?"

Raquel nodded. "My first would have been twelve, almost a teenager." We sat in silence for a time, remembering the children we'd never had.

When Alyssa started kindergarten, Margaret found out she was pregnant again. Though happy for her, the pain of what I'd never had, and would never have, began to gnaw at me. After I finished helping the last woman for the day, I locked my office door and returned to my desk. I pulled out my Bible from the middle drawer and began to flip the pages, seeking comfort.

I found myself in Revelations, which struck me as odd since it was hardly ever preached about. Most of the words bounced off my muddled brain and fell away, but chapter 21 reached out to me. 'He will wipe every tear from their eyes. There will be no more death or mourning or crying or pain.' The words soothed my troubled spirit as I remembered that our time here on Earth was only temporary and eventually there would be a new Earth and God would restore perfection to it.

I closed my eyes and opened my heart. "Lord, I'm hurting today. I know I made the choices, but it's painful to watch the joy around me and not know the feeling. Please take away my jealousy. Fill me with love for those who are rejoicing and patience to wait for the time when I can see Isaac and Henry again. And Lord please help me continue to be a witness and help spare other women from what I'm going through now. Amen."

As the words flowed out of my mouth, a peace flowed in. It didn't erase the sadness completely, but it softened the sting.

At Alyssa's eighth birthday party, we took several of her friends to a movie. Margaret had hired a sitter so she could join us, and the three of us sat in back row of the darkened theater whispering quietly.

"We just got word that Pastor Dan is retiring," Margaret said, reaching in the giant tub of popcorn we were sharing. "Please pray that Tony gets offered the job. We'd really like to stay here, but he is feeling the calling to be a head pastor now."

"Of course we will," Raquel agreed. "We would hate to lose you guys, and he would be an amazing pastor for the church. Don't you think Sandra?"

"Absolutely," I said, but my mind was on the little girls in front of us. Several of them were wearing crop tops showing their bellies, and it bothered me. They were so young and probably thought nothing of it, but it reminded me of my own youth when I dressed that way to get boys to look at me. It had been the beginning of a slippery slope, and I didn't want these girls to go down it.

I added the concern to my prayer journal that night. Though time had improved many things, what it hadn't improved was morality. More TV shows than ever promoted premarital sex, affairs, or multiple partners. I wondered when the first show would promote abortions, and the thought saddened me. Closing my eyes, I opened my heart and gave my worries to God.

When Alyssa turned twelve, my life turned upside down again.

"Cancer?" I couldn't process the word.

"Breast Cancer," Raquel stated again. Her face was paler than normal and dark circles encased her eyes.

"How long have you known?" My brain was whirling a million miles a minute, but I couldn't concentrate on any of the thoughts flying through it.

"Just a few days," she sighed and ran a hand through her dark hair. "It's early, so there's hope, but . . ." she trailed off.

We had both been in the medical business; we knew that cancer death rates were pretty high.

I grabbed her hand. "Have you told Greg and Alyssa yet?"

Tears sparkled in her eyes, and she sniffed. "No, I wanted to tell you first, for practice. What do I tell them?"

"The truth. Then we find the best doctors, and we beat this. Do you hear me?"

She nodded, but her eyes were empty, and I wondered if she had "fight" in her.

I sat with her as she told Greg and Alyssa that night, and we all cried. Then I took Alyssa to bed so Raquel and Greg could discuss options.

"Aunt Sandra?" she asked as she crawled into bed. "Is my mother going to die?"

I rolled as close to her bed as I could and caressed her hair. "Not if I can help it, Alyssa. I'm going to be praying every night, and we are going to get your mom the best care we can."

Although fear filled her bright green eyes, I marveled at the steady voice that asked if we could pray right then. We closed our eyes, and I asked the Lord to save my friend for the sake of her daughter.

A few months later, I sat with Alyssa again as Raquel and Greg attended a chemotherapy session. She was curled up on the couch with a book, and I sat in my chair reading through my Bible.

"Aunt Sandra, why do you go to the clinic all the time?" She stuck a finger in her book to hold her place and shut the cover, turning her inquisitive eyes on me.

I pursed my lips as I thought about how I wanted to answer her. "Well, honey, because women have been misled to believe that babies aren't living, and that they have no options if they get pregnant. I go there to try and talk to women, to show them other options, to keep them from killing their babies."

Her eyes grew wide. "They kill babies? Why? Babies are cute, and they can't harm anyone."

I nodded sadly. "I know, Alyssa, but people don't think about that. They are told it's just a clump of cells, so they convince themselves it's okay. They are told that people will hate them for getting pregnant out of wedlock, so they convince themselves it's okay. They believe they don't have the money to raise a child, so they think they are doing a service to the child. There are lots of reasons, but none of them are good. None of them make it okay."

Alyssa's brow furrowed. "I get the stigma from getting pregnant out of wedlock. It really does exist; I've seen it at school, but why can't women just put the baby up for adoption? It sure seems like someone would want the baby."

A small smile stretched across my face, and I chuckled. "You are so smart for your age. It's too bad more women don't think like you. In fact, there are many, many couples who are waiting for babies to adopt, but women don't think about that. They think about the fact that they don't want to gain weight or they don't want to be inconvenienced for nine months."

"Well, that just seems selfish," Alyssa said shaking her head. "Nine months isn't that long, and you can always lose the weight. When I get older, I'm going to be like you, Aunt Sandra. I want to help save babies too."

"You can now, you know."

Her eyes widened, "I can? How?"

"You can pray for them." I pulled out my prayer journal. "See, I write down the description of the women I see every day, and then I pray for them. You could do the same thing, only without the description. You could just pray for women everywhere to know the truth and to meet someone who will help them."

"That would be amazing," she said, "Can I have my own prayer journal?"

"Absolutely." I smiled as she returned to her book and made a mental note to ask Pastor Tony where he had gotten the prayer journal so I could give one to Alyssa.

Greg and Raquel arrived a few hours later to pick up Alyssa. A pink scarf covered Raquel's bald head. Still, I was startled every time I saw her without her trademark long dark hair.

"How did it go?" I whispered as Alyssa packed up her things. Raquel forced a smile, but I could see the pain in her eyes, surrounded by the dark circles that had become a regular feature. I patted her hand, "I'll keep praying my friend." She squeezed my hand, and then Greg and Alyssa helped her out.

I said an extra-long prayer for Raquel that night before turning out my light. When I woke the next morning, I had a vague memory of a dream of Isaac. It hit me that he would have been graduating this year. Again the weight of grief saddled itself around my neck, and I prayed for God to remove it and to help me find joy in the day.

I dressed and headed to the clinic. As I took up my usual spot, one of the workers was just coming up the walkway. She was younger than the rest and didn't have that hardened look about her yet. Her brown hair was pulled up in a ponytail showing off her slender neckline.

"Why do you sit out here every day?" she asked as she drew even with me.

I cocked my head. None of the workers had spoken to me since the first day, so I was a little surprised by her question. "Years ago, I made the worst mistake of my life here. My son would have been graduating this year, but I threw his life away, and it haunts me every day. I had no one tell me of the possible risks, and I don't want other women to go through what I do."

She bit her lip, "But some of them are so horrible to you. I hear what they say through the doors sometimes, and some are still talking about you when they come in."

I smiled, "Matthew 5:10-12 says 'Blessed are those who are persecuted because of righteousness, for theirs is the kingdom of heaven. Blessed are you when people insult you, persecute you and falsely say all kinds of evil against you because of me. Rejoice and be glad, because great is your reward in heaven.' So it doesn't matter what they say about me here on earth. I know I am doing the right thing, and I know the reward for me will be in heaven."

"Do you really believe in heaven?" Her eyes glanced left and right as if making sure none of her co-workers were eavesdropping.

"I do. I've had dreams of my son and my late husband. I know it's real. Even more, I know God would be saddened by what you are doing here."

She took a step back and clasped her hand at her neck, "But I don't perform the abortions. I just manage the desk and file the claims."

"Do you set appointments?" I asked her.

"Of course."

"Then you are an accomplice. You are helping those women commit murder, even if you aren't the doctor destroying the life inside them."

Her eyes grew wide. "Oh my gosh. I never thought about it like that. I just figured it was an easy job, and it pays really well. I'm not sure how I feel about abortion, but I never thought I was helping it. Do you think God will forgive me?"

"Of course he will, my dear, but remember he also told the sinners he met to 'go and sin no more.'"

A light dawned in her eyes and her words tumbled out slowly, "So it's not enough for me to just repent. I have to find another job, don't I?"

I nodded. "If you truly want forgiveness you do."

Her hand went to her mouth and she bit on a fingernail. "It's so much money though. It's paying my way through college."

My heart went out to the girl facing the age-old dilemma of money versus following God's will. "You have to decide ultimately. God gave you free will, but remember that our time on earth is not forever, and your soul is more important than money."

She nodded, but I could see the battle still raging in her mind.

"What's your name?" I asked her as I pulled out my journal.

"Tonya, why?" she asked.

I opened the leather cover. "I'm going to pray for you Tonya. Prayers for clarity and for a new path."

"Thanks," Tonya said, glancing at her watch. "Oh, I'm late. I better get in there."

As she walked inside, I began praying in earnest for her. I was very afraid that money might win the battle of her heart.

Alyssa's thirteenth birthday party was smaller than we all wished it would have been. Raquel was still feeling ill from chemotherapy and could only attend for an hour. Margaret and I planned most of it, but the absence of her mom weighed down on Alyssa, and after just two hours, she declared the party over and left the room.

"I'll stay with them; you go with her," Margaret said to me before turning back to the shocked faces of six other girls.

I followed Alyssa down the hall and found her curled up under her desk, where the chair tucks in. The chair had been pushed aside, and Alyssa had brought her pillow and curled up in the space.

"Alyssa, come out."

"I don't want to," she said. "I don't care about a stupid birthday anyway; I just want my mom to get better."

"We all do baby, and we are praying very hard that she does, but she needs you to be strong. It's hard on her not being able to see you all the time, so when she does, she needs to know that you are okay."

A sniffle escaped her nose, and her hand wiped tears off her cheek, "But I'm not okay, Aunt Sandra. What if I lose her?"

"First of all," I said, "we aren't going to lose her yet. But secondly, when she goes, remember that she is going to heaven where there is no pain, so she'll be cancer free and pain free when she goes. And I know you'll miss her here; we all will, but you will get to see her again one day. That's what keeps me going when I think about my Henry and my Isaac. I know that I will get to see them again one day, so it makes the time here without them more bearable."

She crawled out from her space. Though her eyes were still red and her cheeks were still wet, she put on a brave face. "You're right, Aunt Sandra. I should be stronger for mom. Did all my friends leave?"

"No, they're all still there with Margaret, and I'm sure they'll understand. Go back and enjoy the time you have with them, okay?"

She hugged me and headed back down the hall. I watched her rejoin her friends before turning the other direction to Raquel's room. I knocked lightly as I pushed open the door. The room was dark as the light often hurt her eyes. Raquel's thin frame lay prone on the king size bed. Her eyes opened weakly as I rolled in.

"Is everything okay?" she asked.

"Not really, my friend," I said taking her hand. "Alyssa is really worried about you. I am too. How are you feeling today?"

"It's not too bad today," she whispered. "I hate that Alyssa is seeing me like this though. Do you think it's my punishment?"

My brows knit together, "Your punishment?"

"For the abortion, remember? Maybe he gave me Alyssa, but not getting to watch her grow up is my punishment for taking the life of her sibling so long ago."

"Hey now," I touched her cheek, "You can't talk like that. I used to think my paralysis was my punishment, but I've come to believe that God doesn't punish that way. You told me that, remember? Our actions have consequences, that's true; maybe abortion increases cancer risks, but that's not the same thing. And you have to keep fighting. We aren't ready to lose you yet."

"I'm trying," she said. "You know in all the time we prepared to become nurses, no one ever told us to prepare in case something happened to us."

I chuckled. "That's true. I know I thought I was invincible."

"Me too." Her eyes closed again, and she struggled to open them.

"Get some rest," I said, squeezing her hand. "I'll come see you again later."

A few months later, Raquel began to improve. Her cancer was shrinking, and her dark hair began growing back in. She spent every moment she could with Alyssa. The two became inseparable. During Alyssa's fourteenth year, Raquel was officially declared in remission. She resumed her job on light duty, working mainly late mornings and afternoons, so I was surprised when she knocked on my office door one afternoon.

She closed the door behind her as she entered and sat down in one of the two office chairs across from my desk. Life had resumed its glow on her face, but there an air of nervousness flitted about her. She crossed her legs and then uncrossed them, leaned forward in the chair and then scooted back.

"What's going on?" I asked her.

She leaned forward again, green eyes serious. "I think I saw her."

"Who?" My brows furrowed together as I tried to figure out who she was being so cryptic about.

"The first one, the sibling, the one I aborted."

My eyes widened, and I leaned forward; she had my full attention. "You think the child you aborted was a girl, and you think you saw her?" I repeated to clarify the information in my own mind.

Raquel nodded and bit her fingernail, uncharacteristic for her. "Actually, there's more. I think I saw heaven or a place in between."

I shook my head. None of this was making much sense. "Raquel, please tell me the whole story from the beginning."

She took a deep breath and blew it out. Her eyes dropped to her hands and then met mine again. "I haven't told anyone yet, but do you remember Alyssa's birthday when I was so weak?" I nodded, of course I did; I had been pretty sure we were losing her that day. "Well, after you left, I fell asleep; only I don't think I was really asleep. I'm pretty sure I died."

My mouth dropped open, but I motioned her to continue.

"I woke up in this field of flowers. The prettiest ones you've ever seen. There was a sea of purple, blue, red, white, yellow. The sun was shining, and I could feel it warming my skin. A soft breeze even blew through making the flowers dance. It was so real. Anyway, I began walking along; I didn't know where, I was just walking, and this woman steps out from behind a tree. It was like looking at a picture of myself when I was twenty, except she had her father's nose. Same dark hair as me, same green eyes. I thought maybe it was me at first, but then she smiled and said 'hi mom.' I fell to my knees, but she came over and hugged me. I asked her if I was dead, and she just smiled. She told me God heard our prayers, and that he was giving me more time. Then I woke up, and I was back in bed."

"Why didn't you tell me before?" I asked her.

She shook her head. "To be honest, at first it was because I thought

I imagined it all. Then I thought I would sound crazy. Once I actually started getting better, I just kind of forgot."

"What made you tell me now?"

"She came back again last night. The girl I met. I dreamt of her again, and she told me my work wasn't finished, but I don't know what that means."

I sat back and smiled. "You, my friend, need to tell your story. Others need to hear what happened to you. Don't you see? What happened to you was a miracle, and not only do we need those today, but your story might be just the thing someone needs to convince him or her that God is real and that he loves him or her."

Raquel sat back and crossed her arms. "How exactly do I do that? I'm a nobody. Who is going to care about my story?"

"You'd be surprised," I said. "Let's at least write it all down, and then we can decide how to go from there."

As Raquel continued to heal, we would meet after work and write down her story. Alyssa would often sit with us and ask questions. Raquel had never hidden her previous abortion from Alyssa and instead had told her about the horrible decision and how much it had affected her life. Alyssa knew about mine as well. We both hoped that even though the world was becoming much more accepting of abortion, that Alyssa never would be after hearing our stories.

Alyssa turned fifteen and got her driving permit. Raquel and I finished her book, which included portions of my story as well.

"What do we do now?" she asked as we read over the final version.

I shrugged and smiled. "I don't really know. I guess we look into sending it out. If God wants it published, it will happen, right?"

"Even if it never gets published, I can rest easy knowing I did what he told me, and it will be there for Alyssa and her children in the future," Raquel said.

When Alyssa turned sixteen, we saw her less. She was often off with her friends.

"I worry about her," Raquel said one evening as we sat drinking tea after dinner.

"Why?" I asked. The ice cubes clanked musically in the clear glass as I took a sip of the cool beverage.

"Sixteen was when I started thinking about sex," Raquel said, tracing a finger around the lip of her glass. "The pressure is even harder for kids these days. I know we've poured into her, but is it enough?"

"She's such a smart girl." I stared into Raquel's eyes. "I think she will be strong, but we'll keep praying for her anyway."

The day after Alyssa graduated from high school, Raquel got sick again. I sat with her in the doctor's office as we awaited results.

The door opened, and Raquel's grip on my hand tightened.

"Ahem, well," – the doctor shuffled around to his desk and sat down – "I see you had breast cancer a few years ago."

Raquel nodded, "I did, and then I went into remission. Is it back then?"

The doctor pursed his lips and nodded. "It is, and unfortunately it's more aggressive than last time. We can try chemotherapy, but I don't think it would help, and you'd just be sick for your last few months."

I could feel Raquel's hand shaking against mine. "Is that all I have left then, a few months?" Her voice came out as a whisper.

"I'm sorry," the doctor said, "I wish I had better news."

I wished that I could hold Raquel up as we walked out. Her shaking intensified as we headed to the car. I unlocked the doors, and she climbed in, eyes staring out the windshield.

"I'm so sorry, Raquel." I touched her arm, and her face turned to me.

"I'm not ready yet," she whispered. "I want to make sure Alyssa's okay."

"She will be, and maybe the doctor's wrong. Maybe you'll live another ten years."

She shook her head. "No, he gave me more time, but that time is up. I can feel it this time, Sandra."

Two months later, I sat next to Alyssa and Greg at Raquel's funeral. She had been right. The cancer had hit quickly, but fairly painlessly. She had been able to have a normal life for those two months before she passed in her sleep.

Alyssa had taken the news hard, even though we'd been preparing her for it. It was her hysterical voice that had called me at seven am a week ago to tell me that her mother was gone. It had taken nearly five minutes for me to understand her, but once I did, I had jumped in the van and hurried over there. Alyssa had lain her head in my lap and let me caress her hair as Greg took care of Raquel. She had cried until her tears were spent, and then she had grown silent. I remembered my own struggle when Henry had died, and I tried to reassure her that it got better, but her head only nodded vacantly.

Even now as we sat at the funeral, she was stoic. No tear rolled down her cheek, and her eyes never wavered from the casket. In my head, I whispered a prayer to God for her, that she would find her strength and not run like I had for so long.

As Greg stood to give his speech, my mind flashed back to Henry's funeral. Had it really been fourteen years ago? Though I knew that I would miss my friend, a little piece of me was jealous of her too. Not only was she seeing Jesus, but she was getting to see the daughter she had given up so long ago. When Greg finished, I wheeled to the front and began my speech.

The emotions whirled in me as I began to tell my thoughts on Raquel. As I recalled some of our funniest times, a smile played across my face, and a tiny trickle of joy filtered in with the sadness clouding my heart. The memories didn't take the pain away though, and more tears streamed down my face by the end of my speech.

Three months later, Alyssa stood before me. "Why are you running, Alyssa?"

She rolled her eyes. "I'm not running. I just can't stay here right now. Her memory is everywhere, and I just need something different right now."

"What you need is your father and to be surrounded by people who love you. You don't need to be throwing yourself into some unknown situation."

"Aunt Sandra, I love you, but I'm not going to argue with you. I'm leaving, and I promise to keep in touch, but I have to go."

I sighed. Her mother's stubborn streak ran strong in her, and I knew I would never convince her. "Okay, Alyssa, please do call me and come back to visit. Oh, and do you have your prayer journal? Please take it with you, and don't lose your connection to God."

She flashed another eye roll, but leaned in and kissed my cheek. "Aunt Sandra, I have it, and I promise not to fall away."

I reached up and hugged her, hoping it wouldn't be the last time I saw her.

18

The Beginning of the End: Thirteen Years Later

I sighed as a wrinkled face stared back at me from the mirror. *When had I gotten so old?* Rolling to my desk, I picked up the prayer journal. I hoped Alyssa was still using hers. She had gotten married a few years back, and I had attended her wedding, but she had never been back to Mesquite. Though she still called at Christmas and a few other holidays, that was about the only time I heard from her. I kept praying that she was still using it and that God would use her.

As I opened the journal, I couldn't help but wonder how much longer I could keep doing this. There had been so many names, so many women. I was glad I had been able to help them, but I was tired, so tired. After my health had deteriorated, I had quit working at the church, but I had started a prayer team, and I continued to sit at the clinic when I felt well enough.

I perused the list, sending a quick prayer for the ones I knew still hadn't chosen abortion and for the ones I wasn't sure on, and then I slipped the journal in my bag and headed to the clinic. As I took up my customary seat by the bench, a brown haired woman I had seen a few days before came up the walk.

"Please don't kill your baby," I said.

The woman turned, and I could see the fear in her eyes. "I'm sorry, but what business is it of yours?"

"Can I tell you my story?" I folded my hands in my lap, "And then I'll never bother you again."

The woman paused. I could almost hear her brain deciding if she wanted to hear. "Fine, go ahead."

I closed my eyes for just a moment asking for the right words, and then the words spilled from my mouth: "My name is Sandra Dobbs. When I was twenty-five, I thought I had my whole life ahead of me. I was planning to be a nurse, but I made the mistake of being intimate with my boyfriend, Peter, and found myself pregnant. I wanted that baby, but we were young; he was a med student, and he didn't have time right then for fatherhood. We fought for a few weeks, but in the end, he won, and pressured me into having an abortion."

The woman's head dropped, and her eyes widened. She twisted her hands together.

I continued, "I knew I shouldn't have been intimate outside of marriage, and though I wanted a baby, I too agreed it wasn't the right time to have one, so I went through the 'procedure.' On one hand, I was relieved, but on the other, guilt plagued me afterwards. I became withdrawn, and Peter and I split up. Soon, the guilt grew so grave that I began drinking to deaden those thoughts, but not heavily – at first. Then I met a wonderful man, Henry, and he started bringing me to church. I told him I thought I had accepted God, but I don't think I really had. I hoped if I acted like everyone else that he would forgive me, even though I couldn't forgive myself. My life seemed fine; Henry proposed to me; and we got married. For several months, I think I was happy, and then things changed. We couldn't get pregnant. After two years of trying, I went to a doctor to see what the issue might be. It turns out the 'procedure' had damaged my ability to ever have a baby."

The woman clapped her hand to her mouth, her knees buckled, and she grabbed the wall of the building to steady herself. Something had hit home.

"Well, my husband didn't know I'd had an abortion before we were married. In fact, I'd never told anyone, but I made the mistake of telling him about it on the way home from dinner that night. He was so upset in finding that out, that he accidentally swerved into oncoming traffic, over-corrected, and sent us careening into a tree. The crash paralyzed me from my waist down and killed my husband instantly. In one night, that "easy" decision I had made five years earlier produced a drastic result. It destroyed my baby and the life I wanted to have. For years now, I have wished thousands of times that I had just kept Isaac."

"You know your baby was a boy?" The woman shivered, and her voice was barely a whisper.

"I didn't at first, but then the dreams came."

"He visits you in your dreams?"

"Nearly every night." Tears sprang in my eyes. "At first, I hated those dreams because having an abortion was 'my choice,' and I didn't like the guilt that greeted me every morning when I woke up. Eventually though, I realized that those dreams were the only link I would ever have to the child I could have had. He would have been thirty-five this year, and sometimes in the dreams I get the sense he would have married and had two or three kids himself. Not a day goes by that I don't regret that decision I made so long ago. Now, I know what happened to me won't happen to everyone, but do you want to take the chance of experiencing that risk?"

I marveled at how God always seemed to put the right people together as the woman shook her head and told me her worst fear was that she wouldn't be able to have children later. Evidently she had done a lot of research and found that what happened to me was not abnormal. I wished that I had researched information for myself before doing my procedure, not that the internet was big then, but maybe I could have found something. I wanted to continue our conversation, but felt odd speaking so personally when I didn't even know her name. "Look . . . um . . . I'm sorry, what can I call you, dear?"

"Callie. Callie Green," she replied, her face still down towards the ground.

My jaw dropped, "Callie Green? Is your mother Melanie Green?"

She raised her head; her eyes were wide, "Yes she is; how did you know that?"

My heart soared. I couldn't believe it. "Your mother goes to my church. She called me a few weeks ago and asked me to pray for you because your fiancé had left you. I've been praying ever since." Then a sobering thought hit me, "Is your fiancé back in the picture then?"

Heat flooded Callie's face, and she stared down at her feet. "I guess. He apologized, and I think he meant it. Have you really been praying for me for weeks?"

Though I was dismayed by the knowledge that her fiancé was back in the picture – as he didn't seem to be a good example – I was still delighted to be meeting her, and I filled her in on the prayer team that I led.

Her eyes widened in surprise, "Why would you pray for a complete stranger?"

And so I told her about God's commission and the call for Christians to pray for one another.

Callie tilted her head and raised an eyebrow. "How do you still seem so peaceful and happy after everything you have gone through?"

My smile faltered as I remembered my morning. I had been doing this so long that as I got up now, I mostly prayed that God would just take me home. Though I loved doing his work, I missed my husband, my son, and my best friend. I decided to be honest with Callie, and so I told her about my lowest moments and how God had helped me through them. Though she didn't accept God that day, I could tell that the words were circling around in her head, and for some reason I felt that her acceptance of God was vitally important. I once again marveled at how God worked through all of us.

Callie appeared a few days later at the clinic to tell me she had accepted Jesus and left her fiancé for good. The joy that filled my heart was unusual. I didn't really know this woman, but I felt some strange bond to her. As we were talking, a young girl exited the clinic.

"Please choose life for your baby," I spoke up. The woman stepped closer, her frightened eyes wide.

"What did you say?"

I repeated the statement, and the girl collapsed next to Callie, who watched the scene with wide eyes.

"I want to, but I'm afraid my parents will be mad. I'm supposed to be going to college in the fall." The girl's head hung in her hands.

Callie laid a hand on her arm, "You still can; there were pregnant girls in many of my classes at college."

Hope filled the girl's eyes. "Do you think so?"

"I know so," I replied, and I told her how parents are there for you, even when you don't expect it. Then I handed her a business card for the closest pregnancy center. I wished our church was still doing some counseling, but they had never hired anyone after I left, and I wasn't healthy enough to do it full time anymore. It gave me hope though, that the girl tucked the card in her purse as she shuffled off.

Callie continued to come by the clinic and sit with me when she could. It had been a long time, and we were very different in age, but I started to feel a connection with her like I had with Raquel. There was such a passion in her for the unborn; it reminded me of myself when I had finally gotten my life together. The only difference was that Callie had saved her baby, and she now got to experience the two things I never did: pregnancy and motherhood.

As tired as I was though, something about Callie and the baby growing inside of her gave me strength to keep going. Perhaps he or she would be another Alyssa for me, a baby I could be close to and share in the joys and sadness. Perhaps it was something else entirely. All I knew was that I was enjoying the renewed spirit I felt each morning when I woke up.

Callie began speaking out about abortion, and I thought back to the words Raquel and I had written so long ago. We had never been able to get the book published, but I felt like Callie's story should be added to it. I rolled to my desk and began rifling through the drawers. Down in the very bottom right hand drawer, I saw the notebook we had filled. Raquel had wanted to type, but I wasn't great with computers, even back then, and so we had hand written every word.

I flipped to the end of the story and read where we had left off. Raquel's death had not been added, but after learning from Callie the correlation between abortion and breast cancer, I felt it was important to our message. Though the words were hard – as they forced me to think back on my best friend's death – I penned them in and began to add Callie's story so far. I'd have to ask her to add more when I remembered.

Callie and I grew close, and my heart grew even more when I met JD, her new fiancé, who was planning to open a pregnancy care center right here in Mesquite. He began the work of remodeling a building, and I prayed even harder. It would be so nice not to have to send women so far away.

When Callie was about eight months pregnant, the unthinkable happened – she passed out at a speaking event and was diagnosed with preeclampsia. She was then told if she didn't abort the baby that she might die. As soon as I received the news, I picked up the phone to call Amanda Adams, a young, spirited high school girl who had a passion for God and was at the top of my prayer chain. With each member of the prayer chain, I prayed for Callie and her baby before hanging up and dialing the next one. After all the members were informed, I called Pastor Tony to ask if we could set up a prayer vigil at the church. He agreed, and Margaret and I began to create a list of members who could be there at different times so the church would always be open.

There were about fifty of us praying at the church when a friend of JD's announced that Callie was in a coma after rejecting the abortion and undergoing a C-section. My own phone vibrated with the same message just seconds later. None of us moved. Prayer was more important now than ever. Margaret whispered beside me that she was going to arrange food for all of us, and I nodded but continued my prayer to God. I would not be eating tonight; I would be fasting and praying as long as I could.

A few days later, I headed to the hospital to see the beautiful baby, Hope. Callie was still in a coma, but I figured I could pray just as easily for her at the hospital as I could at the church.

As I entered Callie's room, I saw her mother, Melanie, rocking the baby. She smiled up at me, "Would you like a turn?"

I nodded, and Melanie rose and placed the sleeping angel in my arms. Her tiny features were flawless against her porcelain skin, and a small smile tugged at her lips in her sleep. I breathed in the scent of baby and sighed. There was nothing like holding a tiny one. “Has she gotten any better?”

Melanie crossed to Callie’s bedside, “No, she mumbled something a few days ago, but since then she’s been quiet.” She smoothed Callie’s hair and adjusted her sheet. “I sent JD home to get some sleep. He was a walking zombie.”

“Looks like you could get some rest too,” I noted the dark circles encasing Melanie’s eyes.

“I will; I promise.”

The door burst open, and a nurse hurried into the room. “You have to see this.” She clicked on the remote until a news channel popped up. A crowd of people praying at a church appeared on the screen. I didn’t understand what we were watching at first, but it soon became clear we were seeing a prayer vigil for Callie, but not at our local church. The reporter explained how they had stumbled across Callie’s story and interviewed her before her surgery. The story had then been picked up by their national affiliate and gone viral. Once again, I was reminded of how big God was and how good he was. I only hoped Callie would get a chance to hear how her story had touched those so far away.

A few days later, I sat again in the hospital room rocking baby Hope. “Callie? Oh praise God. She’s awake,” Melanie shouted. Callie’s eyes opened and focused straight on the petite bundle in my arms. I rolled closer and held out Hope to Melanie who scooped her up and placed her beside Callie. JD, Callie’s husband, entered then, and I rolled back to allow the joyous reunion. I closed my eyes and prayed thanks to God.

“I can’t believe I missed so much of her life. Oh, I’m so sorry Sandra, I wasn’t thinking,” Callie said.

"It's okay. I understand how you feel. I'd give anything to see my baby now." The pang once again pulled at my heart.

"Oh, I almost forgot. Sandra, I saw him," Callie exclaimed, and her face lit up. She began to tell us of her experience while she was in the coma. She had been shown what her life would have been like if she'd had the abortion – it was eerily similar to my life, but then she had been shown how many lives she had touched since speaking out about abortion. I was reminded of Raquel's similar experience the first time she got sick. "Anyway, the angel told me I had to come back to finish the work I was called to do, but I asked him if I could see Isaac first. He agreed, and Sandra, he was so handsome. He has warm brown eyes and caramel skin and a dimple in his left cheek."

Tears welled up in my eyes. It had been so long since I had seen his face clearly. Though I had dreams of him nearly every night, he had become a vague shadowy figure in recent years, and I longed to see his face again.

"We should probably let everyone know you're awake now," Melanie said.

"Let's do that in the hall," I suggested. "These two need a few minutes to get reacquainted, and mother and daughter need that too."

Melanie followed me into the hall, and we began the work of calling or texting everyone we knew to relay the good news. When we had finished, I asked Melanie to tell Callie I'd be back tomorrow, and I left the hospital.

Long ago, I had dabbled as an artist, but I hadn't picked up a brush since the procedure. In fact, when I lost the house, I had lost all the art supplies I had. As I drove to a local supply store, I made a mental list in my head of what I would need.

I rolled through the store, picking up brushes, paints, and canvasses. After checking out, I loaded the supplies in my van and drove home. The need to paint lay heavy on my heart, but I had one more thing to do. I placed the items on the small kitchen table and rolled to my bedroom. After I lost the house, I had packed only a few things, but I knew one of them was a picture of Peter and I. I hadn't known why I had kept it, maybe as a reminder of the child we had given up, maybe for sentimental reasons. Whatever the reason, I knew it resided in a box buried in my closet.

Tossing aside clothes, I dug in the back until I found the old cardboard box. I wiped a light coat of dust off the lid and opened the box that had been sealed shut for years. Under several pictures of Henry and I, I found what I was looking for: a picture of Peter and I at a hospital function shortly before I found out I was pregnant. I touched his face, remembering how handsome he had been, and I wondered briefly what he was doing now. Then I remembered my purpose in finding the picture, and I returned the lid to the box. As I was returning it to the shelf, I saw my old sketch pad on the shelf as well. I had no memory of taking it, but there it was, so I grabbed it as well.

When I returned to the table, I closed my eyes to remember the description Callie had given, then I studied the picture and picked up a pencil. My hand began to flow back and forth across the sketch pad, and lines began to emerge. A face appeared, a combination of myself and Peter, but with a smile original to him. The pencil continued to scratch across the surface, adding depth and shading. The scratching slowed and then stopped, and my heart stopped. Though I hadn't seen what Callie had, I knew that I was looking into the face of my adult son. I set the sketch pad on the table, and then I turned to the canvas and opened the paints. A chill ran down my spine as I dipped the brush for the first time in thirty-five years.

A few weeks later, I tucked the portrait I had drawn of Isaac, grabbed the baby gift for Hope, and headed over to Callie's place for her baby shower. There were already a few other people there when I got there, so I tucked the portrait in my bag, deciding to wait until there was more time. Melanie took the gift I proffered and showed me to the table to grab a snack. Amanda stood chatting with another girl from Callie and JD's pregnancy center. They had opened it just shortly before Callie's collapse and diagnosis, and Amanda had been interning as a counselor. She filled me in on her college plans as we munched on snacks until Melanie called the party together.

"Well," Melanie began, "thank you all for coming. Obviously the baby is already here," Everybody smiled at Hope who was fast asleep in Callie's arms, "but we thought this would also be a great time to get together and celebrate Callie's return to us."

We all clapped and smiled. "Of course, we did bring some things for Hope," Melanie continued and picked up a present. Callie stood and brought the sleeping baby to me. Though surprised, I smiled and opened my arms. It must have been obvious to her that this little angel already had a hold on my heart.

I tried to pay attention as Callie opened the gifts for Hope, but my attention kept getting pulled back to the angel in my lap. Long dark lashes framed her eyes, and her mouth would open and close as she dreamed. As I ran a finger down her face, a smile tugged at her lips. It brought a smile to my own face, and I felt the familiar tug on my heart.

When Callie had finished opening the gifts, she came and took Hope to feed her. People started leaving, but I had a reason to stay, so I tried to busy myself with helping clean up until Callie returned.

"I wanted to say thank you," I said, touching her arm when she finally returned.

"For what?"

I grabbed the bag off the back of my wheelchair and pulled out the portrait I had drawn. As I unrolled it, Callie gasped. "Did you see him?"

I smiled, "Is it him then?"

"It's perfect," Callie's fingertips grazed the portrait.

"I use to draw a long time ago," I began, "and when you told me about Isaac, I knew I had to try to draw his portrait. I used your description and an old picture of Peter, his father, and myself. I was hoping I'd get it close to the real thing."

"You got it spot on," Callie squeezed my arm.

"Thank you for asking to see him and for giving me the description. I'll be ready to meet him when Jesus is ready for me, but until then I now have something to look at. I can never thank you enough, Callie."

"I'm so happy I could help you," Callie smiled back. "And I'd also like to ask you to be Hope's godmother. She is going to need strong female role models, and I can think of no one else I'd rather have."

Tears sprang to my eyes. "I'd be honored. I had a god-daughter once, but she's all grown up now."

As I drove home that night, I thanked God for the wonderful people he had put in my life. Though I had lost my husband and my son, I had been filled with love from others around me, and Callie and Hope gave me a renewed spirit and the desire to keep doing God's work.

I resumed my post at the clinic the next day; only this time I had a stack of business cards for JD and Callie's center. I no longer had to send women all the way to Dallas, and because they had a part-time counselor, there was also someone to help the women if they needed courage telling their partner or their parents. It began to be a well-oiled machine.

Amanda graduated and moved to Lubbock, Texas to go to college. She still wanted to be a part of the prayer warriors, and so we continued to speak once a week, but I missed seeing her bright red hair and freckled face in church. Of course, she returned some weekends and holidays, brightening our lives with her smile.

Alyssa called me when they adopted a baby. I hadn't even known they were having trouble conceiving, but maybe she had spared me that knowledge because of my own situation. I drove out and spent a few days with them, enjoying my first god-daughter, her husband Neal, and the tiny girl they had adopted. I couldn't believe how God had worked that all out.

Hope continued to grow and be a light for both myself and Callie. Every time I looked at her, I tried to imagine her not being in our life, and I couldn't. If only women could see past the nine months. If they could just pause and really take stock, then more might make the choice Callie had done and save their children.

Callie never stopped smiling. For someone who hadn't been sure she was ready to be a mother, the role fit her to a tee. She continued to do speaking events when she could, bringing Hope with her, and when she was home she helped JD at the clinic or came and sat with me.

When Hope turned two, Callie found out she was pregnant again. "I hope it's a boy," she whispered as we watched Hope play. "Not that I wouldn't love another girl, but I think it would be nice to have one of each, and JD could probably use some more testosterone around here."

"I heard that," he said from his chair a few feet away.

"Have you thought of names if it's a boy?" I asked.

Callie's eyes sparkled, and she took my hand. "We're thinking of Henry for one of the names, would that be okay with you?"

Tears filled my eyes and spilled down my face before I could stop them. "Callie, that would be wonderful."

"Sanda, why you crying?" Hope had snuck up while we were discussing and now stood at the base of my wheelchair.

I picked her up and placed her on my lap. Her blond hair waved from the slight breeze. "I'm just so happy angel."

A smile stretched across her face, and she placed a hand on either side of my face. "Me too, Sanda. I love you."

I hugged her close. "I love you too Hope."

19

The Final Chapter

When I got home that night, I gazed at the wedding picture of Henry and I. The familiar pang of regret crept in and tugged at my heart. We had had such big dreams, but no children had ever filled our house. Henry had never had the chance to be a father, and though I had helped raise Alyssa and I now had Hope to see, it wasn't quite the same for me either. I had never gotten to nurse a baby or rock them to sleep after a bad dream or hear them call me mommy. Emotion crawled up my throat, threatening to choke me. Grabbing my Bible, I held it close to my heart, whispering a prayer for peace. It took a while, but finally the pain and regret subsided, and I turned out the light.

The next morning, I woke to the sun shining brightly in my window. I shielded my eyes, and turned my head until I could open them. The clock on my nightstand showed ten thirty. I couldn't believe I had slept so long.

My stomach rumbled, and I climbed out of bed and rolled into the kitchen to make some food. On the way, I passed the portrait I had drawn of Isaac. *Would I ever see him again? Or Henry?* Henry had never returned in my dreams, and though I often dreamed of Isaac, he had never been as clear as the time I had seen Henry and him together. His face had always been hazy in my dreams as he grew up, and I missed seeing him clearly.

Sighing, I opened the fridge and pulled out some eggs to scramble. A pain erupted in my chest, and the eggs fell to the floor, cracking and spilling yellow ooze on the floor. I grabbed my left side, struggling to take a breath. Spots began to appear in my vision, and I tried to move my arms towards the phone but they refused to budge, and then the world went dark.

Light filled the area, and the breeze tickled my skin. I opened my eyes slowly to adjust to the bright light. A glowing being, robed in white, was to my left. Long blond hair surrounded his pale skin and fierce blue eyes. As we soared up, my house grew smaller and smaller in the distance. My heart galloped. I was going home. I'd finally get to see Henry and Isaac again.

We continued up through the clouds and then the gates, gleaming a pearly white, came into view. My breath caught in my throat. It was more beautiful than I ever could have imagined. The gates swung open as we reached them and the glare of gold greeted us. Shimmering people filled the area, and I craned my neck to glimpse Henry or Isaac.

"In good time, daughter," the angelic being beside me said. The words came out with great reverence and command. Around us a chorus of praise erupted, and people declared "Great is the Lord."

"Am I going to see Him?" I asked. Though it was what I had

wanted for more than thirty years, suddenly the thought dried my throat and filled me with apprehension. What if I wasn't found worthy? The angel nodded, and we continued further into the city of gold. The knot of fear grew the farther we went.

"Do not be afraid, daughter."

The crowd continued to part for us, and soon a gleaming golden throne came into view. I raised my hand to shield the brightness of it. When we stopped in front of the throne, I dropped to my knees and placed my face on the ground. I could not look at the powerful figure radiating heat and light.

"Welcome Sandra Dobbs," the voice boomed. "Arise, my daughter. You have done well, my faithful servant."

I stood, but still couldn't fully take in the glory of God before me.

"A place has been prepared for you, but I know there are some people you would like to see first."

My heart soared, and the being beside me turned me around. My eyes adjusted once the brightness was behind me and no longer in front of me. Henry came into sight first, looking exactly like I remembered him even though decades had passed. I ran to him, and he embraced me.

"I'm so sorry," I said into his chest. "I waited so long." He caressed my hair and shushed me.

"I knew. I've been watching. I didn't blame you."

My eyes widened up at him. "You were watching?"

"Of course, I will show you where you can watch too, but first . . ." – he stepped aside. My parents stood behind him. They had passed shortly after Alyssa moved off, but I had had the privilege of leading them to Christ before they did. I hugged my mother first and then my father, who was more joyful than I could ever remember. Raquel was next, and a beautiful woman was next to her.

"Sandra, I'd like to introduce you to my daughter, Arianna,"

Raquel said as we separated. I held out my hand to the woman, but she pulled me in for an embrace.

"Thank you for what you did for my mother," she said. "Without you, she might never have made it here." I smiled at her, glancing around at many other people I had known in life. Finally, I spotted the one I wanted to see most. A few people down the line stood a tall man. I recognized him immediately from the portrait I had drawn. The people fell away, and a silence descended as they watched.

I stepped forward, and he took a step as well. "Isaac," I breathed.

A smile lit up his face, "Hi mama."

He was no longer the baby or even the six-year old that I remembered best. He was a grown man, and he was so handsome. "I'm so sorry, Isaac. I'm so sorry I never gave you the chance to live."

"I know mama." He folded me in his arms, and finally, my heart felt complete.

Later Raquel, Arianna, Henry, and Isaac took me to a special place. Near the edge of the pearly gates was a table and chairs. I raised an eyebrow and shook my head, "I don't understand."

"You will; just wait," Henry said. We sat down around the table, and the opaque surface slowly cleared. Suddenly I could see down on Earth. The view opened first on my house, but someone must have found my body for the house was empty. I could see my Bible sitting on my nightstand. The table clouded over, and then it cleared again. This time I could see Callie and JD. She held my prayer journal and tears streamed down her face. JD put his arm around her, and she leaned into him. Then their voices carried up.

"I know she's in a better place, but I'm going to miss her so much," Callie sobbed.

JD stroked her hair. "It's okay to miss her, but just think right now she's probably up there with Henry and Isaac."

I smiled at my boys. A pang pinched my heart for my friend though. I wished I had gotten to say goodbye to her.

"You're right," Callie leaned her head on his shoulder. "She's probably holding him right now." She wiped the tears from her face. "What are we going to tell Hope though?"

"We'll tell her the truth, and when she's older, maybe we'll give her the journal, and she can carry on the work.

The view shifted to little Hope asleep in her bed. Another pang as I realized I'd never hold the sweet little angel again. I bit my lip, "Does it get easier to watch?"

"Not really," Henry said. "This part is a little like it was for you on Earth I guess. You still missed us right?" I nodded. "Well, they will go on missing you too, and you think about them, even up here, but you can check in on them from time. You can watch Callie and JD and little Hope grow, at least until it's time."

"Time for what?" I asked.

"The rapture," Henry said. "When Jesus says it's time, all the believers will come and join us here in Heaven. None of us know when, but watching the turmoil going on down there, we are starting to feel it might be soon."

"Let's show her the other thing," Isaac said. His brown eyes twinkled, and he clapped his hands, almost like a little boy.

"What other thing?" I asked.

"Watch," Raquel said, and I turned my attention back to the table. The surface clouded over again and then zoomed out. All the people became tiny specks, but some of them twinkled. In fact, a lot of them twinkled.

"Why are some brighter than others?" I asked.

Raquel smiled. "Those are the ones you saved. All the women and babies over all the years, and the ones that shine extra bright are the ones you brought to Christ as well."

"There's so many," I said. The image zoomed out a little more to where all we could see was the United States and there were lights twinkling all across it.

"You saved a lot of babies over the years," Raquel said and squeezed my hand.

I nodded, "We both did."

We smiled at each other, and then Henry and Isaac grabbed our hands as well. Though I missed my friends on Earth, I knew they would be coming soon. As I glanced at the friends around the table with me, I knew that this was where I belonged, and that the best was yet to come.

The End

RESOURCES

Free prenatal care if you put your baby up for adoption:
http://www.adoptionstar.com/birth-
parents/yourpregnancy/prenatal-care/
The loss of fertility after abortion: http://www.lifenews.com/
2012/11/30/abortion-is-a-war-on-women-death-
infertilityemotional-damage/
Dreams after abortion: http://www.afterabortion.com/
dreams.html
Pray to end abortion app: https://www.humancoalition.org/
Abortion stories: http://www.abort73.com/testimony/
Adoption: http://www.pregnantpause.org/adopt/wanted.html

Please reach out to someone if you find yourself pregnant unexpectedly. There are resources and loving couples who would love to raise your baby.

Made in the USA
Charleston, SC
04 November 2016